Millbury Public Library

DIS(

How to Succeed in Murder

Also by Margaret Dumas
Speak Now

How to Succeed in Murder

Margaret Dumas

Poisoned Pen Press

M
DUMAS
M

5-06

*Poisoned
Pen
Press*

Copyright © 2006 by Margaret Dumas

First U. S. Edition 2006

10 9 8 7 6 5 4 3 2 1

Library of Congress Catalog Card Number: 2005934987

ISBN: 1-59058-260-8

Poisoned Pen Press
6962 E. First Ave., Ste. 103
Scottsdale, AZ 85251
www.poisonedpenpress.com
info@poisonedpenpress.com

Printed in the United States of America

Acknowledgments

To my family, and especially my parents, thanks for your continued love and support—and for buying all those copies of the first book.

To Denise Lee and Erick Vera, thanks for putting up with my early drafts and rampant insecurities.

To the gang at the day job, thanks for understanding that when I stare off into space during meetings I'm not being rude—I'm just planning another plot twist.

To the Every-Other-Thursday group—Ann Parker, Claire Johnson, Carole Price, Janet Finesilver, Gordon Yano, Colleen Casey, Michael Cooper, and Rena Leith—thanks for all the maddening and picky comments that made the book so much better.

To Rob and the gang at Poisoned Pen Press, and especially Barbara Peters—who isn't nearly as evil as she thinks she is—thanks for everything!

Chapter One

I'm not terrifically impressed by high-tech geniuses. For one thing, there are so many of them. In San Francisco, it's pretty much impossible to drop by your local Tully's for a Latte Macchiato without bumping into a hypercaffeinated computer whiz who thinks he's just a hundred lines of code away from changing the world as we know it.

Please.

So when my husband Jack told me we were invited to lunch with Morgan Stokes, the *Cappo di tutti cappi* of geekdom, I was underwhelmed. And maybe a little whiny.

"Jaaaack," I groaned. "Do we have to?"

"You're the only woman I've ever met who can give my name four syllables." Which didn't exactly answer my question, but since he said it while stepping out of a steamy shower wearing nothing but an engaging frown I sort of lost track of what we'd been talking about.

Jack looks good when he's wet. But then, Jack always looks good.

He's in his late thirties, which is *much* older than me—I'm only in my mid-thirties—and he has the sort of tall, dark-eyed, chiseled-jaw stuff that reminds me of Gregory Peck in his prime. A sarcastic, sometimes maddeningly secretive Gregory Peck, but my very own classic leading man, nevertheless.

We'd only been married seven months, and we'd barely known each other six weeks before the wedding. So it was probably perfectly natural that my husband could still make me abandon all my plans for the day just by reaching for a towel.

I got to the towel rack first. "I don't think you'll be needing that."

"Is your plan to make us late for lunch?" he asked, dripping.

"With any luck, we'll be late for dinner."

He rewarded me with one of those grins that make me glad I'd gotten over a lifetime of commitment issues and said "I do" to the man.

A while later I opened my eyes and looked at the clock.

Damn. We still had time to haul ourselves out of bed and make the lunch appointment.

I reached over and poked Jack in the arm. "Jack, you can't take a job with this guy."

"Who said I was going to take a job?" He adopted a tone of wounded innocence.

I didn't buy it for a second.

"We said we'd go away as soon as the last play of the season closed," I reminded him.

"We did say that," he agreed.

"That was a full four days ago!"

"But Charley." He kissed me on the nose. "We just got here."

He had a point. We'd moved in to the house exactly two weeks ago, on New Year's Day. I use the term "moved in" loosely, since the only furniture we possessed was the massive bed we currently occupied and a battered desk lamp that Jack had been dragging around the world since his college days.

Finding the perfect house had been a harrowing experience. The endless decisions involved in the process had been enough to make me stay happily in a hotel suite for the rest of my life. What neighborhood? What style? What size? What the hell did I know about real estate?

But thanks to Jack's persistence and a genius realtor, we'd found the perfect place. It was made of white stone, with classical, or maybe Edwardian, or possibly Georgian architecture. I didn't know how to label it, but I loved the high arched windows and the little balcony over the front door. And the Pacific Heights location meant it had postcard-worthy views of the San Francisco Bay.

After all the long hours I'd been putting in at the Rep, the non-profit theatre company I funded and managed, I hadn't been in a rush to take on the job of settling into the big empty house. Settling has never really been my strong suit. And now that the last play of the season had just closed after a surprisingly successful run, I felt I was due for a honeymoon.

It was either that or go furniture shopping.

"Jack." I sat up in bed and looked around for my clothes. What had I been wearing? I wrapped the sheet around myself and followed him into his closet. "Sweetie, remember all our plans? Remember Maui? Remember scuba diving off the Great Barrier Reef? Remember a little cottage in the South of France? Remember…" I could barely remember all the things we'd talked about.

"Remember Tuscany!" I shouted at his retreating back.

"Sure I remember, Charley. All those trips sound great." He was moving swiftly to the hallway, and I knew I'd never keep up with him on the stairs while still wound up in my sheet. Luckily, he's a gentleman, and he waited at the door with an expression of amused lechery until I flung on a robe. Then, perfectly reasonably, he continued. "If you just tell me when and where you want to go, we'll go. But—" he cut off my anticipated whoop of victory—"I don't think we're going anywhere before lunchtime, so we might as well meet with Morgan Stokes."

Damn.

As we pulled up outside One Market, I consoled myself with the thought that at least we'd have a fabulous meal. The restaurant was a power dining establishment owned and operated by one of San Francisco's most celebrated celebrity chefs, and its dessert menu contained a grown-up version of a banana split—involving hazelnut ice cream and a crunchy caramelized effect—that could induce grown women to chuck their diets and live for the moment.

Another consolation was that I'd taken the event as an opportunity to debut a new cashmere sweater dress that clung in just the right places and, mercifully, nowhere else. The jewel-red color worked well with my darkish hair and winter-pale skin, and a fabulous pair of Dior stiletto-heeled boots brought me almost eye-level with Jack—optimum kissing range, which could come in handy after lunch.

After we were seated and assured that Italian fizzy water was on its way, I resumed my line of questioning.

"So if he isn't going to offer you a job, why are we talking to this dweeb anyway?"

Jack looked momentarily pained, probably because the dweeb in question ran one of the most successful software companies in the world. "He wants to hire the firm to look into something at his company."

The firm, unimaginatively named MJC (Mike and Jack's Company), was the computer security startup Jack had formed with his former Navy buddy, Mike Papas, soon after we'd gotten married and come back to the Bay Area.

We'd met while we were both living in London. Me, studying with a British theatrical company, and Jack, doing heaven-knows-what on behalf of the United States Navy. He'd claimed to be a meteorologist, but since you have no way of knowing when a weatherman is making things up, that was a little hard to verify.

Jack's past was something of a mystery.

And that's something of an understatement.

Now I batted my eyes at him. "If Morgan Stokes is such a smarty-pants, what does he need with you two?"

"Because a smarty-pants knows when to call for reinforcements," he batted back at me as the water and menus arrived.

"Right." I raised a skeptical eyebrow. "And I'm sure the only interest this guy has in you is your stellar ability to analyze computer data."

Jack was impervious to suggestion. "That's Mike's stellar ability. I just help with the heavy lifting."

"Right," I said again.

I had extremely good reason to believe that Jack had spent his military career as an undercover operative working clandestinely for Naval Intelligence, where he had picked up some very impressive skills. But Jack still stuck to the meteorologist story. This despite all evidence—in the form of his behavior when faced with a maniacal killer weaving an elaborate plot of revenge in the weeks following our marriage—to the contrary.

In public, I humored him. Privately, I held the belief that Jack, his friend Mike, and a third partner, Gordon, had been the Navy's covert-operations dream team. A real smarty-pants would be interested in MJC for those talents.

Reading my mind, or at least part of it, Jack asked, "How's Gordon doing with the restaurant?"

"He's found the place he wants," I said. "It's on Union Street. We'll be able to walk to it." Although walking back home, uphill, was another story.

"That's handy. How's Harry taking it?"

I grimaced. "Not well."

I'd met Gordon when he'd taken a job as private chef to my Uncle Harry, something Jack had arranged so his colleague could quietly keep a watchful eye on my family. I'm the first to admit that my uncle, a grown-up delinquent who takes both fine living and personal security to alarming extremes, generally needs some watching.

Gordon had immediately become indispensable to Harry. He had an almost-miraculous knack of showing up exactly when you wanted him with exactly what you needed—whether that was a dry martini or a surgical kit.

Harry, never a man to keep his feelings hidden, was still working through the grieving process over Gordon's defection. He'd reached the denial stage, believing Gordon's venture would fail and he'd come back to Harry's Hillsborough mansion eventually, bringing the secret of the perfect Bloody Mary with him.

But anyone who'd tasted Gordon's salmon *en croute* knew his restaurant wasn't going to fail.

"Gordon thinks the place only needs some minor renovations and a new look," I said. "He asked me if I know any good interior designers."

Jack may have chuckled, but he turned it into a throat-clearing so smoothly that I wasn't sure. He raised his eyebrows innocently, not bringing up the fact that a very large, very empty house was waiting for me to decorate it.

"Just because I've only had the painters slap on one coat of Beach Sand semi-gloss so far doesn't mean I'm not going to turn the house into a showplace," I answered his unspoken comment.

I was a little touchy on the subject of decorating. I had plenty of ideas for different fabulous looks, but they all seemed to vanish whenever I walked into a furniture store, or—God forbid—one of those home-improvement warehouses.

"Anyway," I told him. "I'm sure Gordon's place is going to be great."

"I don't doubt it," Jack grinned. "Even if Harry's his only customer, he'll never go out of business."

It was true. I looked at my watch. "The boy genius is late for lunch."

"I know." A flicker of something—worry?—flashed across Jack's face. "And Stokes has a reputation for fanatical punctuality. I heard when he took over Zakdan he put a thirty-minute limit on all meetings, and if someone wasn't there exactly on time they were fined."

I shuddered. "Thank God I never had to have a real job." Especially one working for Morgan Stokes.

As I was reaching for my glass, a thought struck me. "Why isn't Mike here?"

"He's out of town." Jack punctuated this sentence with a look that said Don't Ask. "He talked to Stokes over the phone a few days ago and thought I should meet with him."

"Oh." I sipped demurely. "So why am I here?"

He didn't miss a beat. "Because my love for you is such that I can't stand for us to be parted."

"Yeah, but really. Why am I here?"

Jack grinned. "Because rumors spread faster than Internet viruses in his business, and if Morgan Stokes was seen having lunch with me in some quiet little place it would look like he was interested in acquiring MJC, and that might affect his stock price. But if we're out in the open in a very public restaurant, and if you're here..." He looked at me speculatively.

"It only looks like he's courting an investor," I finished for him.

"Not just any investor," Jack pointed out.

So I had been dragged to the world's most boring luncheon simply because I had—through no fault of my own—a couple zillion dollars.

"I'm your beard," I said. "I'm your rich beard."

Jack patted my hand and allowed a twinkle to creep into his eye. "And a lovely beard you are."

Funny how just when I was completely exasperated, I found myself wanting to rip off Jack's clothes and have my way with him. But he was spared that indignity by the arrival of a disheveled entrepreneurial genius.

Morgan Stokes stood at the doorway, seemingly unaware of the January chill he was letting in behind him, and I knew it was Morgan Stokes not only because he was wearing a leather bomber jacket with the Zakdan corporate logo over his heart, but because every head in the restaurant turned to look at him.

Jack made eye contact with him, and he came over to the table. I know these digital types have the reputation of living on cold pizza and sleeping under their desks, but this specimen looked particularly bad. Dark circles under the eyes, hair that was genuinely messy, not just fashionably unkempt-looking, and an overall air of twitchy desperation.

He was about 5'6", with a slight build that wasn't helped by concave posture. When I'd seen him on TV, he'd always appeared youthful and energetic, more like the eager new intern than the seasoned CEO. But today it looked like he was recovering badly from a well-delivered blow to the gut.

"Morgan Stokes." He held out a shaky hand.

"Jack Fairfax." Jack helped the guy into his chair. "This is my wife, Charley."

Stokes turned to me and, alarmingly, I saw tears in his eyes.

"Your wife," he said faintly.

I was at a loss for words. Could whatever was going on at his company have turned him into this much of a wreck?

"Sorry." He cleared his throat and made a visible effort to pull himself together as he shrugged off his coat. "I know we scheduled this meeting to talk about the security issue at Zakdan." He straightened, his voice gaining strength. "But something has happened that takes precedence over everything else."

Jack flicked a look my way before answering. "If you have to go, we can reschedule."

"No!" Stokes said loudly. People at surrounding tables didn't bother to disguise their curiosity. "No," he repeated, attempting to bring himself under control. "I need to talk to you, but not about Zakdan."

He took a deep breath.

"It's my fiancée. She's been murdered."

Chapter Two

Jack acted quickly. He shot me a look that cut off the exclamations of surprise and sympathy I was about to make and shoved a menu into Morgan's shaking hands.

"The Channel Two news team is at the table in the corner and looking very curious," he said softly. "Try to get hold of yourself. Look at the menu."

Morgan's glazed eyes shifted from Jack to the oversized document in front of him. He blew out his breath. "Thanks."

"Can you talk about it?" I hid my face behind my menu and spoke out of the side of my mouth.

Morgan looked up at me, then quickly down again. He nodded once.

Jack cleared his throat. "I didn't know you were engaged. Had it been announced publicly?"

Morgan stayed focused on the daily fish selection. "We didn't tell anyone. Clara worked at Zakdan." Again his eyes darted up to meet mine. "Not directly for me, of course. There was never anything questionable or unprofessional about it. We just decided early on that it was nobody's business but ours. Clara doesn't—didn't—" He nearly lost his composure again but took another breath and continued with a flicker of pride. "She didn't want people to say that Clara Chen had gotten ahead by sleeping with the boss."

"What did she do at the company?" I asked.

"She was Vice President of Client Knowledge." He saw the blank look on my face and elaborated. "It's another name for Tech Support."

"Oh," I nodded. "The people you call when things go wrong with your computer."

"It used to be just that," he said, and I saw a brief spark of animation cross his face. "But Clara totally changed the model. She expanded the knowledgebase, and developed this whole new approach…" His voice faltered. Eyes back to the menu. "She was brilliant."

The waiter appeared and Jack ordered for all of us. Eventually whatever it was arrived, and we pushed it around on our plates, acutely aware of curious eyes watching every move we made. But the empty routine of the meal seemed to calm Morgan, and he was eventually able to tell us what had happened.

"Clara was working late last night. I talked to her at about ten. I was flying back from the Boston office and wasn't due in until after midnight. I called her from the plane and she said she had just finished up writing her annual employee evaluations and she was on her way to the gym before going home."

"The gym is close to the office?" Jack asked.

Morgan shook his head. "Not the one she goes to." He back-tracked for my benefit. "We're on Townsend, south of Market, near the train station."

I knew the area. Ground Zero for the hip high-tech scene, where just about every old brick building in the neighborhood had been torn down and replaced with a glass palace, or retrofitted into retro offices.

"Clara didn't like the club that's just down the street," Morgan continued. "They don't have a pool. So she belonged to a gym downtown—WorkSpace."

Morgan didn't seem to notice the look that flickered across Jack's face, but I realized Jack was as surprised as I was at the news that he belonged to the same gym as the murdered woman.

"So she left the office for the gym sometime after ten," I said encouragingly.

Morgan nodded. "They swipe your membership card at the front desk when you check in, and their computer shows she got there at 10:47."

The woman had clearly been more dedicated to her exercise regime than I had ever been.

"Was that normal for her?" Jack asked. "To go for a workout that late at night?"

Morgan nodded quickly. "She worked crazy hours—we both do. But she didn't like going straight home from the office. She said a swim cleared her mind, and a steam relaxed…" He faltered, looking down at his plate. Then he cleared his throat.

"They found her in the steam room."

Jack gave him a moment to collect himself. "What exactly do the police think happened?"

"The police?" Morgan's voice turned harsh. "They think she slipped on the tiles and hit her head on the bench."

I could believe that. Steam rooms, at least the big ones in gyms and spas, are usually wet and slippery places. And I know some women who insist on putting lotion on while steaming, making the tiles even slicker. But slipping was one thing, and hitting your head so hard you'd die from it was another.

Morgan was still speaking. "The gym closes at midnight. They make an announcement at 11:30, and again at 11:45, but apparently they aren't very strict about checking everywhere to make sure everyone's gone."

I interrupted him. "You mean you don't have to swipe your card when you leave?"

Morgan shook his head. "You do, but it's meaningless because their system doesn't match up the entrance and exits at the end of the day, so it doesn't tell them who's still there. And they must have assumed everyone had left because the last couple of employees took off a little after twelve. The cleaning crew showed up at one, and it was them…" His voice rasped and he took a quick gulp of water. "They found her when they went to clean the steam room at 1:30." His face became even paler as he continued. "She'd bled to death on the floor."

Horrible. She must have been knocked unconscious by the fall. At least I hoped she had. It would be even more horrible to think of her lying helpless as she realized the gym was closing and everyone had left her alone to die.

"You don't believe she slipped?" Jack asked.

Morgan shook his head. "I don't believe someone as athletic as Clara—with her grace—" He focused on Jack, staring into his eyes intently. "I don't believe she'd just slip and not be able to catch herself. I think someone killed her."

Jack looked at him steadily. "I can't imagine—"

"No!" Morgan cut him off loudly. Once again heads turned to see what was happening at the table.

Morgan continued in a low, urgent tone. "No, you can't imagine what I'm feeling. But my feelings are not clouding my judgment. So if you're about to say I need to give it time and I'll eventually accept what the police believe, you're wrong. I don't. I won't."

I knew what was coming next, and one look at Jack told me he did too.

"I want you to find out who killed Clara."

Jack studied Stokes for a moment. When he spoke his voice was kind but firm. "The sort of security work Mike and I do at MJC isn't geared toward criminal investigation—"

I snorted, which caused Morgan to fix a laser-beam look on me. Jack gave me a look of an altogether different variety. I pretended the snort had been a sneeze and reached for my water.

My husband looked heavenward briefly and continued. "We can reschedule to talk about the original problem you wanted to look into, but as far as a murder investigation…we're just not that sort of firm."

I was surprised at how much Jack's refusal disappointed me. I'd gotten a little bubble of excitement thinking about tracking down another killer with Jack. Particularly one who—this time—wasn't trying to kill us. But Jack was probably right. We really had no business looking into anything the police were calling an accident.

Morgan Stokes didn't agree. His eyes narrowed and I saw something of the steely backbone that must have been necessary for him to hang on to the position he'd reached in a cutthroat industry. He focused on Jack. "I don't know where you got the idea that I'm a man who'll take no for an answer."

It was a battle of wills, and it ended in a draw. Eventually Morgan agreed to a meeting with Jack and Mike in a few days to discuss Zakdan's original problem, and Jack finally agreed he'd look into Clara's death and see if anything seemed fishy to him—without getting in the way of the police investigation.

I didn't agree to anything, but I made a silent promise to myself that I'd steal a peek at whatever information Jack got and make up my own mind about what had happened to Clara Chen.

We pantomimed a happy ending to a successful business lunch for anyone who was still watching us, and parted ways.

In the car on the way home, Jack cleared his voice a couple of times and frowned, clear signals that he was about to say something I wouldn't like.

"Charley," he began, "I don't want you to think, just because I said I'd ask a few questions, that I believe there was anything suspicious about that woman's death."

"Of course not, Jack."

"Stokes has been under a lot of strain, even before this. I just thought I might be able to give him a little peace of mind."

"Sure," I agreed.

"And even if I did find something I thought was odd, I certainly wouldn't take it upon myself to investigate it."

"Of course not," I said again.

"I'd just point it out to the police and let them handle it."

"Absolutely."

I let him drive in silence until we pulled up in front of the house, then, "Jack?"

"Hmm?" He cut the engine and looked at me.

"What makes you think she was murdered?"

Chapter Three

Another day, another lunch.

I'd made plans to meet the gang at the SFMOMA cafe. The museum was hosting a retrospective of some photographer from the thirties, and my friend Brenda had been adamant that I go see it with her.

It would probably be like most things Brenda dragged me to. I'd think *yuk* in advance and then love it when I got there. One of these days I'll wise up and start trusting her.

I found her staking out a tiny metal table and chairs in the crowded restaurant. She was wearing a full skirt, drapey sweater, and shoes that looked like they were designed for maximum comfort by some practical Nordic walking enthusiast.

"How come you get to play on a school day?" I greeted her.

As a professor of Women's Studies at an elite East Bay college, Brenda's time was more flexible than most people who have real—meaning non-theatrical—jobs, but a free weekday afternoon was something rare even for her.

"Isn't it great?" She put her bag down on an unoccupied chair just as a heavily badged refugee from some Moscone Center conference was about to snatch it. "I only teach morning classes this semester, so I'm free in the afternoons. Well, technically I'm supposed to be working on a paper for the journal, but—" She made a face. "How are you?"

I made a face back at her.

Brenda saw our friend Eileen at the door and waved her over. Eileen wove through the noisy cafe purposefully, speaking sharply into a cell phone and wearing a suit that cut a fine line between dominatrix and librarian.

"I wouldn't like to be on the receiving end of that call," Brenda murmured.

Eileen snapped the phone shut, tossed it into her bag, and muttered, "When will these people learn I'm always right?" before giving Brenda a quick hug.

My turn next. She pulled me sharply towards her, then released me with a slight shove. Eileen's signs of affection could sometimes leave bruises. "I mean, what is it with my clients? They want me to manage their money and then they get mad when I tell them they can't spend it."

As one of her clients—she'd been my financial manager for years—I wondered if I should be insulted.

"I'll trade you an annoying client for a dictatorial dean any day." Brenda was currently embroiled in a ferocious battle over some minor point of academia that eluded my intellectual grasp. But I was sure if I understood it, I'd be on her side.

I was just sitting down when I heard a loud, prolonged sigh, followed by the words "Good God I'm bored" drawled from somewhere behind me.

I turned. "If it isn't the Thin White Duke."

Simon Bannister, the Artistic Director of the Rep.

"Hi, Simon," Brenda and Eileen greeted him.

As the end of the season had approached, Simon had taken to moping around town and perfecting those long, pitiful sighs. He was normally up for anything—or anyone, describing himself as "omni-sexual"—but lately he'd assumed the part of a world-weary British expatriate, circa 1938, complete with unseasonable white linen suits.

The look worked well with his lean frame, blue eyes, high cheekbones, and floppy blond hair, but I was finding it all a bit, well, *theatrical.*

"I didn't know you were joining us," I said.

He waved dismissively and dropped into the fourth chair at the table. "Nothing else to do, darling. I'm absolutely stupefied with boredom."

He saw the looks on our faces and amended this statement. "Not that it isn't enchanting, as always, to be with you three charming—"

"Yeah, yeah, yeah." Eileen held up her hand to cut him off. "It's a love fest. What are we eating?"

"I knew you'd be crunched for time so I ordered salads and goat cheese tarts all around," Brenda said. "We're number 265."

I looked at Simon. "Sweetie, listening for our number will give you something to do—after you go get us all some iced tea."

He looked at me darkly. "This is what my vacation has come to." But he got up to fight his way through the crowd to get us the drinks.

"What's his problem?" Eileen asked.

"Since he bought the loft, he doesn't have any money to go away for a break," I explained. "He's feeling sorry for himself."

Simon had done what every San Franciscan dreams of by hugely overextending himself to get into the housing market. He'd bought a trendy faux-industrial loft near the ball park and had been deliriously happy until the arrival of his first mortgage statement.

I felt a little guilty, as I always do when my friends have financial woes, because I have more money than I could spend in several lifetimes, and all I did to get it was have the right set of parents. But Simon had refused my offer to fund his vacation with a simple "Not the done thing, darling," so now I figured he was moaning more out of habit than anything else.

I knew Simon's window of opportunity for getting away from the Rep was the same as mine. We would both have to be deep into the process of planning the next season by late March, and no matter what we did until then, we'd have to squeeze in reading and evaluating countless plays in hopes of finding the perfect companion piece to the three works we'd already chosen.

When Simon drifted back to the table Brenda looked at him sympathetically. "Don't worry, Simon. You'll be happy you bought a place when tax time comes."

"That's what everyone says," he answered. "But now I'm bound by poverty to stick around for the rainy season and I'm simply gagging to get away somewhere and get a tan."

"Grow up," Eileen said briskly. "You're an idiot if you want to trade a sound investment in on a couple of sun-drenched weeks in Maui."

Simon apparently only heard one word.

"Maui," he moaned.

"Oh, stop it," I told him. "You've only been on vacation five days. You can't be that sick of it yet."

"Darlings, I tell you I'm positively dripping with *ennui*."

We did the only reasonable thing and ignored him.

I turned to Eileen. "Speaking of vacations, how was your trip with Anthony?" Anthony was Eileen's ten-year-old son, the sole happy product of the third in a string of four disastrous marriages.

"About how you'd expect a week in Telluride with a pre-teen sports fanatic to be."

"Wasn't it winter there?" Simon was clearly appalled. "I mean, the real kind? With snow?"

Eileen grimaced. "His latest passion is snowboarding."

"You actually took the child across state lines so you could both freeze to death?" Simon demanded. "That's obscene."

"Not obscene, just very, very cold." Eileen looked at the scandalized Englishman to her left. "I know you won't believe it, Simon, but I had a great time. The only problem is that getting away made me realize what a rut I'm in. I think I'm just about as bored as you are these days. I'm so sick of my clients—"

"Thanks," I said.

"Except for you, Charley." She patted my hand absently.

Gee, swell.

"Maybe it's just post-holiday letdown." But she didn't look convinced.

Brenda spoke up. "Well, whatever is going around, I've got it too. You won't believe what I've just signed on to do in the spring."

We heard our number called. "Don't say one word about it until I'm back with the food," Simon ordered. "I can only afford to live vicariously these days." He delivered a pitiful gaze and went off to the counter.

I looked at Eileen. "How can you be bored? You're never bored. Haven't you got your usual fifteen balls in the air? Aren't you still the poster girl for Women Who Have It All? Don't you still work out every day to keep your size-four figure despite taking advanced pastry classes at the Culinary Institute?"

"In the spare time you have after structuring multi-billion dollar deals during the day and coaching Anthony's soccer team in the evenings?" Brenda finished for me.

"And his science club, and his computer group, and let's not forget—"

"Oh, shut up, the two of you," Eileen said. And then she did something I've never seen her do before. She stared into empty space and sighed.

Brenda and I exchanged looks of amazement.

"Do you know," Eileen confessed, "I got an order from Amazon three days ago and I just dumped all the books out onto the coffee table and left them there."

"Oh, sweetie, that's not good." Of course, for anyone else on the planet it would be perfectly normal. But Eileen is a woman who takes organization to an extreme. Her spice rack should be studied by graduates in library science. For books to go unsorted and unshelved in her home was unthinkable. "What's the matter?"

Brenda, far more astute than I will ever be, asked, "Who's the guy?"

Eileen was just sighing again as Simon returned with two enormous trays of dishes. He thumped them on the table. "What did I miss? I always miss the good stuff!"

"I think we're just getting to the good stuff." I reached for a pizza-like cheesy thing.

"It's nothing," Eileen said. Then, looking at Brenda, "There's no one. I haven't even had a respectable crush on anyone in ages." She passed around salads loaded with pear slices and bits of glazed walnuts. "I can't even talk about it. I'll fall asleep in mid-sentence. That's how boring my life is."

"Fine," Simon said, his mouth full of baby greens. "Brenda, what horrible thing have you agreed to do?"

Simon is not exactly what you'd call a sympathetic listener.

Brenda grimaced. "I'm taking nine students to five countries for three weeks."

"Yikes!"

"By yourself?"

"When? Where?"

Eileen broke through our babble with the most obvious question. "Why?"

Brenda chewed thoughtfully. "One answer is that the Comparative Lit professor who was supposed to take them has chronic fatigue syndrome and won't be able to go. So they were looking for volunteers…" She shrugged.

"Good for you!" Eileen proclaimed. "*Carpe* whatever. Life's too short. I mean, I saw something in the paper today about this woman who went for a midnight workout and ended up falling down and bleeding to death in a steam room. Can you imagine? You never know when—what's the matter with you?"

I was choking on my salad. "It was in the paper?"

"Don't tell me you know her?" Eileen asked.

"Darling, have you stumbled across another body?" Animation sparked Simon's features for the first time in days.

"Charley, you didn't!" Brenda scolded. As if it would have been my fault.

"I didn't," I agreed. "But I did have lunch with her boyfriend yesterday."

That added some drama to the conversation. I quickly told them about meeting Morgan Stokes the day before and what he'd had to say about the death of his intended.

"Are you going to investigate?" Simon had rediscovered the use of his spinal column and was perched on the edge of his seat. "What does Jack think?"

"He didn't tell Morgan, but he does think there's something funny about the whole accidental-slip scenario."

"Funny how?" Eileen demanded.

"Was she killed?" Brenda asked.

"I don't know," I admitted. "But Jack belongs to the same gym and he says the tiles on the steam room floor—at least on the men's side—are non-skid. And," I raised my eyebrows significantly, "the bench thing you sit on hasn't got any sharp edges."

"So she was murdered!" Simon said, delighted. "Darling, what are we going to do first? Should we—"

"Hold on a minute." I cut him off. "Jack hasn't even looked into it yet. Who knows? It could be—"

"It could be fun!" Simon insisted. "You're the one who got to do all the shooting and everything the last time—I want in on the action!"

"It isn't a game, Simon," Brenda said. "A woman is dead. Have a little…" She saw the vague puzzlement in his eyes and gave up.

"She was going to marry Morgan Stokes?" Eileen asked. "What did he tell you about her? What was her name?"

"Clara," I told her. "Clara Chen."

Brenda froze, her fork halfway to her mouth. "Clara Chen?" The color drained from her face. "Was she our age? Did she go to Berkeley?"

"I don't know," I said. "Probably. Morgan's in his mid-thirties so she was probably… Sweetie, what is it?"

"I think I knew her," Brenda said, dazed. "I knew her at Berkeley."

Chapter Four

I came home bursting to tell Jack about Brenda's connection to the murdered woman. But, when I found him in the kitchen surrounded by three cardboard boxes filled with pots, pans, gigantic spoons, and a variety of miscellaneous steel objects that I wouldn't be able to identify if my life depended on it, I admit I got distracted.

"You just missed Gordon," he greeted me. "He brought us some equipment."

I picked up a metal thing with a large handle and a mysterious purpose. "For what? Beating off intruders?"

Jack grinned and started opening cabinets. "That's a potato ricer."

I stared at it. "Does it make potatoes or rice?"

"It makes mashed potatoes. You like mashed potatoes, don't you? Won't it be nice to have them whenever we want?"

I've always had mashed potatoes whenever I want, and I've never had to resort to using medieval torture devices. "Why isn't it called a potato masher?"

Jack plucked another implement out of a box. "This is a potato masher."

I blinked. "Okay. Never mind. Where did Gordon get all this stuff?"

Jack was opening empty drawers and pantomiming movements from drawer to sink, then from cabinet to stove and back, seeming to find meaning in it all. The kitchen was large and filled with light. The cabinets were painted creamy white, with shiny black marble countertops, and appliances glistening in brushed steel. It was all perfectly lovely and I saw no need to clutter it up with cooking paraphernalia. I hovered by the large center "prep" island to stay out of my husband's way.

"Some of them are Gordon's castoffs," he told me. "Now that he's got the restaurant, he's going through everything he's picked up over the years and weeding out what he doesn't need anymore."

"Uh huh." There was a certain fascination in watching Jack. He always moved quickly, and seemingly effortlessly. I realized his pantomime act was an attempt to figure out the place for each object that would allow him the greatest economy of movement while he worked in the kitchen. "So it was all Gordon's?"

Jack flashed me a grin. "Maybe some of it was Harry's."

"We're setting up house with my uncle's purloined kitchen-ware?"

"Do you mind?"

"Hell no. Why didn't Gordon raid the liquor cabinet while he was there?"

"I asked him the same question about the wine cellar." Jack turned, and before I knew it he'd swept me off my feet and plopped me down on the island countertop. He pinned me there, with one hand on either side of me, leaning in close. "How was lunch?"

"Oh!" I pushed him away and remembered why I'd rushed home. "You'll never believe me! Brenda knew Clara Chen!"

"What?" Jack's playful mood vanished instantly.

"She went to Berkeley at the same time as Brenda," I told him. "Clara was taking classes in Computer Science and Business, of course, and Brenda didn't know many geeks, but they were in a couple of political action groups together and got to be pretty good friends. Assuming it's the same Clara Chen."

Jack nodded and moved away to lean on the counter opposite me. "Stokes emailed her bio today. She graduated from Berkeley thirteen years ago."

Jack's confirmation that it was really Brenda's former school-mate who had died two nights ago was almost unnecessary.

From Brenda's description of the bright, driven young woman she'd known, I'd had little doubt that her Clara had gone on to become a Vice President at Zakdan.

"Brenda said she was a major academic star. Brilliant. She tried to talk Clara into doing grad work in law or the humanities, but Clara was set on a technology track."

"It paid off for her," Jack said. "She worked at two other companies before coming to Zakdan. Even in the worst times of the high-tech crash she seems to have been a hot commodity, heavily recruited by other firms."

"Do you think someone was trying to steal her away from Zakdan?"

"She'd gotten offers, Stokes was sure of that. But she never showed any interest in them. She was already a VP at Zakdan, and Stokes was about to promote her again, to Executive Vice President. He was also going to give her fifty percent of his shares of the company when they got married."

"I'm guessing that's a lot of shares."

"I checked the stock price. As of today, they'd be worth about three hundred and forty million dollars."

"Yikes. And he was just going to give them to her?"

"He said he wanted them to be full partners in everything they did."

I thought about the devastated man we'd met just the day before. "How's he doing?"

Jack paused. "About how you'd expect."

"Jack." I had to approach the next topic carefully. "Had he told people about his plans to promote Clara, or about the stock?"

I looked up to find Jack regarding me with an unreadable face. "Why?"

I was utterly nonchalant, picking up a spoon from the box next to me. "I just wondered."

"You mean you wondered if anyone had a motive for killing her."

Ah ha! "So you do think she was killed!"

Jack frowned. "Charley, we're not getting involved."

"We already are involved."

"Okay, then we're not getting more involved. We're not detectives and we're not going to—"

"Who did he tell?"

"Charley!"

"Oh, come on, I'm not going to do anything about it. But I know he told you who else knew about the promotion and the stock." I waited expectantly.

Jack blew his breath out in exasperation. "Then can we drop it?"

"Of course." I used my most reasonable voice.

"He only told the Chief Technology Officer, Lalit Kumar, and the Executive VP of Engineering, a guy named Jim Stoddard."

"Lalit Kumar and Jim Stoddard," I repeated. "What are their stories?"

"They have no stories," Jack said firmly. "There are no stories, and there are no reasons for us to talk about this. It's none of our business."

"Right," I said. "You're right. Let's leave it up to the police." I removed all expression from my face. "What are you making for dinner?" Something with a side of mashed potatoes, no doubt.

I ignored the way he was looking at me and gave my husband a bright, trustworthy smile. Then I left him to make some calls.

"I'm so glad you called!" Brenda was on my doorstep at noon on Monday. "I mean, I was so upset about Clara after we talked on Friday, but I didn't know what to do with that energy—it was so good to have something constructive to focus on."

She came into the foyer lugging a satchel bulging with papers, her oversized coat swirling around her shoulders and her long straight hair sliding out of its clip. "I found out so much—" She stopped suddenly and looked around.

"Charley, you don't have any furniture."

"I know." I grabbed my purse from its place on the floor.

"No, but I mean…" She looked through the arched doorway to the large living room, then backtracked across the entrance hall to open the doors to what would eventually be a library and a dining room. "Charley, I knew you hadn't *decorated*, but I thought you'd have something—there's not a stick of furniture in here!"

"We have a bed," I told her.

"But it's been *weeks!*" She turned around, as if expecting to see a set of leather club chairs materialize. "Where do you live?"

"We have a bed," I said firmly. "Now come on. We're going to be late."

Brenda stopped squinting into empty rooms. "Oh! Right!" She suddenly seemed to notice that I was standing at the door, coat buttoned and bag in hand. "Where are we meeting Eileen?"

"At her office."

"I thought you hated going to her office." She stepped outside, and I closed the door behind us.

"I do. But desperate times call for a trip to the financial district."

◇◇◇

Brenda spent the trip downtown trying to get at the deep underlying psychological issues that might explain why I hadn't bought a sofa yet. Which was my own fault—I thought we should wait until we were at Eileen's office to talk about Clara Chen's death.

"Finally!" Eileen jumped to her feet as her assistant ushered us into her office. "What took you so long?"

"Don't ask." The last thing I needed was for them to tag team me on my supposed ambivalence toward putting down roots. We needed to focus on serious matters. "How much time have we got?"

Eileen checked her slim wristwatch. "My calendar is clear until three. Come on, I've set things up at the conference table."

Eileen's office was huge, with sleek minimal furniture and acres of uncluttered space. The conference table was positioned in front of a floor-to-ceiling window offering a calculated-to-impress-clients view of the Transamerica pyramid and a bit of the Bay Bridge beyond it. I knew Eileen was important at her firm, but the view spoke volumes about how important.

It was all very nice, but something about the crisp efficiency of everyone we'd passed on the way from the elevators, and the tidy stacks of manila folders on every flat surface, and the general buzz of purposeful dialogue made me feel as though I might break out in some sort of rash. Places of business usually affect me that way.

There were four neat stacks of color-coded folders on the conference table, aligned in perfect symmetry. Brenda plonked her overflowing satchel down in the middle of them. "Okay." She looked at us.

"Okay," Eileen said.

"Okay," I agreed. "Now, what have we been able to find out about Zakdan?"

Chapter Five

Eileen is a financial genius. She has one of those brilliant heads for business that land people on the covers of magazines that are too tedious to even think of reading. So I had every expectation that she'd be able to come up with a detailed analysis of the financial position of Morgan Stokes' company with one hand tied behind her back.

But I never thought Brenda would turn out to be an investigative mastermind. I'd suggested that she log some internet time over the weekend, reading up on Zakdan, the Chief Technology guy Lalit Kumar, and Jim Stoddard, the other executive that Jack had mentioned—as well as Morgan Stokes himself and anyone else whose name came up along the way. I hadn't expected her to compile an encyclopedia.

She pulled a three-inch stack of papers, bound with a giant black clip, out of her bottomless satchel. "Do you guys know why it's called Zakdan?"

I shook my head.

She grinned, stuffing everything but the stack of papers back into her bag and slinging that onto one of the buttery leather chairs that lined both sides of the table. "In the late eighties, two guys from the Computer Science department at Brown started fooling around with an idea for a programming toolkit to help engineers build graphical applications for the PC more easily." She saw my blank look and waved her hand. "It doesn't matter what they did. The point is, their names were Zak Bridges and Dan Maceri."

"Zak and Dan?" Eileen's eyebrows went up.

Brenda's grin got wider. "You got it."

I pulled her pile of papers toward me. "This is all about Zakdan? And you got it all in one weekend? Do you keep a team of hackers working for you in a basement somewhere?"

Her eyes flashed. "This isn't even half of what I found. Everything is online these days. And—while from a civil-liberties point of view I'm shocked and appalled by the amount of personal information that you can find on just about everyone—a good search engine sure makes investigating someone easy."

Wow. Duly noting her moral compunction, Eileen and I stared at her. "Do we have to read all this," I asked, "or are you going to give us the good stuff?"

First she gave us the dull stuff. Apparently Zak and Dan had been awfully successful with their initial set of tools—which as near as I could tell were bits of computer programs—and had bundled them into a hugely popular product.

"I've never heard of it," I said. "How can it be hugely popular?"

Eileen almost refrained from rolling her eyes and suggested that the Zakdan offerings were probably more well-known among people who'd majored in subjects other than English Literature.

Brenda continued.

The next Zakdan goldmine had involved games. They developed another set of tools that made it a lot easier to program computer games. Apparently just about every blood-splattering, engine-revving, demon-hunting game on the market had bits of Zakdan technology at its core.

Then they turned their attention to the emerging needs of web-site developers. Since this was right about the time when everyone and his brother had decided to get a web site, they'd made another fortune. That's when the two had gone their separate ways, taking their separate millions.

"They got out just before the whole internet bubble burst," Eileen marveled. "They couldn't have timed it better if they'd popped the thing themselves."

"Are you sure they didn't?" I asked. "It sounds like they were smart enough to."

"Charley, the high-tech crash was precipitated by a variety of economic and market—"

"Stop!" I held up my hands. "Please—not Internet Economics 101." I turned to Brenda. "Just tell me what happened to Zakdan next."

Eileen's sigh indicated I was turning my back on a priceless learning opportunity, but she nodded to Brenda.

"That's when Morgan Stokes was named CEO," she told us. "He had a fairly rough time at first, because the bottom was dropping out of the market and a lot of the most senior people left when the founders took off. But in a way he was lucky, because with every other firm in the business having massive layoffs, he was able to hire in some of the best talent as they became available."

"Like Clara Chen," I said.

"Yes." She paused for a moment, as we remembered the reason we were interested in all of this.

Brenda cleared her throat. "A few of the old guard stayed on. Some of them are still there. But most of the exec staff joined at about that time."

"And what are they all doing for their millions now?" I asked.

"Moving beyond the PC," she told me. As if I knew what that meant. "The same ideas they brought to web development, they're now bringing to platform development for devices."

I swallowed. "Can we try that again in English?"

"Cell phones. Digital cameras. Digital music players. All the portable devices that people use to communicate and share data."

"Like my Palm thingy." At least I'm not totally out of the technogear loop, thanks to a gift from my husband.

She nodded. "Exactly. Zakdan makes a development platform that lets other programmers build applications on a huge variety of devices. And not just toys. They work on handhelds that doctors use for patient data, and major companies use to manage inventory. It's fascinating, really."

"Uh huh." Fascinating in a way that made my brain hurt. I looked at them. "What else have we got?"

"No dirt on my end," Eileen said regretfully. "I looked into every aspect of their financial outlook over the past four years and there's nothing. They're healthy, and seem to be well-run. They got into trouble with the IRS a while ago for using temporary workers in full-time jobs, but a lot of companies do that. You pay the fine and deal with it." She ran her hands across the color-coded folders. "I have their tax filings, their earnings statements, their annual reports, and transcripts of their analyst calls if you want to go over them."

Not with a ten-foot pole. "Never mind," I said. "If you say they're in good shape, they're in good shape."

She shrugged. "As far as I can tell."

Brenda spoke up. "I couldn't find anything suspicious about any of the people involved there either." Disappointment was clear in the little vertical line between her eyes. She pushed her glasses up. "Morgan seems like a great guy. He gives a lot to charity—I mean, not on the scale you do, Charley, but—"

I waved my hand for her to go on.

"He went to Brown, and he's endowed a scholarship there in the Computer Science department. He bought a beautiful house for his mom outside of Philadelphia, and he's sending a nephew to college. He seems genuinely nice, and of course we know he's brilliant. Clara probably would have been happy with him." She looked up at us. "It's so sad."

Eileen reached for Brenda's printout. "What about anyone else at Zakdan? Could she have made any enemies?"

"I don't know. We'd need access to their personnel files to know if she'd fired anyone or anything like that. Oh!" Her eyes brightened. "I did get one whiff of scandal. That guy you told me to look up—Jim Stoddard?"

I nodded. "The other executive vice president."

"Right. He's had a couple of DUIs in the past few years. That might be something."

"I'd be happier if he had a meth lab in his attic," Eileen said. "Or a prostitution ring running out of his garage. Something good and juicy."

We looked at each other. We had nothing juicy. We had nothing.

◇◇◇

When Brenda dropped me in front of the house—too depressed at our lack of progress to even come in and talk about my lack of furniture—I saw someone had left a package on the front steps. On closer inspection, it wasn't a package. It was a stack. A stack of plays. At least fifteen of them.

I struggled to unlock the door and slide them across the threshold while dialing Simon on my cell phone.

"What the hell is this?"

"Hello to you too, darling," he answered. "What the hell is what?"

The stack toppled over and the manuscripts slid into an untidy pile on my walnut inlaid floor. Or was it maple? I'm sure the realtor had told me, but who could keep track? "This stack of plays that were waiting on my doorstep. Didn't you leave them?"

"Ah. No, that would have been Chip."

Oh. Chip. That made sense. Ever since I'd let him start directing plays at the Rep, the workaholic Chip had become even more obsessive than he'd been as our stage manager. He was a great guy, but he really needed to get a life outside the theater.

"That boy needs to get laid," Simon said.

"I was just thinking something similar myself."

"Do you know he's going through our entire slush pile? Been at it ever since closing night. It's unnatural."

"What do you mean, our entire slush pile?"

"Just what I said, darling. Everything."

Ever since our first season, aspiring playwrights had been sending their unsolicited masterpieces for our consideration. Since we only mounted an average of four productions per season—and most of them classics—the odds were not in their favor. We'd rejected hundreds, usually not even giving them a brief glance before tossing them into overflowing boxes in a corner of an office. The slush pile.

Simon was still talking. "...says you said something about wanting to work with new a playwright next season. Throw over the classics for something a bit more—are you listening to me?"

"Of course, sweetie." As much as I needed to. "So he's narrowed the slush pile down to this?"

Simon produced a particularly elegant snort. "He's barely scratched the surface. But he wants us to read these, and meet on Friday and tell him what we think. Mind you, I could tell him—"

"Never mind, Simon," I cut him off. "We might as well. It doesn't look like either of us is going to make it out of town for a real vacation, so we might as well get a jump on next season."

He paused. "I hate it when you're right."

"In this case, Chip's right. Talk to you later."

I'd re-stacked the manuscripts while talking to Simon, and now I picked them up and looked around the empty entrance hall, thinking that a table of some sort might be a very handy thing near the door.

I decided to take the stack upstairs to the room I planned to use as my office. There were no handy tables there, either, so I dropped the manuscripts in a corner and looked around, hoping a brilliant idea for the perfectly designed home office would magically appear. No such luck.

Leaving, I glanced across the hall to the room Jack had chosen for his own office and froze. When had he had time to buy furniture?

I went in. He'd set up a desk, where a computer was humming away happily. He'd also gotten a very high-tech looking chair.

These were angled in front of the window to let the light fall on the desk without getting any glare on the computer screen. A variety of moving boxes were scattered around, mixed in with piles of books and other work-related odds and ends.

Jack's partner, Mike, had started their company in a rented space down in Palo Alto, but it looked like Jack already had a fully functional satellite branch of MJC on the second floor of our house.

I went to his desk in disbelief. Not only was he set up, it looked like he was working on something. There were papers and files on the desk, pens scattered around, and little notes on little notepapers.

It took me a minute to realize what I was looking at, probably because I was so stunned to be looking at anything at all. But when I did recognize it, there was no way I wasn't going to read it.

Jack had Clara Chen's autopsy report.

Chapter Six

My self-restraint was incredible. Not that I'd shown any hesitation in tearing through the folder to find the results of Clara Chen's autopsy. That had been a given. No, where I showed restraint was in not bringing up the subject with my husband.

At least, not right away.

He came home to find me lounging innocently on our bed, reading a bad play set largely in the back room of a stripper bar. Jack called out something or other and vanished into the closet, only to emerge thirty seconds later looking crisp and put together in a clean white shirt and black jeans.

"Charley, are you about ready?" He rolled up his sleeves and turned his head to see the title of the script. "*Pole Dancer Diaries*? I hope you're doing research for next season and not looking for a new hobby. Although—"

"Chip sent a stack of plays over," I informed him, ignoring the speculative look in his eye. "Am I about ready for what?"

"It's Monday, remember? Dinner at Harry's?"

Damn. I'd totally forgotten we'd agreed to go visit my uncle.

Jack must have seen a look on my face, because he sat on the bed and plucked the pages from my hands. "It won't be that bad. Besides, we haven't seen him in a while and I think we've both learned it's best to know what he's up to."

True. My uncle, a semi-reformed madman who'd misspent his youth quite vigorously, had settled into his middle years reluctantly, trading in doobies for Cubans, and tequila shots drunk from the navels of beach bunnies for…well, I hoped he'd traded them in.

When my parents died just after my fourteenth birthday, Harry had become my guardian. Back in those days, Harry ran his house as something of a cross between the Playboy mansion and a militia encampment. Perhaps not the best atmosphere for an adolescent getting over the worst trauma of her life, but neither Harry nor I had had a choice.

Harry had taken the term "guardian" to appalling extremes. I was sent to high-security private schools and camps, and I was never without a bodyguard or—when I rebelled against that—private detectives tasked with keeping tabs on me and reporting everything I did back to Harry.

There had been years filled with suspicion and mistrust. And although Harry had mellowed considerably in recent times, particularly since Jack had come along, I didn't wholly believe my uncle's fundamental nature had changed.

He was usually up to something, and since that something was fueled by a dangerous combination of energy and paranoia, it was best to keep tabs.

"Oh, all right." I realized thoughts of Harry had momentarily distracted me from my mission for the evening—finding out how Jack had gotten that autopsy report. "Just let me jump in the shower first."

"Fine." Jack leaned back against the headboard and crossed his legs at the ankles. "I'd say I'd wait for you downstairs, but since there's nothing to sit on—"

"Then my plan is working," I said, throwing him my best sultry over-the-shoulder look. "If there's no other furniture, I can keep you in bed all the time."

"You are an evil genius," he admitted.

When I got out of the shower, I wrapped myself in a towel to make my way across the room to the closet. Jack's eyes were closed. He looked completely innocent. Not in the least like a man who'd tell his wife he wasn't interested in a murder and then promptly go out and lay his hands on a coroner's report.

I scanned my wardrobe for an outfit that would put Jack in a talkative mood. Something that would reduce him to putty in my hands.

And I learned something: A thirtysomething woman whose highlights are in need of a touch-up and who hasn't been to the gym in quite some time should not stand in front of a full-length mirror in her undies when she's plotting a seduction. Even if the undies are La Perla.

To hell with it. I'd get the information out of him the old fashioned way—by tricking him. I threw on a pair of jeans and a cashmere hoodie before fleeing the closet.

Jack was sitting on the edge of the bed, rubbing his face.

"Long day, sweetie?" I sat beside him to pull on a pair of Jimmy Choo boots that I hoped would give my thrown-together outfit the illusion of style.

"Very long." He turned to me. "You look great."

I wasn't even wearing makeup. How could I not be crazy about this man? Still… "Did Yahata have much to say?"

"Not really—"

"Ah ha!" I leapt to my feet, which was a tactical error given that I only had one boot on, but I persevered. "You *did* see Inspector Yahata today!"

I'd trapped him into an admission, and I was flush with victory.

He held out his arm to steady my balance. "Of course I did. Who do you think gave me Clara Chen's autopsy report?"

Oh.

◇◇◇

"Jack, don't you even try to tell me that you were going to tell me about having that report!" We were in the car, heading for Harry's, and I was on a roll.

"Of course I was going to tell you. Although I should have known you'd read it before I got back—"

"And that's another thing—how did you know I'd already read it?"

"Because I went to the office before I came upstairs to the bedroom, and I could tell someone had been there." He glanced over at me. "Since I didn't think a burglar would have been interested in an empty house, I assumed it had been you."

"You're not going to distract me with house decorating talk."

"I'm not trying to. I'm just saying I could give you some pointers on rifling someone's desk without leaving tracks."

Which could come in handy someday, but I wasn't going to be distracted by that, either.

"Never mind. Just tell me when you and Inspector Yahata got so cozy. It wasn't so long ago he was warning me that you might be a murderer."

Our first encounter with the unnervingly observant representative of San Francisco's finest had been shortly after finding a body in our hotel room, so I really didn't hold it against him that he'd been suspicious about Jack's mysterious past. What I couldn't forgive is that whatever Yahata had learned about my husband—which had been enough to make him suddenly bend police procedure to include Jack in an ongoing investigation—still remained a mystery to me.

"I hardly think 'cozy' is the word to describe anything about Inspector Yahata," Jack said dryly.

True. The detective had the ability to send an electric shock through a room merely by glancing around it. Cozy he was not.

"Well, whatever. Why did he give you Clara Chen's autopsy report?"

"Because I asked for it." Jack took the Broadway exit off Highway 101, turning toward the rarified zip code of Hillsborough, where Harry lived in high style and near-seclusion.

"Seriously? He isn't asking you to look into it?"

"Pumpkin, why would a homicide detective ask a private citizen to look into anything? And beyond that, didn't you read the report? There's nothing to look into."

"That's what they say," I sniffed.

"'They' meaning the medical examiner's office and the police force? The skilled professionals who concluded that Clara Chen's death was accidental?"

"Well." I shifted in my seat. "Yes. But did you tell Yahata about everything Morgan Stokes told us? About how she was an athlete and wouldn't have fallen like that? About how she was in line to get a major chunk of power at Zakdan?"

"Charley." Jack came to a stop at a red light on El Camino. He turned to face me. "Morgan Stokes is a grieving man. Of course he doesn't want to believe these kinds of things can just happen. But they do. You know they do."

He was right. I knew all about accidents. Like the one that had taken my parents and left me in the care of my lunatic uncle.

I blinked. "Jack, seriously. Do you believe it was an accident?"

He looked at the stoplight. "I believe there's no proof it was anything else."

We drove the rest of the way in silence.

Harry's rambling pile of stucco and tile looked even bigger than usual in the cold January night. I'd been coming there for twenty years, but I could still swear I heard the guitar solo to "Hotel California" whenever I saw the place by moonlight.

Only a few of the windows were lit in the front of the house, and Harry hadn't put a light on over the massive oak doors.

I shivered. "It's spooky out tonight." The surrounding eucalyptus trees were whipping in a suddenly strong wind.

"Don't worry, this neighborhood is way too expensive for anything really scary."

Jack rang the bell and I considered telling him about the time I'd accidentally walked in on Harry, three cheerleaders for the 49ers, and chimpanzee named Sam. Now that had been scary.

When there was no answer, I dug around in my bag for my keys. I unlocked the door calling my uncle's name.

We entered the great room, which, without Harry in it, seemed even larger than usual. It stretched the length of the house, with comfortable clusters of Mission style furniture arranged in groups across the wide expanse of plank floor.

"Harry!" Jack called. He moved forward to turn on a light. The room was dim, amber-shaded lamps providing only occasional pools of glowing light. It reminded me of a deserted museum you'd see in a horror movie, all quiet right before the monster leaps out.

"Do you think he's all right?" I suddenly felt guilty for not calling Harry more often. He was alone now in his giant house. His only daughter, pushing thirty and still acting out her teenage rebellion, had run off again months ago and hadn't been heard from since. This time Harry—uncharacteristically—hadn't hired private detectives to track her down.

I'd been so busy with the Rep during the season that I hardly ever spared him a thought. He'd been such a source of annoyance for most of my life that it was jarring to think of him all by himself and getting older. And even more jarring to find myself feeling a little sorry for him.

Poor Harry. He must be so lonely. He must be so—

"Well Goddamn! I didn't hear you two come in!"

He crashed through the door from the dining room with a fat cigar in his mouth, wearing khaki cargo shorts and a loud tropical shirt. He held up two large bags of what looked like take-out Chinese food. "Great! Perfect timing! The dumplings are hot and I hope you're hungry!"

"Hi, Harry," I managed to say before he'd deposited the food on a coffee table and crushed me in lung-squeezing hug.

"Charley, you've lost weight!" Which is what he always says. "And Jack! Good to see you, boy!" He stopped short of hugging my husband. Instead they engaged in a vigorously male handshake.

"Harry, you're looking—"

"The same," he cut off whatever Jack had been planning to say. "I never change. Don't tell me anything different or I'll start to feel old. And what's the percentage in that, right?" He winked broadly and moved to the bar, an enormous carved structure that had once been the altar of an earthquake-damaged church.

"What are we drinking? I've got duck with plum sauce, crab stir-fried in garlic and white wine, that shrimp with black bean sauce that I know you like—" Another wink was aimed in my general direction. "—Two kinds of noodles and every appetizer on the menu." He held up a bottle of rum. "What do you say we make a batch of mai tai's?"

Okay, so much for feeling sorry for him.

Harry was right. He never changed.

Chapter Seven

Jack lit a fire in the oversized stone hearth while Harry mixed drinks and kept up a non-stop monologue. I went off in search of plates during his description of the very tasty shredded snake meat soup he'd had on his last trip to Shanghai, pausing at the door to tell him no, I didn't think we should lobby to get it included on the menu at King Yuan.

I returned to find my husband and my uncle sitting in front of the fire, drinks in hand, chatting amiably. It was a tableau that never failed to amaze. I'd been completely prepared for these men to hate each other on sight when I'd brought Jack home after our wedding. The fact that they got along—even seemed to understand each other on some level—was a little unsettling. It implied I didn't know one of them as well as I thought I did.

"Tell me we're not still talking about snake soup." I set the stack of dishes, napkins, and serving spoons on the low table between them, nudging aside the steaming cartons of food they'd taken out of the bags.

"No." Jack handed me a mai tai—complete with little paper umbrella. "Harry was telling me why he didn't hear us at the door."

Harry smiled broadly and raised his glass. "I was working. And whenever I'm working I have the delivery guy come to the back door. So he doesn't interrupt my work. Usually I keep working while I eat, but this is a special occasion." He rattled his ice cubes.

From the number of times he'd used the word "working" in that explanation, I gathered I was required to inquire, "What are you working on?"

"I thought you'd never ask." He set his glass down and put up his hands, palms out, in a "just visualize this" gesture.

"I'm writing a play."

Oh, my God.

"…I mean, I saw all of your plays last season, and I just thought 'Goddamn! I could do that! I have some stories to tell!'"

I realized Harry was still talking. I must have gone into some sort of dissociative fugue state for a moment.

He was giving Jack one of his trademark winks. "You'd better believe I have some stories to tell."

"I have no doubt," Jack said evenly. I looked at him. Only the slightest twinkle in his eye betrayed how very amusing he was finding this conversation. That twinkle would cost him later.

"…so I've got all that figured out." Harry was looking at me, glowing with excitement.

"All what?" I asked, still dazed.

"The plot!" he exclaimed, reaching for a carton and digging in to the noodles it contained. He passed it to me. "Eat something—you've got no color in your face."

I blinked several times, fast. "Harry, you can't just write a play. I mean you can't just pick up a pencil one day and decide—"

"I bought a laptop," he announced, tearing the wrapper off a pair of wooden chopsticks. "I even got this program that takes care of the formatting and everything."

I looked to Jack for backup. He shrugged. "Well, Pumpkin, if the man bought a laptop…"

I considered impaling them both with chopsticks, but decided the ones that had come with the takeout weren't sharp enough. I turned back to my uncle.

"Harry, have you ever even read a play?"

"Well, sure." He found the carton with the crab in it and inhaled deeply, a look of pure joy on his face. "Ah, crab season.

My favorite time of year. Jack, you've got to try this." Then he returned to my question. "I mean, they made us read all kinds of Shakespeare and shit when I was in school."

Shakespeare and shit. Lovely. I was about to launch into a minor rant when the next thing he said stopped me short.

"Of course, I understand there's probably lots of technical stuff I don't know. So I think the best thing to do is get a collaborator."

I froze. "A collaborator?"

"Yeah, you know, like Rogers and Hammerstein."

"If there's a God," I said carefully, "you'll tell me you're not writing a musical."

"No, no, no." He waved with his chopsticks, sending bits of crab shell flying. "But you know what I mean. Lots of plays were written by more than one person."

Sure. Comden and Green. Kaufman and Hart. But not Harry and anyone. And certainly not Harry and me.

He was still talking. "…just a little help with the language and things."

"Oh," I said acidly. "It will have language?"

He wouldn't be deterred. "So what do you think, Charley? Will she want to?"

She? "She who?"

He sat back and spread his hands. "Brenda, of course."

Oh, hell.

"Okay, Jack. You can cut it out now. I get it. You think this is hilarious." We were halfway back to the city and he hadn't stopped laughing for miles.

"Oh, come on—it's cute," he protested.

"Cute? Nothing Harry has ever done could be considered cute."

"You don't think it's cute that he has a crush on Brenda?"

"Harry doesn't have crushes. He has conquests. And Brenda isn't going to be one of them." It was a fate I wouldn't wish on my worst enemy, let alone my best friend.

"Hey, Charley." Jack's tone softened. "You know there was a little something between them a while ago, and it wasn't just on his side."

I hated it, but he was right. Brenda had stayed at the Hillsborough house with Harry and my cousin during a period of time when it would have been dangerous for her to go home. I'd known she'd gotten to be fond of him. But I'd told myself—rigorously and repeatedly—that's all it was. Just fondness. Like you'd have for your eccentric uncle, assuming he was simply eccentric and not a paranoid delusional nutcase.

"Anyway, it doesn't matter," I said. "Because she's taking a bunch of students to Europe. And by the time she gets back, Harry will probably have moved on to his next whacko idea."

"Um, about that…"

His tone sent little drops of dread sliding down my spine. "What?"

"I mentioned Brenda's trip to Harry. When you were putting the leftovers away."

"Okay…" I braced myself. "And Harry said…"

"That maybe he should change the setting to Paris and tag along with the trip."

This was not good.

◇◇◇

"Brenda, I have to talk to you."

I waited on my end of the line while I heard her make waking-up-and-looking-at-the-clock noises. I'd called her from the bedroom as soon as we'd gotten home. Jack was checking his email before coming up, but I didn't have much time.

"Charley, it's after midnight," she informed me.

"Sorry, it's just that…" It's just that I'm completely freaked out by the thought of you and Harry? That probably wasn't the best approach.

"Charley, what's going on?"

I told her something guaranteed to get her interest.

"I found out the coroner has declared Clara's death an accident."

It became very still on the other end of the line for a moment. Then she spoke. "So what are we going to do about it?"

"What?" I thought I heard Jack on the stairs.

"Charley, we have to do something. What are we going to do?"

Excellent question. I thought fast.

"Are you busy tomorrow night?"

"I have a faculty meeting until six. What's the plan?"

"I think we should go for a late-night workout."

I heard a sharp intake of breath. "Can we do that?"

"Why not? Jack's a member of WorkSpace, and it shouldn't be a crime for us to go check out a gym."

"Oh, but Charley—"

I did hear Jack. "Brenda, I have to go. I'll call you tomorrow."

I hung up the phone and managed to grab a random manuscript from the floor before Jack appeared in the doorway. I flipped the pages nonchalantly.

"Any interesting messages?" I was innocence personified.

He looked at me with a certain wariness. Or maybe that was only my imagination. "Not much. Anything interesting going on up here?"

I widened my eyes. "Here? In the bedroom? Without you? Never."

I think he bought it.

The next morning I found myself leaning out the third-floor window and shouting to the figure below.

"What are you doing here?"

Simon looked up. "Ringing your doorbell, darling. Do you think you might answer it?"

I looked up and down the street. Shouting out windows was probably frowned upon in Pacific Heights, but the last thing I'd expected at nine-thirty on a Tuesday morning was an energetic Englishman on my doorstep. Particularly since this Englishman hadn't shown signs of energy in weeks. I closed the window and hurried down the stairs.

"Good lord, darling, I thought you'd be up and about by now." He pecked me absently on the cheek and pushed past me into the entrance hall. "I mean, if experience is any judge, by the time I'm up the world's up." This was spoken with the certainty of a man at the center of his universe.

"I had a bad night." I wrapped my robe a little more tightly around myself and tried to put the images that had haunted me all night out of my mind. Visions of my uncle pursuing Brenda across Europe, nightmarishly mixed in with visions of women bleeding to death on steam room floors.

Simon snorted. "Don't get me started on the subject of bad nights. Not unless you want to hear about the very charming piano player I met at the Redwood Room last night."

I didn't, which didn't seem to matter.

"Gorgeous, talented, and quite surprisingly athletic," he went on. "But also the victim of some congenital sinus abnormality resulting in snores that could peel the paint off the walls."

"Simon, as interesting as this is…why are you here?" I yawned.

"My God," he said, circling the entrance hall and looking into rooms. To the left of the door was an arched entryway into a large, lovely room. Hardwood floors and a perfectly proportioned fireplace. A series of windows looking into the front yard. "Not a stick of furniture," he marveled. "Brenda was right."

"Brenda!" Now he had my interest. "When did you talk to her? What did she say?" Anything about Harry making a nuisance of himself? Or about our planned expedition to the scene of Clara Chen's death?

"Only that you were either paralyzed by indecision…" He crossed the hallway and looked into the den and dining rooms, much as Brenda had done the day before. "…or exhibiting some sort of denial on a scale hitherto—"

"Oh, come on!" I slammed the dining room door, my relief at Brenda's apparent discretion overpowered by my irritation with her fixation on interior design. "I have no dark psychological issues. I just haven't been shopping yet."

"Exactly." Simon arranged himself on the stairs. "Which is why I'm giving you ten minutes to go put on some clothes—" He squinted at my face. "—and some makeup. Then we're going shopping."

I stared at him. "I can't go shopping!"

"Why not?" He raised his eyebrows eloquently.

"I have things to do!"

"Such as?"

Damn him. The last thing I wanted was Simon insisting he could accompany us to the women's steam room at WorkSpace.

"Such as reading all those plays," I said triumphantly.

"Don't bother. They're all rubbish. I read them yesterday."

"All of them?" That was fast work.

He sighed. "Have you forgotten that my life is as empty as your pathetic parlor? I had all day stretching in front of me." His expression sharpened. "And it's not as though you invited me along on your girls-only detective day at Eileen's office."

Oh. That stopped me. "Brenda told you about that, too?" I sat on the step next to him. Hardwood floors are cold on winter mornings. "I guess you heard we didn't come up with much."

"That's not the point! Charley, I told you if there was going to be any detective stuff I wanted to be in on it."

"It wasn't detective stuff. It was internet research."

"Nevertheless—"

"Simon, I promise you that at the first sign of donning trench coats and skulking down back alleys, I'll call you." Which carried no commitment to tell him about donning towels and skulking around locker rooms. "In the meanwhile…"

"Yes," he said briskly. "In the meanwhile we're going shopping. And you now have exactly eight minutes."

Fine. I wasn't going to meet Brenda until nightfall anyway. If Simon wanted to perform a one-man decorating intervention, I could deal with it—on one condition.

We were going shopping south of Market.

Right near Zakdan, Inc.

Chapter Eight

I returned in triumph. Simon had dragged me through every inch of the San Francisco Design Center. I'd seen oriental rugs and French provincial buffets and classical revival fainting couches and modern urban settees.

And I'd studied the exterior of the Zakdan building from every possible angle. But my husband didn't need to know that yet.

"Jack!" I yelled as I came in. "I've been shopping!"

"I know." He appeared at the top of the stairs. "I got your note. Come on up."

"Jack, I really think I'm getting somewhere. I mean, I looked at a ton of stuff and I really feel like things are coming together." I bounded up the stairs and grabbed his hand, intending to pull him up the next flight to the bedroom.

"That's great, Charley." He pulled me the other direction, and I realized he was heading for his office. "There's something—"

"Jack—how do you feel about shabby chic? It's when you buy really expensive stuff that looks like it's been rotting in a barn for a hundred years, and—"

"Whatever you want, Pumpkin. But first—"

"Or we could go for all clean lines and geometric shapes—think the W hotel—and stay with a neutral palette and dark finishes and uplights..." I'd picked up a lot of lingo on the expedition. "What do you think?"

I stopped him before he got to the door, and leaned against the wall in the most provocative pose I could manage—given that

I still wore last year's quilted Burberry coat and I was carrying the world's heaviest shopping bag. "Wouldn't that be sexy?"

His eyes darkened. "I never really thought about it that way." He moved closer. "But if you say so—"

I nodded. "I say so." He got within necking range, so I dropped the shopping bag and went for it. I ran my hands up his arms. He smelled good. He smelled like…veal marsala?

"Hi, Charley. Oops!"

I opened my eyes and saw Jack's partner, Mike, ducking back into Jack's office. I looked up at my husband, who was doing a poor job of hiding his amusement. "Well." I straightened the Burberry. "You at least have to give me credit for some improvement. I used to scream when your friends suddenly appeared out of nowhere."

Gordon suddenly materialized behind Jack and I screamed. But it was just a little one.

"Please excuse me, Charley. I was trying out a few recipes and thought I'd bring something up for you and Jack." Gordon came as close to looking flustered as I'd ever seen him.

"Would that something be veal marsala?"

His expression cleared. "Are you hungry?"

Suddenly I was famished.

The three of them were clearly in the middle of something. There were stacks of folders, half a dozen thick binders, and three laptops in the office. Jack had installed some shelving and unpacked a couple boxes of books, but there was still a lot of stuff scattered around, including the remains of an impromptu picnic. The guys had apparently been sampling Gordon's menu while spread out on the floor.

Gordon smoothly removed some paperwork from Jack's desk and set a place for me in front of the one and only chair. I heard him mutter something about "at least one person sitting like a civilized human being" as he went about it, but he had fully recovered his considerable composure.

The three men were roughly the same age—late thirties or so, and when I'd first met him I'd thought Mike looked a lot like Jack. They were both tall, and had similar builds, but after knowing him a few months I had to admit that Jack's business partner was a geek to his probably-computerized core.

Sadly, although Mike had the raw material of a hunky-brainy type, he apparently had no interest in cultivating the look. Instead, he had the appearance of a man who cut his own hair with dull scissors and dressed without benefit of a mirror.

Gordon, on the other hand, was impeccable. He was slighter than the other two, and his hair was thinning at the crown. He was a study in control, and I had to admit that when I'd first met him I'd cast him in the role of a mild-mannered serial killer. Luckily, I'd been wrong.

Although he clearly had no moral reservations about the murder of baby cows—and smelling the veal dish I put aside mine as well—Gordon had turned out to be surprisingly soft-hearted. He could even put up with Uncle Harry.

"What are you guys working on?" I asked innocently, taking off my coat and trying not to drool as Gordon composed a plate of baby root vegetables, roasted new potatoes, and veal, then ladled the rich mushroomy sauce over it.

Nobody answered me.

"I'm rethinking the plate." Gordon placed the meal before me. "I'd been thinking classic white with a one-and-three-quarters-inch rim, but now I'm not sure if it needs a little something more."

I took a bite. "It needs nothing."

"Of course, in the restaurant I'll do a dusting of fresh parsley, and that will add visual interest…" he mused.

I'll stack my foodie credentials up against any other self-respecting San Franciscan, but I've never fallen into the trap of valuing presentation over taste. "It's amazing," I assured him. "You're a genius."

"He knows he's a genius," Mike said. "He just wants to be a successful-restaurant-owning genius."

"Unlike you," Gordon replied. "I suppose you want to be a bankrupt computer-security consultant?"

Mike ran his finger around the one-and-three-quarters-inch rim of his plate, then licked it. "Nope, I'm pretty much in it for the money."

"How's it going?" I asked. "What are you working on?" Not that I didn't have my suspicions.

"Zakdan," Mike said. "It's fascinating. They're—"

I was too busy giving my husband an "ah ha!" look to pay attention to what Mike found so fascinating.

Jack interrupted his colleague using his best it's-no-big-deal voice. "We're working on the computer glitch that Morgan Stokes first approached Mike about."

Oh.

Well, still. "Is that all you're working on?" I enquired suggestively.

Mike was oblivious to my prompts.

"It's really interesting," he told me. "They noticed a pattern in the issues being reported to tech support over the last six months or so. At first I didn't see it—it's very intricate—but it's there. There's something going on with the code and it isn't random."

"Tech support?" I looked from Mike to Jack. "Isn't that the department Clara Chen managed? Only it had a fancier name." Something about clients.

"Oh." Mike suddenly looked nervous. "Um—I mean…" He found something worth studying on his empty plate.

"Yes." Jack was watching me carefully. "Stokes told us it was Clara who first noticed the pattern."

Again, it took every ounce of self-control to refrain from shouting "Ah ha!"

"But," Jack continued, "he also told us he was absolutely sure she hadn't said anything about it to anyone else. So if you're thinking what I think you're thinking…"

"What? You mean that someone killed Clara Chen because she discovered a conspiracy at Zakdan?"

Jack closed his eyes briefly. "Something like that."

"Come on, Jack—it's a motive!" I looked to the other guys for support. Gordon suddenly became fascinated with the flame under his chafing dish and Mike gave his plate even more attention.

"It might be a motive," Jack said evenly, "*if* it turns out that the glitch in the software was deliberately engineered and not just a bug—which we haven't established. And it might be a motive," he continued before I could respond, "*if* the person who engineered it knew that Clara had noticed something."

"But." Mike gave me a half-hearted smile. "Since Morgan Stokes is the only one who knew she'd noticed something, he'd be the only one with a motive to kill her."

"And then only if he'd been the one to engineer the bug," Gordon concluded. "In which case he'd hardly have hired these two to investigate it."

"So, Charley." Jack stood, and something in his body language triggered the other two to start looking around for their jackets. "We still don't have anything solid to go on."

I could accept the facts. I nodded in agreement, and said one word.

"Yet."

Jack told Gordon that we—meaning, I assumed, he—would clean up and return his catering paraphernalia to him later. So later that evening my husband and I formed a cozy little picture of domesticity at the kitchen sink.

Jack washed, I talked.

"Simon and I drove past Zakdan today. It's right down the street from the Design Center."

"I know. Mike and I went there yesterday."

"Yesterday? You didn't say anything about it." It was actually nice, watching Jack with his sleeves rolled up, flexing his forearms in the sudsy water.

"You didn't ask." He reached for a towel. "Which reminds me—what did you do yesterday?"

I swallowed. Not that I wanted to lie to my husband about going behind his back with Eileen and Brenda to look for nefarious goings-on at Zakdan, but… Okay, yes. I did want to lie about that.

"Brenda came over for a while," I said. Which wasn't a lie. "And gave me serious grief about the lack of comfy chairs in the living room." Also completely true. "That's why she sent Simon over to ambush me today." Utterly truthful, and a nice segue into a completely different and much safer topic. "Oh! I haven't shown you what I bought!"

"I assumed it was being delivered," he said. "Something in modern lines with geometric shapes?"

"That was just an idea. Meet me in the dining room."

I dashed upstairs and recovered the world's heaviest shopping bag. Then I went to the dining room to find Jack waiting, leaning against the wall with his arms folded and a gleam in his eye.

"Wait…" I turned my back to him so I could remove my treasure from acres of tissue paper without him seeing it. "I really wasn't sure—it was between this and a life-size ceramic rooster, but I thought this was just—" I turned around and held it up.

"It's a…" He furrowed his brow.

"A candlestick." I brought it closer. "It's an antique, wrought iron candlestick from France. See the fleur-de-lis?"

"Now that you mention it."

"It's going to set the tone for the whole look in here. What do you think?"

He took the candlestick and examined it, his expression unreadable.

"Jack? What do you think?"

He cleared his throat. "Well, it's clearly superior to any ceramic rooster I've ever seen."

I took it from him and set it on the floor in the center of the room. It was exactly right. "There. It will be just perfect when I find the right table." I beamed at Jack, then looked back at it. "The dealer said it was really rare to find one this old that wasn't completely rusted."

Jack stood behind me and wrapped his arms around my waist. "It's one in a million," he said. "Just like you."

Chapter Nine

While Jack finished up in the kitchen, I went upstairs and tried to invent a plausible reason for meeting Brenda late that night. And for doing so alone.

Sometimes it comes in very handy to be involved in the theatre.

"There's this thing tonight," I told Jack, after finding him back in his office. "It's sort of an experimental, avant-garde play."

"Sounds fun." He tapped a few keys and the screen changed. "When do we leave?"

"It should be amazing," I said. "Even though it is only a student production put on by some of the kids in one of Brenda's classes."

"Oh."

Did I sense a decline in his interest? Please?

"It's performed in real time—and real space—around the city," I went on. "It's more performance art than traditional theatre…about how the mainstream media has corrupted the true meaning of the feminist movement. One of the characters is a womb, which is played somehow by a talking watermelon."

If that didn't do the trick…

"Um, tonight?" He scrunched up his face. "I may need to do some work."

"Oh," I said with profound disappointment. "Are you sure you can't come with us? Some of it is performed in mime…"

At which news Jack firmly but regretfully declined the offer.

Mission accomplished.

Brenda picked me up around ten thirty, and we got to the gym a bit before eleven, which is just about the time Clara Chen had gotten there on the last night of her life.

The lobby looked like it belonged in some upscale modern hotel. There were sleek chairs arranged around flat-screen televisions playing all sorts of sporting events. An espresso bar at the far end of the room was just closing. They had all the amenities, apparently, except security.

The girl at the front desk wore a white WorkSpace polo shirt and was perkiness personified. She hit us with a "you can do it" smile as soon as we were in the door.

I didn't have a membership card, so I'd planned on talking our way in with a story about wanting to look around the place a bit before deciding whether we wanted to join. But Brenda took control of things as we approached the desk.

"I can't believe you invited me here and then forgot your membership card," she declared loudly.

I stared at her.

The girl behind the counter spoke up. "Oh, did you forget your card? That's okay, everybody does it. Lots of people leave them in the locker rooms by accident, and then they don't even know it until they come back again, and then they're all like 'hey, where's my card?' and I'm like 'are you sure you had it with you when you left?'"

She blasted me with a dazzling smile. "Do you have any ID? All we really need is a driver's license."

Brenda gave me a "what are you waiting for?" look, so I handed over my license.

The girl, whose nametag read "Tiff," twirled her ponytail with one hand while she scanned my card with the other.

"There you are." She studied the computer screen. "Family membership. Gosh, Mrs. Fairfax, your husband comes here all the time, but this looks like your first visit. Is this your first visit? Because all the trainers are gone and you should work with a trainer on your first visit." Her eyes clouded over at this predicament.

"That's okay," I told her. "We just want to grab a quick steam before you close. I don't really need to be trained for that."

She beamed; training crisis averted. "Okay! Great! And is this your guest?" She gave Brenda a smile that said WorkSpace loved guests, then turned back to me. "You can bring in a guest twice a month for free, but you're supposed to use the coupons that we send out with your flyer every month. Are you getting the flyer? Do you have a coupon?"

I vaguely recalled seeing the occasional envelope from the gym in the mail, but I'd never opened one.

"I must have forgotten that too."

Tiff waved her hand. "Never mind." She grabbed a card from a stack on the counter and handed it to Brenda. "Just fill this out. It'll be our little secret." She winked. "How many towels do you guys want?"

Brenda filled out the guest card, which Tiff tossed into a drawer before we took our towels and followed her directions to the women's locker room.

There were three women just leaving when we got there. They all seemed to have been in the same Pilates class, and were discussing posture and ab strength as they passed us on their way out. Then we were alone.

"This is really nice," Brenda murmured.

It was. They clearly went in for the swank spa look at Work-Space. I could understand why Clara had preferred coming here instead of the generic twenty-four hour place that was just down the street from Zakdan.

The lighting was flattering, and the long vanity contained tidy wicker baskets filled with anything a person might possibly forget to put in her gym bag. The aisles were wide, with gleaming wooden benches down the center and hair-and-makeup stations at the ends.

We turned down an aisle. All the locker doors were slightly ajar. I opened one and put my purse in it.

Brenda had gotten quiet. Both of us knew what we were going to do next, and neither of us wanted to do it.

"Brenda, we don't have to—"

She shook her head. "No. We're here. It's why we came."

She opened another locker and started peeling off her clothes.

When I was wrapped in a towel and my clothes were all hanging in my locker, I tried to close the door. It refused to shut all the way. I opened it again and realized the bolt on the door was extended, preventing it from closing.

"Did they give us keys?"

"I think…" Brenda produced her guest card and inserted it into a slot at the top of the handle. There was a clicking sound, and the bolt retracted. She closed the door. "Ta da."

"Oh, it's like a hotel key," I realized. I popped my temporary membership card in once to unlock mine, then closed the door and swiped the card again to lock it.

"Hey, how did you know Jack got a family membership here?" I asked as I tried to figure out where to put the membership card. Towels don't have pockets. "Did he say something?"

"No, but it seemed like the sort of thing he'd do."

"Why? Does he think I'm fat?" Flattering lighting or no, those walls were covered with mirrors, and—

"Don't be an idiot," Brenda scolded. "He thinks you're perfect. And he—"

But further defense of my husband was cut off by an announcement over the loudspeaker system. It was eleven thirty, and the gym would be closing in half an hour.

I met Brenda's eyes. It was now or never.

We followed a sign pointing the way to the women's steam room and dry sauna facilities. Both of us hesitated in front of the steam room.

As soon as I opened the door we were engulfed in the white mist that came spilling out. We went in, and when the door closed behind us I could barely see Brenda through the hot wet fog.

This is where Clara had died. This claustrophobic tiled room with two ledges for seating, and only one door out.

"What's this?" Brenda's voice was shaky, but resolute.

She was pointing at a large red button on the wall near the lower seating ledge.

"A panic button?" I guessed. Could Clara have used it to call for help?

Brenda pushed it, and we immediately heard a loud hiss as more steam came pouring out of nozzles in the walls.

"Not a panic button," Brenda coughed. "Can you breathe in here?"

Not very well. I felt the ledge where Clara had hit her head, trying to keep from seeing the scene in my mind. The edge didn't feel too sharp to me, but it was undeniably hard.

"How slippery does it seem to you?" I tested my foot on the wet tile floor to get a sense of how easily a person might slip.

Then I looked over to Brenda and realized what a bad idea this had been.

I caught her just as her legs went out from under her, and half-dragged her out of there, apologizing for bringing her along in the first place and telling her we were leaving immediately.

"No," she said, gasping for air. "We're staying. We came this far." She sat on a bench and looked at the door to the steam room. "Just not...not where Clara..."

She took a deep breath.

"Just not in there."

So after taking a few moments to collect ourselves, we moved to the dry sauna instead. It was just as small and just as hot, but without the steam, and without the feeling that Clara's ghost was watching us.

We sat on the slatted wooden benches and didn't say much for a while. At eleven forty-five we heard the second announcement about the gym closing.

Brenda still looked shaky. She needed a distraction, so I blurted out the first thing that popped into my head.

"I bought a candlestick with Simon today."

She blinked. "A candlestick?"

She seemed less than impressed, but maybe it was just the circumstances. At least she sounded a little more like herself.

"An antique French candlestick," I elaborated.

As a distraction, that seemed to do the trick.

"That's it?" she said. "An entire day's shopping and you bought one lousy candlestick?"

Okay, maybe it did the trick too well.

"It isn't lousy." I wrapped the towel tighter. "And I made a lot of progress in figuring out what I want."

"Charley, I can't believe you. I mean, I know your fear of commitment is epic—"

"It is not!" I protested. "At least, not once I figure out what I want to commit to—look at the Rep!"

"Well, sure, the Rep. It's perfect for you. It's always changing."

Your friends always know how to hit you with the truth.

"What about Jack?" I countered. "I'd call getting married a commitment."

"Which is why I had a glimmer of hope that marrying Jack and buying the house might mean you'd grown up, but—"

"Grown up? Since when do you have to buy custom upholstery to be grown up? What is it with you and furniture? Why do you care about—"

"Because I want you to stay!" she yelled.

"I am staying!" I yelled back. Then, "What?"

She clapped a hand over her mouth.

"Brenda, what are you talking about? Where do you think I'm going?"

She exhaled slowly, and took a minute to do her getting-centered thing, before answering.

"Charley, I know you weren't crazy about the idea of buying a house, and I know you want to go away for your break. I just don't want you to go off somewhere again and not come back. I want you to stay."

"Brenda, I—"

But she was on a roll. "I want you and Jack to be happy and live here and raise babies and—"

"Babies!" I suddenly had a hard time getting my breath. "Who said anything about—"

"Okay! Maybe not babies right away. But I want you to have a home. I want you to have roots and be connected here. I know Jack has lived all over the place, and you—"

"Hey, Brenda, just slow down for a minute." The room was starting to spin. I reached for a washcloth from a stack on the bench and wiped my face before answering her.

"We're not going anywhere. And even if we did, we wouldn't come back because of a house full of furniture. We'd come back because of you, and Eileen, and the Rep, and—God help me—even Harry. Okay?"

She sniffed. "Okay."

Good grief. You just try to do a little simple detecting with someone and all of a sudden your entire life comes under scrutiny.

Brenda spoke up. "I'm sorry for yelling, Charley. I'm just feeling a little fragile. I mean, when I read Clara's obituary and realized how we'd lost touch… I just don't want that to happen with you."

"That's so not going to happen with me," I assured her. "Unless you start talking about babies again."

She didn't, thank heavens. "Okay. I'll give you a year or so on that one."

Definitely time for another change of subject. "What did the obituary say?"

"About what you'd expect. 'Brilliant, successful'…the funeral is on Saturday."

"Are you going?"

"Will you come with me?"

"Absolutely." Funerals are not exactly my thing, but I'd go to support Brenda, and maybe just to check out the crowd and see if anyone looked suspicious or guilty.

"Thank you." She looked around the room. "What time do you think it is?"

I didn't have to answer, because Tiff chose that moment to throw open the door.

"Hey, you sillies! Didn't you hear the announcements? It's midnight! You'd better get out of here! You wouldn't want to be locked in all night, would you?"

Thus endeth the stakeout.

"Well, that was singularly uninformative." I buckled my seatbelt as Brenda started the engine of her little Saab. It had started raining, and the car began to fog up almost immediately.

"It wasn't a complete waste. At least we found out how bad the security is, even if they have added a spot check to make sure everyone's out at night." She shivered, either from the freezing rain after the hot sauna, or from the thought of her friend having been killed.

Tiff had told us that the spot check had recently been added to her night shift duties, because someone had had "an accident" a few days ago.

"Charley, do you think the killer had to be a woman?" Brenda switched on the windshield wipers and looked at me.

The same thought had crossed my mind. "Based on where Clara was killed, I suppose I'd assumed so before we went in there," I told her. "But it was awfully deserted, wasn't it?"

She nodded. "I looked at the notice board, and the last exercises classes end at ten. So even if people hang out and take showers and saunas and everything, it's probably just as empty every night at eleven as it was tonight."

"And the men's locker room is right next to the women's. I mean, it probably wouldn't have been hard for the killer to slip out one door and slip in another after he'd given Clara enough time to get into the sauna. I don't think Tiff, or whoever was at the front desk that night, can even see around the coffee bar to the locker room doors."

"The killer might even have asked Clara how long she was usually in there, and if she's usually alone." Brenda was getting more excited.

"Especially if he was someone she knew."

"Do we think he was someone she knew?"

"Oh." We had no idea. But…"Aren't most people killed by someone they know?"

"I suppose." Brenda was looking slightly deflated again, but she shook it off to sum up our findings.

"So we've learned that the killer could have been a man or a woman, and that the gym has increased security since Clara died."

"At least that's something." I looked out at the empty parking lot. "But I think I've just realized something else."

"What?" Brenda pulled out onto a deserted street.

"Morgan Stokes said Clara left for the gym around ten that night, but according to her membership card she didn't get here until 10:47."

Brenda nodded slowly. "That seems like kind of a long time, if there was no traffic."

We looked at each other.

"Check your watch," Brenda said. "We're going to Zakdan."

Chapter Ten

It took us sixteen minutes to reach the offices of Zakdan, Inc.

Which left roughly half an hour of Clara Chen's time unaccounted for.

Brenda pulled to the curb across the street from the Zakdan building and squinted up through the drizzle. "There are still lights on."

"Morgan did tell us that people work late here. Look at how many cars are still in the garage."

There was a parking garage below the building, and we could see through the grating that at least a dozen cars were still there.

"Hey, someone's coming!" Brenda grabbed my arm.

A thin man in a black raincoat had come through a door at the back of the garage.

"An elevator must go straight down to the garage," I said. "Can you tell who it is?"

"I don't know anyone at Zakdan," Brenda said. "I haven't even met Morgan—Oh! Charley! I do know who it is!"

"Who? How?" She'd gripped my arm so tight I was losing circulation.

"It's the Chief Technology Officer! Oh, what's his name? Lalit...Kumar! Lalit Kumar!"

"It is?" I strained my eyes. "How can you tell?"

"I got his picture off the internet when I was doing the research. Look! I'm sure it's him!"

Now that he got a little closer, I recognized him from the dossier Brenda had compiled on all the Zakdan execs.

"I wonder what he's been doing here until almost one o'clock in the morning." Brenda was a little breathless, and she still hadn't let go of my arm.

"I don't know," I said doubtfully. "Working? Although when I think about people working all night at software companies, I assume it's the programmers, not the executives."

"Me too."

"He's getting into the Jag." I watched him unlock the car and toss what looked like a laptop bag into the back seat. Then he reached into his coat pocket and pulled out a cell phone.

"Is he calling someone?"

"No." I squinted. "I think he's answering."

"Who calls a person at one in the morning?" Brenda asked.

"Stay here." I was out the door before Brenda could yell at me, and I dashed across the dark, wet street as quickly and quietly as I could. I took a position at the bottom of the driveway, hidden by a concrete pillar, and peeked around through the bars of the electronic garage door.

Brenda's question was a good one. Who would call at that hour? And who would make Lalit Kumar as angry as he looked, now that I got closer and could see his face?

The CTO was clearly not happy with what he was hearing. I couldn't make out everything he said, but I did hear snatches.

"No. No way."

"Forget it—I'm not getting involved."

"How dare you!"

I took another peek at that, in time to see Kumar bring his fist down on the roof of his pricy sports car.

"Dammit, this is the last time!" With that he slammed the cell phone shut and opened the door to his car.

I sprinted back across the street to Brenda, gesturing wildly for her to start the car. I threw myself in the passenger's seat, panting and dripping.

"Quick! He's leaving!"

"Get down!" She ducked down and pulled me with her. The Jaguar's headlights illuminated the interior of Brenda's car as it pulled out of the garage. As soon as it was dark again, Brenda released her grip on me and scrambled to get moving.

We didn't even discuss it.

We followed him.

Brenda pulled a U-turn on Townsend and waited until Zakdan's Chief Technology Officer had crossed Fifth Street heading south before she put on her lights.

"I can't believe you did that! What if he'd seen you?"

"He didn't see me," I protested. "And I had to do it to find out who was calling him."

"Who was it?"

"I don't know," I admitted. "But whoever it was got him pretty ticked off and talked him into something he didn't want to do."

"What?"

"I don't know, but we're probably going to find out if we don't lose him."

I watched the taillights ahead of us through the rainy windshield. We were practically the only two cars on the road.

I thought back to what I'd overheard. It could have been anyone, asking him to do anything.

"I'm going to be awfully disappointed if he's just going home to his wife and kids," I said.

Brenda shook her head. "No, he isn't married. I remember all about him from the research we did, because I was thinking he might be kind of perfect for Eileen."

I stared at her. "You're matchmaking during a murder investigation?"

She shrugged. "Not actively, just for future reference."

"You mean in case he doesn't turn out to be a murderer," I clarified.

"Anyway." she ignored me. "If I recall correctly, he lives in North Beach, just like Eileen."

"Brenda—"

"My point is," she cut me off. "He's not going home."

He wasn't. He'd taken a left on Potrero, heading uphill, and now he took a right on Sixteenth Street. He was heading for the Mission district, which was a good thing for us because the neighborhood had enough bars and twentysomething residents to still be hopping in the middle of the night.

Brenda let a car come between us as Lalit made a left onto Valencia. We followed.

"Where do you think—" But I didn't have time to finish the question, because the silver Jag came to a stop ahead of us, double parking in front of a darkened restaurant.

"Yikes! What should I do? Should I pass him? I can't—"

But I grabbed her arm before she could finish. "Pull in! Pull in! Pull in!"

"Charley! What? Oh!" She saw the space I was pointing at and slammed the wheel to the right.

It wasn't the safest maneuver, but it got us parked about half a block behind Lalit's car. Okay, we were illegally parked in someone's driveway, but I had a feeling we wouldn't be staying long.

"Now what?"

Good question. "Is he getting out?" I asked. The rain was coming down harder and I had to squint to see what was going on.

"No. He's put his blinkers on. I think he's waiting for someone."

The block had several bars, and all of them had clusters of people out front, huddling under scant awnings while they stole a smoke. I scanned the groups, but nobody seemed to be taking notice of the idling sports car or its occupant.

"Charley!" Brenda dug her fingers into my arm again. She pointed to a figure dashing across the street, a newspaper held overhead to keep off the rain.

"Who is it? Where did he come from? Is he—"

"I can't tell." Brenda pushed her glasses up and strained forward, putting the wipers on high. "I'm not even sure it's a guy. Oh!" She dropped my arm and reached for the gearshift. "He's getting in!"

The figure had crossed in front of the silver Jaguar, but the brief glare of headlights was of no use. Lalit, apparently expecting company, opened the passenger door from the inside, and the figure vanished within.

"He came out of one of those bars," Brenda said. "He must have been watching for the car."

I glanced to the other side of the street. The bars were all busy, with the usual crowds in front. Nobody seemed to be chasing after Lalit's passenger. "I thought you said you weren't sure it was a guy." I gripped the dashboard as Brenda swung the car out into the flow of traffic again.

"I'm not. What was he wearing?"

I rewound the scene in my mind. "Black jeans and a black leather jacket?"

She nodded vigorously, keeping her eyes on the cars ahead. Two had gotten between us and our quarry. "I think so too. Could you see anything about the face?"

"Nothing. He's taking a left!"

He was, so we did, and we kept following him as he made a series of turns that took him out of the Mission and across Market Street. I was so busy trying to keep my eyes on the low set of taillights that I didn't even pay attention to the streets we were taking until things started to look familiar.

"Brenda, are we going to Pacific Heights?" At least I thought I recognized my own neighborhood.

"We're in Pacific Heights," she told me. "I think we're going to the Marina."

It looked like she was right. We crested the steep hill, crossing Pacific, and saw the lights of the waterfront Marina neighborhood below us. There was now only one car between us and Lalit, and with a stop sign on just about every corner, it was getting easier to keep our eyes on him.

I hoped that didn't mean it would be easier for him—or his unknown passenger—to keep an eye on us.

"Can you see if they're doing anything in the car?" Brenda asked.

"I see their heads, and I think I see the passenger's hands every now and then. Do you think they're arguing?"

"I don't know. Maybe he's just one of those people who talks with his hands?"

"You said 'he' again."

"But I'm still not sure. Maybe when we get down by Lombard the streetlights will be brighter."

Lombard was a busy street, the main artery between the Golden Gate Bridge and Van Ness, which cuts across the city to the freeways that come up the peninsula.

"If he takes a left on Lombard he's probably going over the bridge," I said.

"But if he goes right he might just be going home." Brenda started closing the distance between us and the car just ahead as we got nearer to the intersection. "I mean, we've just come from the other end of town, so why would he double back? A right would take him over to North Beach."

"If he was just going home from the Mission there are a lot easier ways to get there," I said doubtfully.

I squinted, straining to see inside the silver Jag as we came to a stop at the last cross street before Lombard. Lalit's car moved into the intersection.

"Brenda! Did you just see that?" I grabbed her arm.

"I did! There was a flash of something!" She shook my hand off and strained with impatience behind the car ahead of us.

"Something metal!" I gripped the edges of my seat. "Was it a gun?"

We crossed the street and made for Lombard. "Do you think it was?" Brenda asked breathlessly. "The light only hit it for a minute—Damn!"

The light ahead had turned yellow. Lalit's car picked up speed and turned neither left or right. It raced through the intersection while the car ahead of us braked for the light.

"Brenda! Go around!"

"I can't!" But she did go around the car before slamming on her brakes at the red light.

"There's nobody coming!" I checked both ways, the seatbelt cutting into my neck as I strained forward.

"Go! Look—he's turning! We'll lose him!"

The Jag had made a left further down the street. If we didn't catch up soon we'd never find it.

"Hold on!" Brenda yelled, and hit the accelerator.

"Wait!"

"What!?"

"Cop!"

She braked, and we lurched to a stop two feet into the intersection. A black-and-white police car was parked on the other side of the street, and the officer inside was looking at us grimly.

"Shit," I muttered through clenched teeth, while giving him a hugely apologetic smile. "If we get a ticket we'll never catch up to him." And I'd never hear the end of it from Jack.

Brenda mouthed "I'm sorry" to the officer, who apparently decided we weren't worth getting out in the rain for. He shook his finger at us, then waved us through as the light changed to green.

"Where did they turn?" Brenda asked.

"The first left, I think." But by the time we got there, there was no sign of the silver sports car.

We drove up and down the blocks for a while, but nothing turned up.

"Should we go back and tell that cop?" Brenda asked.

"Tell him what? That we've been following a perfect stranger all over town for no particular reason?" At least, I figured, that's how it would seem to the cop.

She took a minute to think about it. "What about the gun?"

"Are you sure it was a gun?" In the absence of adrenalin, I was starting to have doubts.

"I don't know," she admitted. "It could have been a cell phone or something."

I nodded glumly. "Anything shiny, really."

She sighed, and turned up a street that would take us to my house.

"Do you want to spend the night? It's awfully late for you to drive home." Pushing two, I realized.

"I'll be fine. Besides, where exactly would I spend the night at your place? On your nonexistent couch?"

She must be cheering up if she was picking on me again.

"What are you doing tomorrow?" she asked.

I winced. "More furniture shopping."

Chapter Eleven

For the first time since our wedding, Jack had gone to bed without me.

I couldn't blame him, considering the hour, and I should have been relieved, considering the steam-room-followed-by-rainstorm state of my appearance—and the fact that nobody would believe an outdoor experimental piece of performance art could run on for four hours.

Nevertheless, it was very strange to slip into bed next to him, causing only a brief grumble and change of position on his part.

I looked at him in the moonlight. If I told him about the night's activities, he might be able to help figure out what had delayed Clara half an hour on her way to the gym the night she died. And he might be able to find out whether Lalit Kumar made a habit of picking people up outside bars and driving around town with them.

He might do both those things. But he was guaranteed to do something else, and that was to tell me to stay out of the Clara Chen investigation. Which, at this point, I was going to do anyway. Particularly since my ideas for detective work were exhausted.

So I decided to think about it in the morning.

In the morning Jack was gone, and Simon was at the door.

Jack's note said he'd decided to let me sleep since I'd gotten in so late. Simon's knock said he wanted to come in and he expected coffee. He drank it while I showered and got dressed.

Simon had spoken to a decorator, who had suggested I stop focusing on furniture and concentrate instead on fabric. "It makes perfect sense," he explained as we scouted for a parking spot in the depths of the Union Square garage. "The types of fabric you're drawn to should tell you what your style is. Whether it's simple stripes or elaborate florals or whatever. So that helps you figure out the style of the furniture, and the colors feed in to the paint choices. It's all perfectly simple."

"Maybe." I'd heard this sort of thing before.

"Of course, you could just do the sane thing and hire my decorator friend and let him worry about it." Simon squeezed into a spot at the end of a row.

"I could," I agreed, getting out of the car.

"But you won't."

"Then it would look like his house, and I want it to look like my house."

"Well, darling." Simon slung his arm around my shoulders and propelled me toward the elevators. "It certainly doesn't look like anyone else's."

Britex Fabrics is heaven, if you're into that sort of thing. Four floors, in a grand old building off Union Square, with contents ranging from faux furs to bridal laces, and about a jillion bolts of fabric in between. We spent an hour looking at fringe and tassels alone—which at least was enough to convince me that I wanted no part of fringe or tassels.

It also reinforced the fact that I really shouldn't attempt this sort of thing after a late night of tailing suspects.

By late afternoon we'd succeeded in amassing a huge pile of upholstery options and thoroughly confusing a very nice saleswoman.

"Well." She surveyed the pile. "I wouldn't have thought of putting the French silk damask in the same room as the tropical monkey print, but I suppose if you're going for some sort of mid-century Polynesian…"

She was trying, I had to give her that.

"I think where we're going is for a drink," Simon told her.

Twenty minutes later, over the sugared rim of a watermelon martini at the Four Seasons bar, things were looking better.

"It's all my fault, darling. I simply shouldn't have dragged you there. I blame my own monumental boredom as much as your inadequacies as an interior designer." He sipped. "I shouldn't have looked to your shopping challenges to distract myself from the vast hollow emptiness of my life."

"Perhaps not." I dug into the silver bowl of nuts between us.

"Definitely not, darling. Not when there's a much juicer distraction just staring the both of us in the face." He waited.

I've spent enough time around actors to know when I'm being prompted for a line.

"What distraction?"

"The investigation into the mysterious death of Clara Chen."

I'm sure, in Simon's mind, sinister organ music accompanied his words.

I knew he'd just moan about not having been invited, so I'd resolved not to mention what Brenda and I had been up to the night before.

"I'm going to Clara's funeral on Saturday with Brenda," I told him. "That's about the extent of the future investigation."

"Right. And what's Jack up to?" Simon's raised eyebrows spoke volumes.

I told him about the bug in the Zakdan software that Mike was exploring. "The problem is, it doesn't provide a motive for anyone other than Morgan Stokes. And I hardly think—"

"Not so fast," Simon interrupted. "It provides a motive for the person who sabotaged the software in the first place."

I downed the last of my candy-colored drink. "Jack would point out that we're not sure the software was sabotaged, and even if it was, the person who did it wouldn't have known Clara was on to him."

"That sounds like Jack," Simon agreed. "But Jack's not here, is he? And besides, who knows if the saboteur booby trapped the software somehow to warn him if his bomb had been detected?"

"Okay." I nodded to the bartender. I was going to need another drink. "First, let's avoid the use of the word 'saboteur' from here on out, all right?"

Simon rolled his eyes. "Fine."

"And it isn't a bomb in the software, it's a bug." He was perhaps the only person in the greater Bay Area who knew less about computers than I did.

"Nevertheless," he persisted. "We should be doing something."

"Such as?" Reinforcements arrived, in the form of watermelon flavored vodka. Simon waited until the cocktail waitress was out of earshot. Then he leaned across the small table.

"Such as going undercover at Zakdan," he hissed.

◇◇◇

I told him he was insane. I told him this repeatedly, over more drinks and an order of mixed Asian appetizers. But the more he kept talking, the less insane he sounded. Which probably meant it was time to switch to coffee.

"But darling, if you just think of it as live theatre, reality-based theatre, a sort of improv in the round…"

Which did sound kind of interesting. I'd given up any delusions about being an actress years ago, but I'd loved all the workshops and classes I'd taken before realizing I had no talent.

"And for the things where we'd need a script—for the technical bits and so on—we could enlist Eileen. You know she could give us enough to bluff our way through a couple of meetings…"

And I knew she felt like she was in a rut these days, so she was likely to agree to the crazy idea.

"In a company that big, if we just act casual, nobody will take any notice of us. Haven't you seen *How to Succeed in Business Without Really Trying?* It's all in the attitude." There was no stopping Simon's fevered imagination. "Eileen could give us a plausible cover story, and once we were inside, we could talk to people and figure out what's really going on, and who might really know something about Clara's death."

I wasn't sure about that, but I thought Simon was right about being able to talk to people. Morgan Stokes didn't think Clara had told anyone else about the pattern of technical problems she'd noticed, but how could he be sure? For that matter, she might have told more people about her engagement, and her imminent promotion.

I doubted many of Morgan's employees would feel comfortable chatting with him about his girlfriend's death. He was their boss, after all. But those same employees might spill their guts at the water cooler with a harmless temp who was going to be gone in a few weeks. One thing I'd learned in the theatre—gossip will out. And how different could an office be?

"Okay, that's enough." I signaled for the check. "This is all starting to sound perfectly logical, which means it's time for us to call a cab and go home."

"But, Charley—"

"No but Charleys. You shouldn't drive."

"Well, that's not in dispute, darling. But—"

I held up my hand. "Okay. I'll think about it."

"Promise?" His eyes lit up.

"I promise."

"Will you talk to Jack?"

Ah. Um. Well. "I'll have to think about that."

Chapter Twelve

I did think about discussing Simon's idea with Jack. Really. But he'd made it abundantly clear that, in the absence of any more data, he didn't think there was anything to investigate. And I had a fairly strong sense that he might not see the immediate benefits of the let's-go-undercover-to-gather-data scheme.

So, somehow, the subject didn't come up.

I spent most of the next day reading bad plays in preparation for Friday's meeting at the Rep. I couldn't imagine what Chip had endured in order to come up with the fifteen he'd sent over, because they were uniformly awful. Never mind the one about the strip club—the absolute worst had to be an excruciating coming-of-age story written by a precocious eleven-year-old.

In blank verse, no less.

I had thought that the stack of manuscripts, while not giving me much hope for the future of the American stage, would at least serve to distract me from dwelling on the idea of infiltrating Zakdan to unmask Clara Chen's killer. But the plan kept percolating in the back of my mind.

Simon's enthusiasm had infected me, and it stuck even after the vodka was out of my system. I liked the notion of reality theatre. And the thought of being able to get some useful information for the investigation was very satisfying.

The more I thought about it, the more I thought we should do it. And soon. The office was bound to still be buzzing about Clara Chen's death—every person there would have a theory about why she died. And I was guessing that "because she slipped" would be fairly low down on the list.

I wanted to hear those theories. If we could get the inside scoop on who really knew about the software bug she'd discovered, and who really knew she was about to be promoted and given all that stock, we'd find ourselves with a list of suspects.

I pictured myself striding into Inspector Yahata's office—Did he have an office? Or was he at a desk in a big open room with lots of people and yelling and phones ringing? Anyway, staging issues aside, I'd stride in and present him with an amazing lead, or some sort of incontrovertible evidence. And then he'd look at me, and…

Oh.

He'd look at me and I'd get that feeling of being a bug under a magnifying glass, sizzling slightly while he examined me. I was getting a little fried just thinking about it. Then he'd tell me, quite calmly, that by messing with the chain of custody or something I'd ruined whatever chance the authorities had ever had to bring the killer to trial.

Maybe I'd better stick to the plays.

Or to finding something to go with my candlestick.

"Early" does not mean the same thing to me that it does to my husband. So on Friday morning Jack was long gone by the time I had showered and made the bed.

This was my morning ritual. I may not be big on housework, but I took a lot of pride in smoothing a fresh set of Frette sheets on the bed every morning, pulling up the duvet and arranging all the pillows just so. I bundled the old sheets and tossed them down a laundry chute, where eventually they were found and dealt with by the cleaning service that Eileen had arranged to come in once a week.

As a result, the hallway linen closet always contained neatly folded bundles that smelled vaguely of lavender, and I got a soothing glow just opening the door every morning. I'd have to remember to mention this to Brenda. She'd be thrilled at any evidence of domesticity.

It was bound to be freezing at the theater, so I pulled on a pair of jeans and a fluffy Eileen Fisher sweater. I went down to the kitchen carrying my shoes. I'd found the echoing sound of heels in the empty hallways to be a little unnerving lately, so I'd taken to wandering around in my socks.

Maybe we should have a house rule that people need to remove their shoes when they come in? That would be easier than finding rugs to muffle all the hardwood floors in the place. I turned the possibility over in my mind as I poured the coffee Jack had left in the pot.

Then I got distracted by a plate of healthy looking muffins on the kitchen island.

I blinked. Had Jack gone out to a bakery? Probably not, because if he had, he'd have gone to the Patisserie on Union Street and I didn't think they produced anything like the brown globular specimens before me.

Then I noticed the bowl. It was freshly washed and drying in the dish rack. And it was accompanied by a measuring cup, a spoon, and a muffin tin.

Good lord, my husband had baked muffins this morning.

I approached them with caution, and picked one up. It was heavy. I sniffed it. Definitely healthy stuff in there. I took an experimental nibble. As I thought, it would take gobs of butter and jam to make it edible.

I opened the refrigerator and located a butter dish. Interesting. The pale yellow rectangle was pristine. Jack hadn't used it. Likewise, the jar of jam was still sealed. I took another sip of coffee and smiled to myself. I was a detective already. I could reconstruct Jack's actions this morning perfectly. He'd made dietetically virtuous muffins and eaten them plain. I lifted the napkin off the plate and counted. Ten, and the muffin tin held twelve. He'd eaten two of them plain.

Further self-congratulation was delayed by the sound of the doorbell ringing.

"Simon?" The kitchen is at the back of the house, so I yelled as I went down the hall to the front door. "Is that you? You're early."

I opened the door. "And you're not alone."

"Charley!" Before I knew what I was looking at, I was swept aside by a six-foot-four, bald, chocolate-skinned set designer. "This place is huge, girl! Why haven't you done shit-all with it?" He performed the by-now-standard routine of opening doors and looking into empty rooms while criticizing me.

"Hi, Paris," I greeted him in return. "I thought you were going to…Paris?"

"I was." He began to unwind a lengthy scarf from around his neck. It looked like it might take some time. "I am. But Simon told me you were in crisis, so I decided to give you my housewarming present early." He nodded to someone over my shoulder.

I turned to find Simon struggling to maneuver an uncooperative piece of furniture through the door. There must have been someone on the other end of it, but I couldn't see who. "Lord, this is heavy," Simon gasped. "Paris, a little help, please?"

I looked back at Paris, who handed me an armful of scarf and said, "Think about a coat rack," before lending a hand.

The gigantic slab of wood was finally angled through the doorway. When they turned it around and set it down I finally saw who my third guest was. Chip. And I finally realized what the furniture was.

"A table!" I ran my fingers along the richly polished surface. "It's gorgeous!"

"It's a handcrafted, solid cherry, artisanal dining room table in a modified Arts and Crafts style," Paris informed me. "Built by my very own Gabriel as a gift from us to you. And by the looks of things, not a minute too soon."

I ignored his last comment and hugged him. "Thank you! It's perfect!"

"Of course it is," Paris agreed.

"And it's heavy," Chip volunteered.

"Oh, thanks for bringing it," I said. "And, um…" I looked at the dining room door.

"Yes, darling." Simon gave me a perfunctory kiss on the cheek. "We'll take it the rest of the way."

Chip was a lot smaller than the other two men. Fidgety and kind of squirrelly. Not what you'd look for in a mover of large furnishings. But he grabbed an end and hoisted, and the three of them got the thing into the dining room.

"Right in the center…yes." I directed, dashing in ahead of them to pick up the candlestick, which had remained in the middle of the floor. "Or…" I looked at the table once it was positioned. "Maybe no. Maybe we should angle—"

"No." Paris buffed a fingerprint away with the sleeve of his long grey coat. "It goes straight down the center of the room. Dead center lengthwise with the middle of the fireplace, and dead center widthwise with the middle of the bay window." He made karate-chopping arm movements to illustrate this axis of perfection. "At least, until you get a sideboard or something that would balance it."

"Or chairs, maybe?" Chip looked around the room.

"I have something better!" I placed my perfect candlestick in the center—dead center—of the table, and stood back to take in the effect.

"Yes, darling," Simon murmured. "Much more original than chairs."

So, instead of meeting to pick the remaining play for next season in the chilly offices of the Rep, we found ourselves having an early lunch on Union Street.

We wound up at Betelnut, sharing a dozen or so small plates of things like chili calamari, hoisin pork in pancakes, and green papaya salad. And since the bar specializes in Asian beers...well.

At one point I remembered my manners and thanked Paris again for the table. "Did Gabriel really make it himself?" I knew Paris' partner was some sort of cabinet maker, but I hadn't realized the extent of his talent.

"Designed it and made it," Paris informed me, not without a touch of pride.

"Could he make more things?" I asked. "I mean, the house is pretty big, and I haven't really—"

Simon's snort cut off the rest of my words. I gave him a squinty-eyed look, and he took a sudden interest in a red lacquer bowl on a small shelf behind me.

"Girl, do you know how long it takes to make a piece of furniture like that?" Paris always brought out the remaining Texas notes in his voice when he wanted to make a point.

"A long time?"

"Let me put it this way—your babies would be having babies by the time he was through furnishing that house."

What the hell was it with people and babies these days?

I took a deep swallow of Tsingtao. "Never mind."

Predictably, it was the single-minded Chip who brought us back to the purpose of the get-together, and it was the borderline-workaholic Chip who stayed back at the house with Simon and me after Paris left us with "I don't care what show y'all decide to put on next year, as long as it has nice juicy sets."

So the three of us got comfortable and indulged in a heated debate about the relative merits—or lack thereof—of the fifteen manuscripts we'd read.

Which is how Jack found us.

"Pumpkin, should I ask why you're in bed with two men?"

This is not something I'd ever expected to hear my husband say, and particularly in such a casual tone. But since the only place in the house to get comfortable was the bed, we'd ended up having our meeting there.

"Jack!" Chip sprinted off the duvet and came close to standing at attention. Despite the fact that he'd merely been sitting, fully clothed, at the foot of the bed, he blushed furiously.

"Hi, Jack." Simon, who had been lounging on his stomach with his head in his hands, merely rolled to his side and gave a finger wave.

"You're home early," I said. I was sitting cross-legged with my back against the headboard.

"Apparently." He came over and put his finger under my chin to tilt my face toward him. "Maybe I should come home early more often." He kissed me.

"Maybe you shouldn't leave in the first place," I smiled.

He looked at Simon. "But then how would you get any work done?"

"There's this new thing called a chair that I've heard is all the rage," Simon told him. "I've been trying to convince Charley to try one out."

"It's a thought," Jack said.

"Really, Jack," Chip volunteered. "We were only talking…"

Jack turned to give him a friendly clap on the shoulder. "Really, Chip, if I thought anything different you'd be dead by now."

Chip attempted a grin. It didn't come out quite right.

"Oh, don't be silly." I eyed my husband. "Give us your opinion on these plays—would you rather spend the evening with an albino in a snowstorm who's dealing with feelings of invisibility, or a young boy confronting his junior high angst against the backdrop of highly competitive slam poetry?"

Jack cleared his throat. "I think I'll leave that to the professionals."

I sighed. "This professional has had it." I closed the last of the manuscripts and faced my director. "Chip, thanks for all your work, but there's no way we're putting on any of these next season."

He nodded. "I thought you'd say that. I'll send over the next batch in the morning. I'd have brought them with me, but the copier was down." He perched on the bed again. "There's one that I think has real possibilities. It's about a logger and an environmentalist trapped in the crown of a redwood tree while—"

"Chip, old man." Simon stood and stretched. "I've been kicked out of enough bedrooms in my sorry life to know when it's time to make my exit."

"Oh." Chip seemed to realize something, then jumped off the bed again. "Oh! Okay. I'll just...we'll just..."

"We'll just find our own way out." Simon took him by the arm and led him to the door. "It's called surrendering the playing field. You'll get used to it."

"'Bye, guys!" I called after them. Then I turned my attention to my husband. "Want to join me on the playing field?"

A speculative gleam appeared in his eye. "Always. But we don't have time for anything but a warm-up if we're going to be on time."

"On time for what?" I stopped in mid pillow-plump.

"Dinner at Bix."

"Oh!"

"With Harry."

Oh.

Chapter Thirteen

I hadn't forgotten another dinner with Uncle Harry. Apparently it was a spur-of-the-moment thing that he'd arranged with Jack that afternoon. Funny how he'd called Jack instead of me.

In any case, as I contemplated which pair of shoes to ruin on yet another rain-soaked night, I consoled myself with the thought that the choice of restaurant was just right for both the weather and my mood.

Bix is an old-school supper club, tucked away in an alley near the financial district, with dim lighting and good jazz in the background. The kind of place where you can imagine guys in fedoras smoking cigars and deciding among themselves who the next governor will be. The kind of place where the bartender really knows his stuff.

It was, I acknowledged, Harry's kind of place.

I slammed the door and shook the rain out of my hair once I got in the car—a black Lexus SUV that we'd borrowed from Harry months ago and hadn't gotten around to returning yet.

"Do you own an umbrella?" Jack asked, flicking my second-hand drops off his jacket.

"Several. I only wish I knew where I put them." I looked back at the big empty house as we pulled away. There were a lot of places to lose things in there.

Jack turned down the steep hill to Broadway and made a right. It was almost eight, so the worst of Friday rush hour was over. There was still a bit of cross-street congestion ahead of us, but our straight shot to the Broadway Tunnel, which makes a swooping cut through one of the steepest hills in the city, was relatively clear.

After about the fourth stop sign, Jack made an irritated sound and adjusted his rearview mirror.

"What's the matter? Ow!"

Jack didn't need to answer my question because I'd just been temporarily blinded by the lights of the car behind us shining directly into my eyes from the side mirror. "That guy seriously needs his headlights adjusted."

Jack was alternately squinting into the rearview mirror and squinting to see the road ahead of us. We were getting to the busier intersections, with lots of pedestrians, and visibility was already bad because of the rain.

"They aren't headlights," he told me. "He's got a row of spotlights across the roof of his truck."

I turned around to look, shielding my eyes. "Isn't it against some sort of law for him to have them on in traffic?" We went through a green light at Van Ness.

"It should be." Jack signaled and moved to the left lane as we approached the mouth of the tunnel.

We had a moment of relief from the glaring lights, then the truck pulled forward, as if to pass us on the right, flashing the bright lights like strobes and blaring the horn.

Jack accelerated instantly, but it wasn't fast enough. Exactly at the point where the tunnel curves, the truck smashed up against us, slamming into our right side as the white tiled wall of the tunnel rushed to meet us on the left.

"Jack!" I grabbed the arm of my seat and held on. I couldn't see anything beyond the blinding lights of truck that was trying to crush us.

Jack fought to keep the car under control, still accelerating as we were being pressed into the tunnel wall. The sound of metal crashing against metal on one side and metal screeching against tile on the other was deafening. Sparks were starting to fly past Jack's head.

"Hold on!" he yelled, wrenching the steering wheel to the left as the tunnel straightened. There was a last ear-splitting metallic squeal as we scraped deeper into the wall, but when Jack gunned the engine we were suddenly free of the truck's pressure.

The truck roared past as Jack slammed on the brakes to avoid crashing into the backed-up line of cars outside the tunnel.

"Are you all right?" he shouted.

"Jack! He's getting away!" I saw the truck—some huge black sort of extra-wide pickup—race through the stoplight while we were still stuck in our lane, the traffic to the right moving too quickly for us to change lanes and follow it.

"Never mind. Are you okay?"

"Yes! Did you see a license plate?"

He shook his head grimly. "There wasn't one."

Jack pulled over as soon as he could, and we took refuge in the tiny driveway of a Chinese greengrocer. We stared at each other. I was shaking uncontrollably, still hearing the screech of metal, still seeing giant purple spots in the shape of the truck's lights bouncing around.

Jack, not surprisingly, looked good. Face slightly flushed, eyes slightly blazing. More like he'd just navigated a particularly tricky stretch of alpine roadway than nearly been crushed to death at high speed.

As soon as I got my breath back, I had one question for him.

"Jack, just exactly who did you piss off at Zakdan the other day?"

I waited. He appeared to be thinking. Then he nodded his head, as if he'd figured something out.

"I was at Zakdan again today," he began.

"*What!* Why? Were you going to tell me—"

"Mike and I went back today." He cut off my questions. "So he could…it doesn't matter why. The important thing is that

I got the call from Harry inviting us to Bix on my cell while I was there."

"Who were you with?"

"Just Mike. We were in Lalit Kumar's office. He was out today. Morgan put us in his office so we could work undisturbed."

I was a little disturbed at the news that Kumar had been out that day. Had he been back to work since Brenda and I had followed him all over town two nights before? But Jack was still talking.

"I don't know how soundproof any of those offices are. I don't remember anyone passing in the hall when I was talking to Harry, but I'll find out who has the offices next to Kumar's, and who might have overheard my side of the call."

Would that mean Clara's killer was one of the Zakdan executives? Because, as far as I knew, the only person who might want to scare Jack away from his investigation was the person who had killed Morgan Stokes' fiancée.

Jack looked at his watch. "Are you hungry?"

"Are you kidding? You still want to meet Harry?" I was thinking of something more along the lines of a quick call to the police followed by a very large martini, enjoyed from behind some barricaded walls.

He started the car. "If we don't show up there will be questions."

"If we do show up there will be questions," I countered. "Such as 'where is your side mirror and most of your car's paint?'"

Jack grinned. "Remind me not to park under a streetlight." Then he reached over and touched my cheek with the back of his hand. "Sorry for putting you in the middle of that, Pumpkin."

Which only made me want to burst into tears and throw myself into his arms. But I'm a big girl, so I told myself I could do that after dinner. Instead I took his hand and held on.

Jack called Mike as soon as we were moving again, to let him know that apparently someone had been noticeably unhappy with their presence at Zakdan that day. I spent the rest of the trip jumping every time a car came near us, but I think by the time we parked (not under a streetlight) and scurried through the rain to the restaurant, I probably looked as composed as I ever do.

"Let's not tell Harry about this," I said as we shook off our coats under the awning outside the door. "He'll want to call in his own personal cavalry, and I really don't think I could deal with that right now."

"Agreed," Jack said. "There's just one thing I need to do before we go in."

At which point he pulled me into one of the most spectacular kisses of my life, swift and intense, leaving me breathless and disoriented and feeling that having nearly been killed was almost worth it, if this was the effect it had on my husband.

Then he turned me around and propelled me into the restaurant.

Harry, unsurprisingly, was already there, and for once he wasn't dressed like an aging beach bum. Instead he wore a sober gray suit that I was willing to bet he'd bought for a funeral. He gave it a distinctly personal flair with the addition of a vintage Hawaiian print silk tie.

He was not alone.

"Brenda!" I couldn't wait to get her off to the ladies room and tell her everything.

"Hi, you two," Brenda greeted us. "Isn't this nice?"

Her glasses were sliding down her nose and her long black hair was, as usual, drawn into a ponytail bound by some hippy device one of her students had given her years ago.

I looked from her to my uncle, who had draped an arm proprietarily over the back of her chair. "Nice" was one word for it. "Suspicious" was another. Maybe our little brush with death wasn't the only frightening aspect of the evening.

Jack held my chair as I slid into the seat next to Brenda. "What's Harry up to?" I hissed.

"Good to see you too, Charley," Harry said loudly. Then, "What's new, Jack?"

"Not a thing," Jack said, just a beat too quickly. He looked beyond Harry. "Well, it looks like the gang's all here."

I followed his gaze over to the door, where Simon had just entered and was making something of a production out of removing his Burberry.

"What's he doing here?" I asked.

"Joining us for dinner." Harry exhibited wide-eyed innocence.

It was just as well the waiter arrived then with Sidecars for everyone. Simon sauntered up just as he was leaving. "Hullo all." He kissed Brenda on the cheek before sitting. "Isn't this nice?"

"Simon, I spent all day with you," I reminded him.

"Well, yes, darling. But that was work. And this is…" He looked at Harry. "Not that I wasn't delighted to get your message when I got home, old man, but…what's the occasion? I gather it's not entirely social?" He grinned with the attitude of someone who would enjoy it immensely when the other shoe dropped.

"Not entirely, no." Harry leaned back and took us all in. "I think this is what you showbiz folks call schmoozing."

Oh, good God.

"Harry's written a play," Brenda told us.

"Yes," Jack filled the ensuing silence. "He mentioned something about that."

"Charley didn't seem too enthusiastic." Harry was speaking to Simon. "So I thought, since you're the artistic director of the Rep, I should pitch it to you directly."

Simon clearly found the evolving situation less and less amusing. He was blinking rapidly and making clever comments like "Ah, Um, Well, Ah…" when Jack raised his glass in a toast.

"To the theatre!"

Hilarious, my husband.

Chapter Fourteen

Almost being killed does amazing things for a person's appetite, and the dinner was everything I could have asked for in upscale comfort food. Little potato thingies topped with caviar (mine) and firecracker shrimp (stolen from Jack's plate) for starters, followed by lobster spaghetti (which I did not share). And I will say this in Harry's defense: The man can navigate a wine list.

I was just beginning to contemplate warm chocolate brioche pudding and a terror-free ride home when Brenda gave a little squeak.

"Oh!" The color drained from her face as she looked toward the door. "Were we expecting…"

What now? We all turned to look.

I swear there was a disturbance in the restaurant's electricity the moment I saw him. It was probably my imagination, or possibly the storm. Nevertheless, I felt the air crackle as he approached us.

"Good evening." He inclined his head slightly and somehow made eye contact with each of us at once. There was a silence, then Jack spoke.

"Inspector Yahata."

The policeman was, as usual, impeccably dressed. There was always something cutting-edge about the way he looked, and if I could put my finger on it I might have chosen a career in fashion instead of the theatre. He was crisp and sharp and angled, from the not-quite-spiky way he wore his hair to the precision of his language.

"What a pleasure to see you all again."

At least he hadn't said "Isn't this nice?"

"Inspector." Harry eyed the detective. "Please, join us." It was possibly the most unwelcoming invitation ever issued.

A small, suitable flicker of regret passed over Yahata's features. "Some other time, perhaps. I fear I have other plans this evening."

Oh, so this was an entirely coincidental meeting. Right.

"Mrs. Fairfax." He turned his attention to me. "I hope you are well? And keeping safe?"

I had a horrible certainty that he knew exactly whose paint job was now decorating the Broadway Tunnel—and he probably also knew precisely where Brenda and I had been at one a.m. two nights before. But I swallowed and gave him what I hoped was a completely innocent smile.

"Absolutely."

"Excellent." He held my gaze a moment longer than was required before turning to Jack. "May I have a word?"

Jack gave me a look that said "Don't even think of coming along" before excusing himself and leading Yahata to a quiet corner of the bar.

Simon exhaled slowly. "Am I the only one who finds that fellow a little…"

"No." Brenda and I answered together.

"He's something," Harry said speculatively, observing the men at the bar. "And unless I'm mistaken—which I'm not—they're up to something."

Brenda grabbed my hand. "Do you think it's about Clara?"

Of course I thought it was about Clara.

"I don't know," I told her.

But I did know Jack hadn't called the detective, which meant Yahata hadn't suddenly materialized simply because someone had tried to squish us on the way to the restaurant.

"Who wants to bet that's the good Inspector's date?" Simon asked, raising his eyebrows in the direction of a woman near the door.

She stood in one of those hipbone-out, one-shoulder-dropped, red carpet poses, as if she were perfectly accustomed to being stared at, and gave her shimmering golden hair—somehow unfrizzed by the rain—the slightest toss.

"Oh, she's got to be." I glanced back to Jack and the detective. They shook hands and parted, Yahata pausing to look in our direction and incline his head again. Then he moved toward the supermodel, and they exited smoothly into the night.

"So." Jack took his seat next to me again. "Who wants coffee?"

We stared at him. Then we all spoke at once.

"Goddamn! If you think I'm going to—" Harry.

"Well, old thing, if you're not going to—" Simon.

"Jack, are the police going to—" Brenda.

"Oh, cut it out!" I spoke the loudest, so I won. Admittedly, it was at the expense of some curious stares from other tables, but whatever. "Jack, if you don't tell us what Inspector Yahata said this instant I'm never speaking to you again!"

"It's really not anything—"

"Jack," Brenda said quietly. "Please."

So he told us.

"Clara wasn't alone?" I stared at my husband. The information from Yahata had left us in a stunned silence, until I summed up the gist of the news. "Someone was with her at the gym?"

"How can they not have known?" Simon asked.

"How in the hell can they not have known?" Harry elaborated.

"How do they know?" Brenda's eyes were huge.

He shrugged slightly. "It was a mistake. One of the officers who was first on the scene took a statement from the receptionist who'd been on duty at the gym that night. Then, after the detectives arrived, the cop and his partner got called away to another incident—a holdup at a convenience store a couple of blocks away."

"Oh, my God—I read about that," Brenda said. "There was a shootout."

Jack nodded. "The cop's partner was wounded, and the robber was killed. So with everything involved in that…"

"Our cop forgot to tell anyone about the statement he took," I concluded.

"Unbelievable," Simon said.

"Un-fucking-believable," Harry agreed.

"And the receptionist is sure she saw someone else with Clara that night?" I asked.

"Positive," Jack confirmed. "She says Clara came in with a guest. But the description could fit almost anyone—an adult of medium size wearing gray sweats, with the sweatshirt hood up. She can't even swear whether the guest was a man or a woman."

"But wouldn't a guest have to sign something? Or fill something out?" Brenda asked, knowing full well they would, since she'd done it Tuesday night.

Jack pushed his wine glass away. "Yes. But they've gone through all the guest cards and none of them list Clara as the member sponsor."

"So it was premeditated," Simon announced. "Whoever the guest was, she—or he, I suppose—covered his or her tracks from the very beginning."

We thought that over as the last of our plates were cleared and a dessert wine was presented for Harry's inspection.

"Isn't there any sort of security system?" I asked Jack. "Closed circuit cameras or something?" I hadn't noticed any, but I hadn't been looking for them either.

He shook his head. "There are cameras, but only in the day care center. The video is fed to screens in all the exercise rooms, so parents can keep an eye on their children during their workout. But that's all."

"People probably don't want to think they're being filmed during their workouts," Simon mused. "Remember when there was all that fuss about Princess Di being photographed at the gym?"

It was the age-old struggle between privacy and security. I sure as hell wouldn't want my spandex-clad ass to be broadcast by somebody's web cam. On the other hand, I would like to think that my potential murderer might be caught on tape, should the occasion arise.

Brenda suddenly sat up straighter. "But, Jack, this is good news, isn't it?" she asked. "I mean, this means the case is still open, right? And that the police are going to look for the killer, right?"

He looked at her. "It's good news."

I caught a whiff of caution in his answer, and suspected that the police probably weren't going to issue any immediate warrants to question every medium-sized adult who owned gray sweats. But the mood at the table had lifted considerably, so I kept my thoughts to myself.

The arrival of the desserts was Harry's signal to take back control of the evening. "All right, then," he said expansively. "There's nothing to worry about. The police will figure out who killed your friend." He patted Brenda on the hand. "They're already making progress and it's just a matter of time." He spoke as someone unaccustomed to contradiction.

Simon sent me a look full of significance—whether it was in regard to the hand patting or the assurances I didn't know. But he went along with it, and after indulging in a single sip of the rather amazing Inniskillin icewine, he stepped up manfully and took one for the team.

"So, Harry. Tell me about your play."

◇◇◇

"How are you holding up?" Jack said the instant we were both buckled up in the battered car.

"You mean aside from the fact that I can't tell whether we just witnessed my best friend and my uncle on a date?"

"Aside from that." He glanced over at me. "Although if you want my opinion—"

"I really don't think I do," I told him. I'd gotten Brenda and Simon alone long enough to tell them about the tunnel incident, but I hadn't had any extra time to try and extract girlish confidences from Brenda.

Not that I'd have wanted them, if they involved Harry.

The rain had let up and the streets were fairly quiet, but Jack kept up a steady rhythm of checking rearview mirrors as he drove. The ones we had left, anyway.

"Did you tell Inspector Yahata what happened to us tonight?"

"Of course," Jack said. "But I'm guessing that truck was stolen, so I doubt there's much they can do about it."

Right. I shifted my position so I could study his face. "What else did you two talk about?"

He put on an innocent look. "Um, remember the news about Clara Chen not being alone that night?"

"I do, and that's a nice try. But I don't see why Inspector Yahata would interrupt what I'm sure was a very hot date just to tell you they have one vague description from one uncorroborated receptionist."

Jack shot me a sideways glance. "And here I was thinking you were distracted by the dessert menu."

"What else did he tell you?"

"Clara Chen's gym membership card is missing."

My mind flashed to the locker room at WorkSpace. "Missing?"

"It should have been with her, or around her, or anywhere in the locker room. The membership cards are the electronic keys to the lockers."

Since I hadn't gotten around to mentioning my midnight expedition with Brenda, Jack thought he was telling me something I didn't know. But I remembered swiping the card through the slot to open the locker.

Jack went on. "Clara's locker was locked but the card was gone."

"So where is it?" I stared at him. "Or, more importantly, who used it to lock her locker? And why did they need to open it in the first place?"

Jack nodded grimly. "That's what Yahata would like to know."

Ah ha!

Chapter Fifteen

A bleak chilly hillside in Colma, the City of the Dead. Clara Chen was being laid to rest. We were gathered at the top of a steep hill, and the tidy rows of headstones—uniformly sized, shaped, and spaced—stretched away beneath us, reminding me of an empty theater viewed from the balcony.

I'd never been to a Chinese cemetery before. There were several things I gradually noticed. The fact that all the headstones had small, oval photographs of the deceased on them. The fact that they were real headstones, upright monoliths rather than the flat slabs that had elsewhere been adopted for the convenience of lawnmowers. The fact that they were lettered both in the front, as you'd expect, and in the back. Every back was the same, the family name in English, and over it a Chinese character carved in a circle—presumably also the family name.

Most of the headstones had matching marble urns on either side, and most of the urns were filled with flowers—real, silk, or plastic. There were smaller urns for incense sticks. And, I realized, there was food.

Most of the graves had at least a small pile of oranges. Some had more, apples and bananas. Some had pink boxes from bakeries or take-out restaurants, plates of buns arranged into pyramid shapes, or piles of little cakes. Offerings for the dead.

I wondered if it was always like this, with so many families visiting, children darting around as if they were on a picnic. Or if weekends were the time to pay respects to your ancestors.

Or if people made a special effort in the weeks leading up to Chinese New Year.

I was standing on one side of Brenda, holding her hand. Eileen stood on her other side. Jack was next to me; I could feel his warmth radiating between gusts of damp wind. I was there for Brenda, but I was trying very hard not to be there.

I looked up at a gray sky filled with gulls. No doubt drawn by the offerings, they would wait until the service was over and the mourners were gone to return to their graveside feasts.

From high on the hillside, looking over the valley, the view was all greenery and rolling hills. At the bottom of the Chinese cemetery, two white stone temple lions guarded the gates, perpetually snarling across the street at a pair of medieval-looking towers—the castle gates of Cypress Lawn.

That other cemetery was very different. Old and overgrown and vaguely gothic, with its sculptures of weeping angels, its crypts and family mausoleums. That cemetery was where San Francisco society had been buried for generations. The Spreckles and the Floods and so on.

People began to move, and I realized the service was over. Jack moved closer and murmured in my ear.

"Are you all right? You were a million miles away."

No, I wasn't. But I wanted to be. A million miles away from the view, down the hill and across the street, into Cypress Lawn and the ornate monuments to the Spreckles, the Floods. And to that other San Francisco family, the Van Leewens.

My parents were buried across the street.

I'd never been to their graves.

"This is where Morgan Stokes lives?" Eileen took in the freshly painted Victorian with a touch of skepticism. "I had him figured for a sleek SOMA loft run by a centralized computer system."

"This is the address," Brenda confirmed, referring to the card Stokes had given Jack at the funeral. He'd told us he was having some people come back to his house after the service, and he'd invited us to join them. "It's lovely."

It was lovely. In a great neighborhood sometimes called Dolores Heights and sometimes called Upper Castro, depending on your realtor, the street where Stokes lived was lined with Victorian-era houses. Some were in better repair than others and most had been converted into flats. His stood out as a testament to what a fortune in renovations could accomplish.

"Should we wait for Jack?" Brenda looked doubtfully down the street. Jack had dropped us off and gone in search of parking.

"He'll be a while," I guessed. "Let's get out of the wind."

The door was answered by Clara's sister. Brenda had met her years ago, and the two moved off to talk with some of Clara's other old friends from her Berkeley days.

"Should we get something to eat?" Eileen asked. We'd found ourselves in a large living room, and people were milling around with plates of food. "There's got to be a buffet table somewhere."

"I'm not hungry," I told her.

"There's a first."

I ignored her. I was busy visualizing each of the guests in gray sweats with hoods. Had someone here been Clara's mystery guest at the gym on the night she died? And if so, who? I discounted all men with facial hair and everyone who was over- or undersized. That left a lot of people.

And I recognized a few. For example, there was a slim guy with a sleek blond ponytail, wearing a black turtleneck with black trousers and scarfing down what looked like an entire platter of marinated shrimp.

"That's Troy Patterson," Eileen said softly, following my gaze. "He's the vice president of Marketing."

Of course. I knew he'd been featured in one of the folders we'd gone over in Eileen's office.

"And that's Millicent O'Malley." I nodded toward a gaunt gray woman in what I hoped was a fairly subtle manner. "She's something big in Engineering, isn't she?"

At the moment, she was looking disapprovingly at a heaping plate of food being rather messily consumed by the pudgy man she was speaking with.

"Right. She's talking to Bob Adams, the head of Quality Assurance."

The head of Quality Assurance dripped guacamole on his shirt, to Millicent's evident disgust.

"And that's the Engineering exec." Eileen shifted my attention to an unhappy looking balding guy deep in conversation on his cell phone in a corner. "Jim Stoddard."

I nodded. He was one of the few who knew about the engagement and Clara's upcoming promotion.

But I didn't find the one person I really wanted to. Lalit Kumar. I hadn't seen him at the grave site either. I knew from Jack that Kumar had missed at least one day of work, and now he was absent from his colleague's funeral.

I sincerely hoped he'd caught a nasty cold that night when Brenda and I had followed him around in the rain—the alternative was something far more sinister.

I was distracted from this worrisome train of thought by a disturbance in another room. Someone was shouting. Eileen and I exchanged looks and followed the sound of the strained voice to a dining room which contained an elaborate buffet and a hysterical young woman.

"How can you all just *eat?*" She was sobbing and shaking, her blond hair limp and her eyes sunken and wild. "Clara's *dead* and you're all just acting like this is some *party!*"

She took a swipe at the table, sending a plate of finger sandwiches over the edge. Most of the guests backed away, looking either embarrassed or shocked.

"Who is she?" I asked Eileen.

"No idea."

"You *bastards!*" she yelled. "None of you gives a damn—"

"Krissy!"

A commanding female voice stopped the sobbing young woman in her tracks. Millicent O'Malley crossed the dining room swiftly. "Control yourself," she ordered. "This is neither the time nor the place."

She gave the impression of a no-nonsense schoolteacher who wasn't about to have her classroom disturbed by raw displays of emotion.

"But she's *dead*!" the girl protested. "She's—"

Quickly, before I saw it coming, Millicent raised her hand and slapped the girl across the face. The sharp sound of it seemed to echo in the room, and the silence that followed it was shocked.

The girl, Krissy, put her hand to her cheek as if she were stunned. She stared at the older woman for a moment, then simply crumpled, falling into her arms and sobbing.

Millicent made soothing sounds and looked around at the gathered guests apologetically as she led the girl out of the room and down a hallway, presumably to somewhere she could pull herself together.

"What was that about?" Jack spoke softly from behind me.

I turned around. "Grieving, I suppose." I looked up at him. "Or guilt?"

"Maybe both. Did I miss anything else?"

Nothing except me sizing up the suspects.

"Not really. We decided not to wait outside for you."

"Very sensible. It's just started to rain." He looked around. "This is a nice place."

"It's lovely," I said automatically. But then I realized it really was. The décor was hip but not off-putting, comfortable but not sloppy, uncluttered but not sterile. "It's perfect."

"Thank you." Morgan Stokes joined us, having made his way through the thinning crowd of guests after the uncomfortable scene was over. He led us back to the living room, seeming to notice his furnishings for the first time.

"This was all Clara's doing. Before we moved in together I was in a huge cold loft with computers everywhere, right down the street from the office."

I caught Eileen's "I told you so" look.

"Clara decorated this?" I asked.

"She worked with a decorator," he said. "But the ideas were all hers." He hunched his shoulders, and for a moment his youthfulness left him and he looked truly alone.

"She must have been…" I didn't know how to finish.

"She was," he said quickly. Then he seemed to come to himself again, and he targeted Jack. "We need to talk. Let's go to my study."

He didn't wait for an answer before turning and walking away. Jack followed him. I looked at Eileen and shrugged, then I followed Jack.

"What progress have you made?"

I slipped into the book-lined room in time to hear Stokes' question. I was startled by the sharpness of his tone.

Jack raised his eyebrows mildly. "As we stated in our report, Mike thinks the pattern of the error flags—"

"I'm not talking about the damn bug," Stokes interrupted him. "I'm talking about Clara's murder. What have you learned?"

"Nothing since we last spoke," Jack replied evenly.

Had he told Stokes about Inspector Yahata's news of the night before? I decided now wasn't the time to ask, and sat next to Jack on a deep leather sofa in front of the fireplace.

Stokes didn't seem to notice I was here. He stared into the fire without moving.

When he finally spoke, there was desperation in his voice. "Do you believe there's a connection?"

"Between Clara's death and the software bug she'd discovered?" Jack asked.

"Yes," Stokes said.

"Yes."

I blinked. I hadn't expected Jack to give a straight answer. They were rather rare, in my experience.

Stokes met Jack's gaze without flinching. "My company is falling apart," he said. "Someone is trying to ruin it, and that someone killed Clara."

They stared at each other some more. Maybe it was a male-bonding thing, but it was getting on my nerves.

"What do you mean, your company is falling apart?" I asked, breaking the charged silence. "I mean, I know you have this bug, but aside from that, isn't Zakdan one of the biggest tech companies around?" I was pretty sure I could remember all of Eileen and Brenda's research correctly, and they certainly hadn't used the phrase "falling apart."

Stokes looked surprised. "Yes, for now, but—" He let out a breath, probably at the hopelessness of explaining things to me.

"But what? You've been profitable for the past twelve quarters. You've exceeded the analysts' projections for the past eight. You came through the dot com crash relatively unscathed and you've got a healthy bottom line for the foreseeable future."

Two pair of eyes stared at me.

"What? I've been talking to Eileen." And apparently listening more than I'd realized.

"I'll bet you have." Jack's mouth twitched.

"Not everything shows up in the financial reports," Stokes told me. "We have to be looking to the future to see where we'll be in two years' time, or five, or ten." He spread his hands. "That's forever in this business."

"So where will you be?" I asked.

"That's the problem." He frowned. "We don't know. It's called a 'vision thing,' and right now we don't have one."

He leaned forward. "Last year the board decided to completely reinvent the company. They hired dozens of consultants to try and establish 'synergy' with the media. We got product placements in the biggest movies and made sure that our tools were used in the production of the coolest videos. We spent hundreds of millions of dollars getting to be a pop culture brand name."

Which was probably the only reason why I'd heard of them. "And?"

He sat back again. "And we found out that fame does not equal fortune. There was absolutely no impact to sales of our core product line."

Ouch.

"So what's this year's reinvention plan?" I asked him.

He rolled his eyes, something you don't see a CEO do every day. "We're addressing the fallacy of the paperless office."

I probably gave him a fairly blank look, because he elaborated. "The biggest paradox in business today is that the more electronic communication increases, the more paper is actually printed and wasted—at tremendous cost. We already make the leading platform for the development of wireless applications, so now we're working on an enterprise level data mining component with a GUI front end..."

Which was right about when I would have dozed off, if Jack hadn't surreptitiously poked me in the ribs. Not that Stokes would have noticed. He was on a roll.

"...Our best people are on it. Jim Stoddard, our senior VP of Engineering, is heading up the thing, and he's using the best and the brightest we've got. MoM has been involved from day one—"

I couldn't let that pass. "Mom? Your mother works at Zakdan?"

"Oh." Stokes smiled briefly. "No. Millicent O'Mally. She signs her emails with her initials, so everyone has always called her MoM."

Wow. The gray-haired schoolmistress who had slapped the hysterical girl was some sort of corporate matriarch?

"Anyway." Stokes proceeded to geek out again. "She's leading a Taxonomy Task Force, and she's brought in a couple of Ph.D.s in Epistemology to analyze all the content from..."

"Fascinating," Jack said. "How's that going?"

Stokes wound down. "Oh. Right. I guess the point is, it isn't going well. We're pouring millions into it, and there's no end in sight. The board still loves the idea, because they like statements that begin with 'If we can solve this problem...'"

"And end with 'the stock will go through the roof'?" I guessed.

"Ignoring the fact that 'if' is the key component to the equation," Jack finished.

Stokes shrugged. "Anyway, that's where we are now."

There was a glum silence.

"Gosh," I said, which caused Jack to look at me suspiciously. "It sounds like your board of directors would listen to any corporate snake oil salesman who came along."

"Not just any," Stokes corrected wryly. "They'd have to be expensive."

I nodded. "But, getting back to the point of this discussion…" Jack's eyes narrowed, but I decided not to notice. "If the software bug and Clara's death are connected, and we can figure out who planted the bug, we'll have found Clara's killer, right?"

Jack opened his mouth, and I realized that pausing rhetorically might not have been my smartest move. I rushed on. "So probably the best way to find out who planted the bug is for someone to go undercover at Zakdan and…" I tried to remember how Simon had phrased it. "Infiltrate!"

"Charley—" Jack said.

"Are you serious?" Stokes asked. "You could do that?" He looked from me to Jack and back again.

"Morgan—" Jack began.

"We could," I said.

And then I held my breath.

Chapter Sixteen

The mood in the car was not sunny.

Eileen had taken one look at Jack's face when we'd emerged from Stokes' study and told us she was taking a cab home. That left me with one grieving best friend and one simmering husband—not the best guest list for a little light conversation.

Brenda, speaking from the back seat, was the one to break the crushing silence. "What's the matter with you two?"

"Nothing." We said it at the same time, and apparently neither of us was believable.

"O…kay," Brenda said. "You know, you guys, I can take a cab if—"

"Jack," I interrupted her. "It's a good idea. Morgan Stokes thinks it's a good idea, and even you have to admit it's a good idea."

He didn't answer.

Brenda, after waiting a few beats, asked, "What's a good idea?"

I turned around to face her. "Going undercover at Zakdan."

Her eyes widened. "Seriously? Jack, you're going under cover?"

"Not him," I corrected. "He's already been to the company with Mike and met a bunch of people. He can't do it."

"Then—"

"Me." I waited for her enthusiastic response.

It took a little too long, and when it came it wasn't exactly what I'd had in mind. "*You?*"

"Yes, me. Why not? It's the only way we can get the real scoop on what's going on." I didn't wait for her reply. "Clara might have had real enemies at Zakdan. She might have figured out some sort of huge conspiracy, and following that up is the best way to find out who killed her."

Brenda blinked a couple of times and looked like she was thinking it over. I turned my attention back to my silent husband. "You know it's a good idea."

He shot me a quick glance. "I never said it wasn't."

Before I could whoop with victory, he continued. "It might make sense for *someone* to go undercover, but that someone isn't you. You wouldn't last five minutes."

"I would so!" Not my most intellectually refined argument, but the one that came out first.

"Charley, you've never set foot in an office and you know nothing about business."

"So what? Eileen can tell me everything I need to get by. And whatever she doesn't know, Mike does. And besides," I rushed on before he could answer, "I don't actually have to do any real *work*, not if I pretend to be a consultant. Morgan just told us they've got consultants parading around the place left and right, so nobody will think anything of it."

I kept going, not giving him a chance to reply. "I'll just hang out and collect the gossip. I may know nothing about business, but I could write a book on gossip. And I'm an amateur compared to Simon."

"Simon?" Brenda and Jack asked as one.

Damn.

"Well, it was kind of his idea," I admitted. "He called it 'reality theatre.'"

"Good God," Jack replied.

"That figures," Brenda said.

"Which doesn't make it any less—"

"Charley, you don't have the slightest idea how to gather intelligence," Jack insisted. "You may be able to get people talking, but you don't have the skills to analyze what you learn, or—"

"Which is what I have you for," I told him. "We'll do a...a debriefing every night after work, so you can tell us what to follow up on the next day." Where I'd come up with the word "debriefing" was a mystery, but I was pretty sure it was the right concept.

"It's not that easy," he insisted.

"It can't be that hard," I countered.

"But it can be that dangerous." Jack's tone took on a note of finality. "If Clara Chen was murdered because of something she'd found out, that means there's a murderer at Zakdan. And if our little escapade on our way to dinner last night was any indication, they're not afraid to kill again. So if you think I'm going to let you go poking around where—"

"Let me? You're not going to *let* me—"

"Stop the car!" Brenda shouted. "Now!"

There's something to be said for marrying a man who's been trained to follow orders. Jack pulled into an illegal space immediately. We were at the tiny Alta Plaza park, deserted in the rain.

As soon as the car came to a halt, Brenda jumped out and ran out onto the grass. When she stopped she doubled over, wrapping her arms around herself. Then she looked up at the sky and screamed. It was a sound that came from her depths, and I'd never heard it before.

"Brenda!" I jumped out and tore through the rain toward her. She held up her hands as I got near.

"Wait," she gasped.

I hung back, and Jack came up behind me. Brenda took a few deep breaths, wiped the rain off her face, and finally looked at us.

"Jack Fairfax, you know damn well that Clara Chen didn't slip and fall in that steam room. She was killed. Now, Charley and Simon and I may not know the first thing about going undercover—"

"You?" I interrupted. "Nobody said you—"

She gave me a look that shut me up. Then she faced Jack again. "But whatever we don't know about it, you do. And between you and Mike you can get us in there and get us out again safely. Don't even think about denying it."

I don't know what he thought about, but he didn't deny it.

"If you're half the man I think you are, you'll do everything in your power to find out who killed Clara and why. And that includes using Charley and Simon and me to get information. So let's stop arguing and get out of the rain and figure out how we're going to do this."

She waited a moment, holding Jack's gaze as the rain dripped down her face. Then she walked past us to the car and got in.

I looked from her to Jack and back again, pushing the wet hair out of my eyes. I'd known her half my life, but I'd never seen Brenda lose it before. It was pretty damn effective.

We were going undercover.

Chapter Seventeen

When I woke up the next morning I reached for Jack. He wasn't there, so I reached for the phone.

I'd barely begun explaining the plan to Eileen when she interrupted me.

"I'm in. When do we start?"

My second phone call took even less effort.

"Yes!" Simon yelled, once he'd woken up enough to understand my call. "Darling, I never doubted you'd come to your senses and realize how brilliant I am. When do we start?"

It seemed to be the question of the day.

For the answer, I went looking for my husband.

"Jack, we can't go on like this."

I'd found him downstairs at the desk in his office. He looked up from the computer screen when he answered me.

"That's a dramatic way to begin a conversation."

"I'm not being dramatic." At least, not any more than usual. I perched on the desk and faced him. I was still wearing the champagne silk and lace concoction that I'd slept in, so I hoped the perch was effective.

"Okay." He leaned back in his chair. "How, exactly, can't we go on?"

"With you all angry about me going undercover."

His eyes narrowed slightly. "I'm not angry about that."

Oh. "Well, then—"

"Would you like to know what I am angry about?"

This conversation was not going the way I'd planned. Something about the tone of his voice. "Um—"

"How about the fact that you discussed this scheme with Simon, in apparently quite a bit of detail, and never even mentioned it to me?"

"Oh, well—"

"Or how about the fact that you and Eileen have compiled some sort of financial dossier on Zakdan, and you didn't bother telling me about that, either?"

"Ah, well, that was really Brenda—"

"Or maybe the fact that I've told you everything Yahata has told me, and everything Mike has found out, and you've been running around with the Scooby gang getting into God knows what and keeping it all a secret from me?"

Damn.

He was right. And he didn't know the half of it—the camping-out-in-the-gym and following-Lalit-Kumar-all-over-town half of it.

I stared at him while I tried to frame something like an apology or explanation. "Jack—"

"Just promise me that all stops now." The look he gave me would have melted all my resistance, if I'd had any.

I nodded. "Okay."

"Okay." He slid me toward him on the desk, and I thought we were about to seal the deal with a little passionate something. But he was just trying to get at the notebook I'd sat on. He flipped it open and grabbed a pen.

"Let's plan this thing."

◇◇◇

Simon showed up two hours later with Eileen, her son Anthony, and six folding beach chairs in assorted lollipop colors.

"They were on sale at Pottery Barn," he explained. "I simply can't take another meeting on your bed."

Jack took three from Simon's arms. "You have no idea how much I appreciate this," he said meaningfully. The two men headed for the living room.

"Aunt Charley, this place is *cool!*" Anthony, with the speed and enthusiasm only ten-year-old boys seem to possess, went tearing from one empty room to another. "Mom, why didn't you tell me to bring my roller blades?"

Eileen looked at me. "If you won't put a few throw rugs down, you have to expect this kind of reaction."

I shrugged. "Next time have him bring his skates." Actually, that sounded kind of fun.

Jack joined us in the hallway and addressed Anthony. "If your mom doesn't mind, I have a new computer game upstairs in my office. It's giving me some trouble, and I seem to remember someone telling me how good you are at computer games." His voice took on a conspiratorial tone. "It's about pirates."

Anthony glanced up at Eileen expectantly, and I realized with a shock how much he was starting to look like her. He'd lost his little-boy roundness and was suddenly tall for his age, and as thin and angular as his mother. It was hard to tell if he had her wavy dark hair, as his was cut so short he looked like a junior Marine recruit, but the eyes were Eileen's dark liquid and his lashes were an absolute crime.

"Go ahead," Eileen told him. "But don't touch anything else in Jack's office."

"I promise." He sprinted up the stairs.

"Maybe we can make an exception for my secret stash of chocolate chip cookies and soda pop," Jack said, following him.

"Within reason," Eileen called after them.

As soon as Jack was out of earshot she turned to me. "He's great with kids."

I did not like the suggestive glint in her eye. "How about a little less with that kind of talk and a little more with the covert strategy planning?"

She grinned. "I'm just saying…"

"What are you saying, darling, and what have we got to drink?" Simon joined us, having arranged the canvas chairs into a colorful circle in the center of the living room.

The doorbell rang. "That'll be Brenda." I turned away, grateful for a change of topic.

I opened the door to find her partially obscured behind two large brown sacks. "I brought bagels," she announced. "What have I missed?"

The bagels—enough to feed an entire squad of undercover operatives, and accompanied by a scallion cream cheese spread that she'd made herself—were surprisingly effective brain food. Jack brewed some coffee, I poured some juice, and we settled into the beach chairs to strategize.

"Eileen should be the team leader," Jack said. "She'll be the only one who talks business to anyone outside the group."

"That makes sense," Simon agreed. "Since she's the only one of us with the vaguest notion of how to talk business."

She was also the only one of us who'd brought a laptop, possibly because she was the only one of us—aside from Jack—who owned one. She'd popped it open and was taking notes in between neat nibbles of poppyseed bagel.

"I've sent an email to work telling them I'm taking some time off," she told us. "Jack, how long do you think we'll be at Zakdan?"

He frowned. "I'd say between one and two weeks. You'll need to dig up whatever you can quickly, before anyone there might expect to start seeing results from your 'consulting.'"

"Got it. Two weeks." She typed a note for herself. "Brenda, can you get that kind of time off?"

"No problem," she responded. "They're so glad I volunteered to lead the spring student trip that they'd say yes to anything right now."

"Great."

Jack continued. "Eileen, Mike wants to give you a crash course on the kind of technical jargon you should know. He had someplace to be today, but he's available tonight if you two want to get together. Is that okay?"

"If he doesn't mind lasagna with Anthony and me, it's okay."

I looked at my husband in amazement. I'd been trying to throw Eileen and his geeky partner together for months, and he'd just casually arranged it as if it were the most natural thing in the world.

He caught me looking at him. "What?"

"Not a thing," I said. "What's my assignment?"

"You'll be the program manager."

"Great! What does that mean?"

"You won't ever talk about the work that the group is supposedly doing. You'll just mutter things about schedules and budgets."

I nodded, relieved. I could mutter with the best of them.

"If anyone presses for specifics, just tell them the information is on a 'need to know' basis."

"Right! What does that mean?"

"It means they should leave you alone."

"Excellent!" This would be a breeze.

"Simon." Jack turned to him. "You're a visionary."

"Thank you, Jack. You know, I've always thought I had a certain knack—oh!" He seemed to suddenly remember the topic at hand. "Oh, you mean on the team—right, naturally, of course." He smiled and blinked a few times. "Sorry. I'm a what?"

Jack refrained from sighing. "A visionary. A big-picture guy."

"Right. So if anybody asks me questions, I say…"

"Tell them they have to take the thousand-foot view," Eileen suggested. "Or maybe just look like you're considering whatever they're talking about and say you'll need to 'tee that up' for discussion."

"I'm sorry?" Simon looked clueless.

"It's a golf metaphor," Jack explained. "And it's good." He turned to Eileen. "Can you supply them with more of that kind of thing?"

"Please, it's all I hear all day." She set the laptop aside and scrunched forward in her chair. "Let's see...if anyone asks you about anything like project goals, just say we need to 'push the envelope.' Or you could say we need to focus on the one thing that will 'move the needle.' And if anyone asks you something in a meeting and you don't have an answer, tell them you want to 'take it off line.'"

"Oh, I've heard that one," Brenda said. "In faculty meetings."

"And there are lots of sports things," Eileen went on. "Team members should 'play their positions,' and instead of looking into an issue, you 'go deep.'"

"It's no wonder, given the male-dominated, patriarchal nature of American business, that sports phrases would be popular," Brenda said.

"Um, sweetie." I waved at her. "Unless you're going undercover as a Women's Studies professor, maybe that's the sort of thought you should keep to yourself."

She looked startled. "Oh, right. Habit." She turned to Jack. "So what is my cover?"

He grinned. "You'll be a human resources representative, specializing in change management. Basically, you're a sympathetic ear for people who are being affected by the proposed changes. You're someone they can confide in about their fears."

"What proposed changes?" I asked him. "I thought we were just faking it."

"That's the beauty of the thing," Jack explained. "As long as you don't define the plan, everyone will assume they're being affected, so they'll all need a sympathetic ear."

"Which makes Brenda Grand Central Station for rumors and backstabbing," I guessed.

"Cool!" She beamed.

"Hang on a minute, Jack," Simon spoke up. "Do you mean to say that we're really going to go in there with one person who vaguely knows what she's doing and three completely bullshit pieces of fluff?"

"Welcome to consulting. Makes you want to start your own firm, doesn't it?"

"Bloody right it does. How much are we charging for this?"

"Lots," Jack told him. "Otherwise they won't think you're worth anything."

Simon sat back in his chair. "I'm in the wrong line of work."

"Okay." I stood and stretched. "Now that that's all figured out, we should talk about costumes. Eileen, you're taken care of, but the rest of us don't have anything even remotely businesslike in our closets."

"Too bad Martha's still out of town," Simon said.

Martha, the costume designer for the Rep, had come out of the broom closet a few months ago, announcing herself as a proud practitioner of Wicca. She'd gone off to Stonehenge on some sort of pilgrimage as soon as the costumes for the last play of the season were complete, and nobody had heard from her since.

"It is a shame," I agreed. "She'd have known just what to wear."

"Oh, for God's sake," Eileen said. "It isn't complicated. Let's just head to Union Square tomorrow, and somewhere between Banana Republic and Brooks Brothers, we'll come up with something."

"You're a genius," I told her. "And before you say anything, I'm picking up the tab for this shopping expedition, and I don't want any arguments."

I looked at Brenda, who had a policy of refusing my attempts at generosity except on her birthday or Christmas, but it was Simon who spoke.

"I wouldn't think of arguing the point."

Brenda made a face and nodded. "It's in a good cause, and I can always donate the clothes to charity when we're done."

Simon looked appalled.

"Now that we've got that important subject taken care of," Jack said dryly, "could we talk over one more tiny detail—like coming up with a pretext for getting you all into Zakdan in the first place?"

I gave him a blank look. "What do you mean?"

He sighed. "So far we've figured out what you'll do when you get in. But we need some sort of scenario that Morgan Stokes can take to the board of directors. He has to convince them you're selling something they want, and we haven't figured out what that is yet."

In the silence that followed we heard faint buccaneer noises from the office upstairs where Anthony was playing the computer pirate game.

Eileen spoke. "You're right, Jack. Even if it's nonsense and we don't do a damn thing once we're there, we have to have a reason to be let in the door."

"I don't suppose Morgan could just tell the board what he's up to?" I suggested.

Jack shook his head. "Until we know who's behind all of this, we don't know how high up it might go."

Again, silence.

"Um." Brenda looked startled that she'd made a sound.

"Do you have an idea?" Jack asked.

"No." She hesitated. "I mean…I have a thought, but it's not about what to do, it's about who could help."

We were listening.

"I mean," she continued. "We know someone who could help. Someone who could approach the board as a huge investor, and then insist that his team of experts do an in-house assessment before he'll commit. Someone who has that kind of money, and clout." She looked at me. "And someone who can bullshit better than the rest of us put together."

Ugh. She was right. I hated to admit it, but she was right.

"Harry."

Chapter Eighteen

My uncle had one condition—that we stop for takeout from Big Nate's Barbeque on the way down to Hillsborough to see him.

As a consequence, vast quantities of ribs, chicken, and cornbread now waited in a warming oven while Brenda, Simon, and I waited in the game room across the hall from Harry's office, where Jack was outlining the plan for him.

The game room, aside from the usual equipment such as a pool table and a backgammon board, held a disturbing array of wall-mounted animals and the sort of weaponry that might have been used to bring them to their current sorry state.

Maybe Harry thought the big-game hunter macho thing the décor implied would land him the babes, or maybe he just hadn't bothered to redecorate since the last in his extensive string of ex-wives had stormed out. In any case, the feeling of being watched by several dozen glass eyes wasn't really helping our stress level.

"He'll do it." Brenda's voice held confidence. Then she looked at me. "Won't he?"

"He's bound to," Simon replied, amusing himself with a fencing foil he'd taken from its display case. "Harry's up for anything." He thrust with the thin blade. "You know that."

I deeply hoped she knew nothing of the sort. But Simon was right in one sense. Harry never turned down a chance to meddle in things. And infiltrating a major corporation with a bogus team of consultants would constitute meddling on the kind of scale he was known to appreciate.

"Hello, Charley."

I jumped a good nine inches off the mocha leather chair I'd been perched on. Harry's voice can do that to me.

He'd entered the room from the door behind me. I turned to find him regarding me with a massive cigar in his mouth and a massive gleam in his eye.

"Jack says you need me." The cigar got a chomp of satisfaction.

"He's paraphrasing," Jack told me, following Harry in and pausing to give me a reassuring peck on the cheek.

Harry made for the bar. "Who's drinking? Simon, I've got an *Añejo Reserva* tequila here that will set us up for that barbeque just right. Can I twist your arm?"

Simon lost interest in the sword. "Twisting won't be in the least necessary, Harry."

"And Brenda?" The cigar was removed to allow for a broad smile. "Can I tempt you?"

Was she blushing? Good God, was she blushing?

"Harry!" My voice produced something closer to a panicked yell than I'd intended, but I went with it. "Would you stop playing bartender for a minute and tell us whether you'll do it?"

He turned to me with a bottle in hand and a maddeningly amused look on his face. "Do what?"

I sighed. I reached for the bottle, took a glass, and poured myself a shot. I downed it looking at my uncle, shuddered briefly, and spoke. "Will you help us?"

His eyebrows went up. "Sure, Charley. All you had to do was ask."

Jack took the bottle from me before I did something drastic with it.

"I only have one condition." Harry lined up four shot glasses on the bar.

"Of course you do." I added my glass to the line.

"You'll need protection."

"Jack and I have already gone over all that. We'll be perfectly—"

Whatever bland assurances I would have made were cut off by Harry's completely unreasonable demand.

"You'll take Flank."

"*Flank!*" Simon protested before I had a chance to close my mouth. "The man's a menace! He practically killed me once just for walking into a room with Charley."

"Well, that is kinda what you look for in a bodyguard." Harry eyed me. "You're taking him."

Flank had been my bodyguard for an unpleasant period when certain people had been trying to sabotage my theatre and kill me along with my husband. He was a handy guy to have around in an emergency. But he was also extremely large and extremely hairy and—unless we planned to enter Zakdan as a team of paleoanthropologists traveling with our own live Neanderthal exhibit—he wasn't exactly going to blend in.

"Harry, it's impossible. Jack, tell him it's impossible."

Jack didn't get the chance.

"Impossible or not." Harry motioned for the tequila from Jack and began to pour. "You're taking Flank or I'm not going to the board of directors to tell lies for you. It's your choice."

"Just what are we supposed to tell people about him? He doesn't exactly look like a computer programmer."

Harry grinned as he passed the shot glasses around. "No, I can't say he does." He paused before handing me my drink. "Maybe a secretary?"

Flank. A secretary.

We were doomed.

"It's awful. It's just awful."

Eileen was referring to the outfit Brenda had on. And I couldn't disagree. We'd met at Saks the following morning to shop for our undercover wardrobes.

We were not having much success.

"I'm not a suit type of person," Brenda explained. Faced with the pinstriped evidence, I found it hard to disagree. "I just don't do tailored well."

"But the point isn't to look good." Eileen spoke as if she were trying to convince herself. "I mean, a lot of women look professional without looking good."

"Eileen," I reminded her. "You're the one who said this was going to be easy."

"It should be," she insisted. "It's not like we're walking down the red carpet on Oscar night. We're just going to work. In an office. People do it every day."

"People, maybe," Brenda said. "But not Charley. And not me." She pulled the jacket off with evident relief. "Why can't I just dress like a teacher?"

Things in the changing room were on the verge of getting ugly when we heard a familiar voice calling from outside in the hallway.

"Hello? Darlings? Where are you?"

"Simon?" I popped my head out the door and peered down the hall. Simon was hovering at the end of the row of dressing rooms, averting his eyes and hollering for us.

"You're supposed to be shopping." I couldn't imagine anything that would prevent Simon from wreaking havoc through Union Square with the shiny new credit card I'd given him.

"There you are. Thank heaven!" He spoke to someone behind him. "Darling, it sounds like we're just in time!" Then back to me. "We could hear you three arguing all the way from the escalator."

"Who's 'we'? And why are you here?" Eileen pushed me out into the hallway so she could get in on the discussion.

"I'm here because I'm always looking out for you, darlings, with never a thought for myself. And today I'm saving you from a fashion disaster. Look who's here!"

He vanished from the doorway, and shoved someone else into the dressing room hall. Someone who was rail thin, five foot two on her best day, and draped head to toe in filmy egg-plant-colored knitwear.

"Martha!"

I'd never been so happy to see a witch in my life. Particularly since the witch in question was the Rep's brilliant costume designer, apparently returned home from her vacation to the top ten Wiccan hotspots of Europe.

"Hi, Charley. I got back a few days ago, so when Simon called this morning and told me about your reality theatre project I thought it sounded fun." She came down the hall to our dressing room, brushing back her hood, or cowl, or whatever it was, to reveal her hair in a long loose braid and her face astonishingly free of the heavy eye makeup I was used to. She looked about fourteen years old. I'd have to remember to ask her if there was a spell for that.

But first, to business. She entered the dressing room and appraised the three of us with a critical eye. "Who's playing who?"

Clearly Simon hadn't mentioned the whole covert ops aspect to the costuming challenge. I explained that Brenda was in the human resources role, Eileen was playing the team leader, and I was a project manager. Martha nodded, tilted her head to the side, and considered.

"You," she said to Brenda, "need to stay loose and unconstructed. If you want people to confide in you, don't wear shoulder pads. I'm thinking Eileen Fisher with Cole Haan shoes."

Brenda nodded as if she knew what that meant.

"You." She pointed at Eileen, gesturing with a twirly finger for her to turn around. "If you're supposed to be in charge, you should be intimidating. You're in suits in every scene…slim-fitting trousers with pointed toe boots…spiky heels…and let's see if we can do some sort of sleek ponytail with all that hair."

Just what had Simon told Martha she was dressing us for? I didn't have time to question her, because her attention was now firmly on me.

"And you're somewhere in the middle. You're not the boss… you don't have a lot to spend on clothes…probably a few good pieces that you got on sale…the rest is Gap and Banana…"

I stopped paying attention. I didn't have to. I was in the hands of a professional.

◇◇◇

"Well, that's settled, then." Simon sat back in his chair with a look of blissful satisfaction.

We were all pretty pleased with ourselves. Once Martha had taken over she'd made quick work of marching us to the proper departments in the proper stores to get the proper costumes.

We'd finished in time for a late lunch, for which she declined to join us, saying something about a prior appointment at the East Bay Vivarium. I didn't choose to speculate about what she might be browsing for at a reptile specialty store. The rest of us had gone on to meet Simon at the Neiman Marcus Rotunda.

He'd had a successful day as well, and was topping it off with a lobster club sandwich. "I wonder how the meeting at Zakdan went."

Jack had called Morgan Stokes from Harry's the night before, and asked him to make arrangements for a board meeting in the afternoon. I looked at my watch and realized my uncle was probably spinning an extensive string of lies somewhere South of Market as we spoke.

"Let's hope he can sell it," Eileen said. "I'd hate to have to return everything we just bought."

Simon choked on a bite of brioche. "You can't be serious."

"It won't come to that," I assured him. "Harry will sell it."

There are some things of which I have no doubt.

"Charley." Simon seemed struck by a thought. "What are we going to do about the Rep while we're...occupied?"

"What do you mean?" I picked at my seafood Cobb salad.

"Well, these two—" He gestured to Eileen and Brenda with a French fry. "—are on vacations from work, but we still have to get through that pile of plays Chip has lined up for us."

Damn. I'd completely forgotten about that.

I looked up at the stained-glass dome of the restaurant. It gave me no inspiration.

"We'll just have to squeeze the reading in where we can," I told him. "That's what we'd do if we'd gone on vacation some-where." I allowed myself one tiny daydream about the untaken vacation, visualizing myself next to a bronzed and mostly naked Jack lying on a beach somewhere.

In the daydream I wasn't reading.

"Charley?" Brenda was looking at me funny. "Are you okay?"

I sighed. "As well as can be expected." I looked at Simon. "Tell Chip to come over on Saturday. We can talk about the next batch then."

"Speaking of the Rep," Eileen said. "Should you two be using false names when we go undercover?"

I gave her a blank look.

"You and Simon have been in the paper more than once, for opening nights and things," she explained. "People might recognize you and wonder why you gave up a life in the theatre to become high-tech consultants."

Simon and I looked at each other. "Do you think?"

He shrugged. "It's not as though we're famous or anything…" He seemed to lose interest in the topic with the arrival of the dessert menus.

"I'm a little more worried about the fact that you and Brenda and I went to Clara's funeral," I told Eileen.

She waved her hand dismissively, over both the dessert selections and my concerns. "That's easy. We weren't actually introduced to anyone from Zakdan, just seen. It would be perfectly reasonable for us to pay our respects to Morgan's fiancée if we'd been working on him with the preliminaries of the consultancy job for the past few weeks."

"I suppose so." We'd just have to find a way of working that into the conversation somewhere.

"Oh!" Brenda sat up suddenly. "But what about the other night? In the car? Do you think the driver of that truck could have gotten a good look at you?"

That was a frightening thought. I'd assumed that the killer's attempt on us had mainly been an attempt on Jack, because of his snooping around at Zakdan. But Brenda was right. Even though the driver might not have set out to kill me, he might have gotten a good enough look at my face to recognize me when I came strolling into Zakdan masquerading as a consultant.

But then again… "It was pretty dark and rainy that night, and everything happened awfully fast. And Jack is positive the truck wasn't trailing us from the house, so the killer wouldn't have seen me getting into the car."

Brenda still looked worried. I can't say I was entirely calm about it all myself.

"Maybe you should go blonde, darling," Simon suggested. "Or what about a fiery redhead? That might suit you very well."

"I'll ask Jack what he thinks." Except I'd probably omit the fiery redhead suggestion. "But I really don't think it's worth worrying about. So don't worry."

Good advice. I wished I'd be able to take it.

Chapter Nineteen

There are a number of images that come to mind when I think of "home." A quiet, book-filled room on a rainy day. Jack building a fire in the hearth. Maybe the aroma of something yummy baking in the oven.

One image that does not come to mind is my uncle, bourbon in hand and cigar in mouth, greeting me at my own front door.

"Charley!" He flung the door open as we trudged up the path carrying our purchases. "It looks like your operation was a success." He stepped aside as I struggled past him, weighed down with shopping bags. Then he reached around me to take Brenda's bags from her.

"It wasn't an operation so much as an expedition, Harry, into the darkest heart of retail." Simon was unencumbered. He'd left his own undoubtedly enormous assortment of purchases in his car. Eileen followed him in carrying the remains of the things Brenda and I had gotten. Her shopping had been relatively light, since she already owned an assortment of power suits, and her few bags remained in her car.

"Where's Jack?" I asked Harry. "How did the meeting go?"

"Come on, Charley." He set the bags down at the bottom of the stairs and took the cigar out to give me a self-satisfied grin. "Have you ever known me to walk into a board meeting and not come out with what I wanted?"

"Not recently," I admitted.

"So we're in?" Simon asked. "It's on? It's a green light? It's a go? We're a—what's the word?"

"Hysterical," I answered, patting him on the arm. "Calm down, okay? It's not like we start tomorrow."

"No." Jack appeared at the top of the stairs, Mike and Gordon behind him. "You start Wednesday."

"Seriously?" I gulped. "That seems awfully soon. I mean, I know we've tossed around a few lines and everything, but I really thought we'd have more time to rehearse, I mean…the day after tomorrow? Seriously?"

Simon's left eyebrow went up. "Now who's hysterical?"

Eventually, aided by a few sample bottles of wine that Gordon had brought from his restaurant, I got a grip. We gathered in the living room, some on Simon's beach chairs and some sprawled on the floor. Harry paced.

"We'll be fine." Simon was suddenly the soul of nonchalance. He gestured to the pile of shopping bags. "At least we'll be dressed for the parts, and the right costume is half the battle."

That was one way of looking at it. A shallow way, but it was something.

Jack spoke. "Remember your best option is to avoid discussing your work—instead you'll try to get the other person to talk. And if you're completely cornered, try to be evasive." He looked at me. "That shouldn't be hard."

I nodded. "Avoid and evade. Got it."

"You know…" Harry took a reflective sip of a fairly excellent Cabernet. "In my experience, everyone in every business is always bluffing to some extent or another. It's like Warren Buffett once told me—'It's only when the tide goes out that you discover who's been swimming naked.'"

He was enjoying this way too much.

"I've always been rather fond of swimming naked," Simon remarked, to no one's surprise.

"And we're not completely naked," Eileen said. "Mike, have you got the books?"

"Um, right." Mike had been scribbling something on a piece of paper. The secret to cold fusion, no doubt. "Yeah." He got to his feet and retrieved a stack of three-ring binders he'd left near the doorway.

I couldn't believe that in all the fuss over shopping I'd totally forgotten to ask Eileen how her dinner with Mike had gone. Whether, between lessons in technical jargon and servings of lasagna, anything interesting might have developed. I couldn't really read much into her expression as she watched him. No obvious wanton longings, but you never know.

Mike passed the binders out to Simon, Brenda, and me. "This should help you," he said. "There are different sections." Each clearly marked with color-coded tabs. If Mike had organized them, maybe he was perfect for Eileen.

"It's a Fake Book," Mike explained. "I thought it might be helpful to use the same concept that musicians do, of a book with just enough of just about any song to get them to the point where they can fake the rest. This book has just enough information to get you started." He grinned nervously. "After that you fake it."

Something told me we'd have an easier time faking a chorus of "Swanee River" than bluffing about high-tech business ventures, but whatever.

"There's a listing of all of Zakdan's current products, ongoing projects, and key players," Mike went on.

"And a glossary of terminology you should get familiar with." Eileen took Brenda's copy and turned to the relevant section.

I flipped through the thing. "There's a bibliography." I looked up. "A bibliography?"

"Oh, uh." Mike looked a little embarrassed. "They're just suggestions. Some of the more popular business books from the last few years. Just in case someone refers to one of them, you should know the titles and have a passing familiarity."

As long as I wasn't expected to understand them all.

"The last part is a primer on office etiquette," he offered. "Things like what's cool and what isn't on company email and, um…" He blushed. "Sexual harassment sort of stuff. Things you'd know if you worked in offices."

Okay, brilliant or not, if the man couldn't utter the word "sexual" in adult mixed company without turning pink, maybe he wasn't quite what Eileen should be looking for after all.

"Office etiquette?" Simon demanded. "And who the bollocks do you suppose needs that?"

"Certainly not you, sweetie," I reassured him. "But—" I turned to Harry. "—if you're still serious about sending Flank in with us, we might need to check into regulations about physical intimidation in the workplace."

Harry stopped his pacing and leaned against the wall, crossing his arms. "The man can't help the way he looks, Charley."

Brenda spoke up. "If we say he's our secretary, we can probably just keep him close to us, so he won't…I mean…so he doesn't…"

"So he doesn't cause a panic in the break room?" Simon asked. "Something suggestive of gazelles fleeing the watering hole as they sense a frisky bull elephant on approach?"

"Something like that."

"At least you won't have to worry about him saying the wrong thing to the wrong person," Jack offered.

True.

In my experience, Flank's verbal abilities were limited to a series of unintelligible grunts—unless he was holding a gun, in which case he was perfectly articulate. And since I didn't anticipate he'd go prowling the corridors of Zakdan with a Walther in his hand, we were probably safe on that score.

Further discussion was interrupted by the doorbell.

"Have we ordered takeout?" Simon brightened.

"We just had lunch," Eileen scolded him.

"That was hours ago!"

Jack rose to answer the door as Gordon spoke up.

"If you like, you can all come down to the restaurant to sample some of the things I'm thinking of putting on the menu." A line appeared between his eyebrows. "I still haven't made the final decisions."

"Excellent!" Simon beamed. "If you need a discerning palate, look no further. I'm your man."

"That's so sweet of you," Brenda said. "I've missed your cooking."

Harry grunted and shot Gordon a dark look. He still hadn't forgiven the chef for leaving his position as Harry's cook and right-hand man. Even if that position had been a cover he'd assumed in order to investigate my family.

Jack came back into the room, followed by an enormous burgundy leather wing chair. The kind of thing you see in old movies of old libraries in old gentlemen's clubs.

"Great!" Harry clapped his hands once, then rubbed them together. "Now I can finally sit down in this place."

A grunt came from behind the chair, and I got an awful feeling that I'd figured out who was carrying it.

"Right here by the fireplace," Harry said, and the chair was dutifully deposited in position. Its bearer straightened to reveal himself.

He looked like the love child of a mob enforcer and a yeti, and he was grinning at me as if he couldn't be happier.

I did my best to smile back. "Hi, Flank."

"I can't believe he did that."

Jack looked at the chair, and I swear I saw his mouth twitch.

"I mean, it's not normal for a person to bring his own furniture to another person's house," I insisted.

"But if we're talking Harry, are we really talking normal?"

It had started to rain, so Jack and I had decided to stay home when everyone else went off to Gordon's restaurant. Jack had stuck something from the freezer into the oven for dinner later. Then he'd built our first fire while I'd gone upstairs to grab the duvet off the bed. We were now comfortably curled up on it in front of the crackling logs.

I sighed and turned my back on the chair, choosing not to remember the tremendous enjoyment Harry had taken in occupying it for the later part of the afternoon.

"I should be reading plays," I said halfheartedly.

"That sounded convincing." Jack pulled on the duvet to slide me closer to him.

"I've got a whole stack to get through. And then there's Mike's Fake Book to study."

"Uh huh."

Something in the way he looked at me made me suspect I wasn't going to get much accomplished. And I was okay with that. But I did have something to discuss with him, just because I'd promised the gang.

"Jack, do you think I should be in some sort of disguise?"

His eyebrows went up.

"Brenda is worried that the guy from the truck the other night might recognize me as the person who was in your car with you."

Jack nodded. "I'm a little worried about that too, but if I really thought he'd recognize you from seeing you in those conditions, I'd lock you in the bedroom and throw away the key before I'd let you set foot in Zakdan."

That was sweet, in a sort of like-hell-he-would way. But since it didn't seem to be an issue, I decided not to get all huffy about it.

"What about using a false name? Eileen pointed out that Simon and I are fairly well known in theatrical circles, so she thought maybe…what do you think?"

He seemed to be giving it consideration. "What kind of a name?"

"Oh, I don't know. I really think just Charley Fairfax is good enough, because anybody who would know me from the theatre would know me as Charley Van Leewen." I still used my maiden name for most things related to the Rep.

"Still." He appeared to be thinking it over. "If the killer knows my name it might not be a good idea to show up using Fairfax."

"Oh." I hadn't thought of that. "Okay, I'll stick with Van Leewen."

"Maybe you should use a different first name," Jack suggested.

"Do you think?"

"Something like Hazel or Brunhilda."

"Gee, thanks." When I had thought about it, I'd been thinking of something more like Hildy Johnson—the fast-talking investigative reporter Rosalind Russell played in *His Girl Friday*. Or maybe Bunny Watson, after Katharine Hepburn's character in *Desk Set*. Something suitably business-ish.

Jack interrupted my thoughts with the last suggestion I would have imagined.

"How about Mina?"

I stared at him.

"No?" He watched me. "You don't like it?"

I didn't like it. I didn't like it when I was born Hermina Van Leewen, in honor of my grandfather. I didn't like it that, however much I preferred to be called Mina, all the kids at school persisted in calling me Herman. I'd liked it so little that I'd legally changed it when I was fourteen, right after my parents died. I chose Charley because, if I was going to be called by a guy's name, it was at least going to be a cute guy's name.

I blinked. "You know?"

He grinned. "I know everything, remember?"

"How?"

He scooted me closer again. "I have ways."

Damn right he did. Which were a little unnerving.

"Do I have *any* secrets from you?"

"Do you need any?"

"This isn't fair," I said. "You get to know everything about me, and what do I get to know about you?"

He tilted his head, close to mine. "Everything you need to."

Right. I have a husband on a need-to-know basis.

"My middle name is Pequod." He looked me in the eye. "Like the ship."

"Your middle name is George," I informed him.

His eyes flashed. "See? I can't lie to you. You know too much about me." The last statement, while false, was spoken in a low whisper and accompanied by a soft bite to the earlobe, so I didn't much care about its veracity.

"I do know one thing."

"Mmmfghbt?" As he was occupied in the general area of my neck, I couldn't quite make out what he said.

"I know this duvet isn't thick enough for the kind of thing you have in mind."

He stopped in mid-nibble. "Then I suggest we go upstairs immediately." He stood and held out a hand. "And if I should feel the urge to call out a name in the heat of passion...?" he grinned.

"It had better be 'Charley.'"

Chapter Twenty

The following day I had a choice. Make the most of my last day before going undercover at Zakdan by studying my Fake Book and burning through as many of Chip's manuscripts as possible, or make the most out of it by sleeping in, booking spa appointments for the afternoon, and making reservations at some decadent restaurant for a quiet little dinner with Jack.

I was just trying to decide which spa appointments to book when the phone rang.

"Charley, I'm working on my opening speech for tomorrow."

It was Eileen, sounding uncharacteristically flustered.

"What speech?"

"Haven't you talked to Jack yet today?"

"He was gone when I woke up," I yawned.

"Don't tell me you're not out of *bed* yet?"

I sat up and put my feet on the floor. "Of course I am. Do you think I'd spend the last day before our operation just lazing around? Give me a little credit."

"Oh, sorry."

So was I. Briefly.

I started stripping the bed while Eileen talked.

"Jack spoke to Morgan Stokes this morning, and Morgan told him that he's arranged an executive staff meeting for first thing tomorrow. So we can meet all the major Zakdan players at once."

"That's great." Then a horrible thought struck. "When, exactly, do you think 'first thing in the morning' might be?"

"Around ten."

Thank God. "Okay, so we'll go to the meeting. What's the problem?"

"Well, obviously, I'm going to have to say something."

Well. Obviously.

"I mean," she went on, "the people in the meeting won't know they've been assembled in order for us to look them over as suspects. They'll be expecting to meet this crack team of consultants. So, however much we can avoid and evade in follow-up conversations, as the team leader I'll be expected to make some sort of opening remarks."

I sat on the bed, a bundle of sheets in my lap. "Damn. I guess you will."

"Which is why Jack called this morning. He says I should prepare a speech."

"I don't suppose he gave you any idea what it should be about?"

"He said I should be vaguely reassuring while vaguely intimidating. Something that conveys a sense of urgency without getting into specifics about what we're supposed to be doing there."

"All subtext and no text." I nodded. "Tricky."

"Then help me! I only know money—you're the one who knows speeches."

"Sure, sweetie." I got up, stuffed the sheets down the laundry chute, and returned to the bed, picking up a bathrobe along the way. "What have you got so far?"

I heard the rustle of paper. "'Good morning.'"

Uh huh. "Well, it's a start."

After an hour on the phone, Eileen had a reasonable draft of the speech and I had a must-have-caffeine-now headache. I went looking for Jack in his office and didn't find him, but when I stumbled into the kitchen I found a note.

C,

Gone to meet Inspector Yahata at the pier in Pacifica.
They think they found the truck that crashed into us.

Maybe you should call Eileen. I think I freaked her out.

—J

Right. At least I'd managed to calm her down. I couldn't say
the same for myself. Now that the whole scheme was becoming
a reality, I had to admit to a tiny case of nerves. Okay, a raging
case of anxiety.

I entertained the brief hope that some evidence in the truck
might lead the police to the killer before tomorrow morning.
But that was probably something I shouldn't count on.

I saw Jack had put fresh grounds into the French press for
me, so I filled the kettle to boil water.

It wasn't that I was nervous about how we'd perform, or that
we'd be dramatically unmasked as spies. I was of the firm belief
that most people go through life too self-absorbed to notice
minor discrepancies in those around them. They're too busy
trying to cover their own discrepancies.

No, what was eating at my nerves was the fear that it wouldn't
work. That, even if we didn't blow our own covers, we might
just be really bad at gathering information. Or even worse, what
if we turned out to be great at getting people to spill their guts,
but we picked the wrong people?

Sure, Clara had been a member of the exec staff, but did that
mean her murderer was one of her close colleagues? Suppose it
was some dweeb in the mail room that she'd turned down for a
date once? Suppose it had nothing to do with the software glitch?
Did high tech companies even have mail rooms?

These were not productive thoughts.

I poured the water into the carafe, grabbed a mug, and took
it all back to the bedroom. After a shower and a pot of coffee
I'd be able to deal. After a shower and a pot of coffee I'd tear
through the stack of manuscripts so they wouldn't be hanging

over my head anymore. Then I'd study Mike and Eileen's Fake Book until I knew everything cold. It would all work out.

All I needed was a shower and a pot of coffee.

"Charley, have you read the paper?" Brenda's voice on the phone was a good octave higher than usual.

"I've been reading plays all morning. Why? What's in the paper?"

I heard her gulp. "Lalit Kumar is dead."

"*What?*" I pushed the scattered manuscripts aside and jumped out of the bed. "What do you mean, dead? Since when? Who—"

"Just listen," she interrupted. "Here's what it says. 'Police are investigating the apparent suicide of local software executive Lalit Kumar. The Chief Technical Officer of San Francisco's Zakdan, Inc., Kumar was last seen Wednesday evening at the Zakdan offices. Concerned friends contacted the police when Kumar failed to appear at a weekend social engagement—' I wonder if that means Clara's funeral?"

I swallowed. "Maybe. What else does it say?"

Brenda continued reading. "'Investigation of the software executive's home revealed no clues to his mental state. His body was found in a remote region of the Presidio, near his abandoned car. At this time, information regarding the apparent suicide is being sought by the SFPD.'" She paused. "Then it gives a number to call if you know anything about it."

I'd held my breath while she finished. "They don't say anything about a connection with Clara's murder?"

"Nothing."

I wasn't sure if that was good news or bad.

"Charley." Brenda's voice was shaking. "They think the last time he was seen was at work on Wednesday."

When, in fact, we'd seen him pick someone up outside a bar in the Mission District and vanish into the rainy night.

"Charley, we have to call the police."

"It's worse than that," I realized. "We have to call Inspector Yahata."

◇◇◇

First, I called Jack. I wanted to give Brenda enough time to come over from the East Bay. And somehow I figured Jack would get less upset over me lying about where I'd been Wednesday night if he heard it from me instead of from the police.

I reached him on his cell phone.

"Are you still with Inspector Yahata?" That thought hadn't struck me until he answered.

"No, he was gone by the time I got there. I just took a look at the truck and confirmed it was the right one."

"It was? So what happens now?"

"The police scraped some paint from our car to send to the lab, but whoever stole the truck did a good job of cleaning it up before ditching it in Pacifica. Why did you want to know if I was with Yahata?"

I took a deep breath.

"Jack," I began. "Do you remember that conversation we had about not keeping anything from each other anymore?"

There was a foreboding pause. "Yes."

"Well, I wasn't exactly keeping this from you, because I really didn't think it mattered at the time, and because I did it before we had our little talk and everything…"

"This is going to be bad, isn't it?"

"No," I said hastily. "No, not really, it's just that…"

I got through it quickly from that point on. It was less painful that way. Just like ripping off a bandage.

With slightly less yelling.

Being questioned by Inspector Yahata was excruciating. Particularly since we had so little to tell.

He and Brenda arrived at the same time, and the three of us sat awkwardly in Simon's beach chairs for the ordeal. At least, Brenda and I were awkward. The inspector seemed to have an uncanny ability to make the chair sit up straighter when he was in it, as if it dared not insult his impeccable posture.

He tapped a small leather-bound notepad with his sleek silver pen. "You can recall nothing particular about the person you saw get into Kumar's car?"

It was not the first time he'd asked that question. The sharpness of his gaze had increased with every repetition, and I had the feeling he would slice me open with it if he said it again.

"It was dark and it was raining, and we were at least twenty feet away," I told him. "All we saw was someone in black jeans and a black leather jacket holding a newspaper over his head."

"Or her head," Brenda offered.

The detective's lips grew thinner. "White? Black? Asian?"

Brenda and I looked at each other and shrugged.

"And this glint of something metallic that you saw the passenger holding before you lost sight of the car—are you sure it was a gun?"

"I thought so at the time," I told him, unconvincingly.

"But when we talked it over afterward, we weren't sure," Brenda explained. "It was so…"

"Dark, yes, I understand. And raining." Yahata held us with that gaze a moment longer, then snapped his notebook shut.

"I just keep thinking that if we hadn't lost him that night he wouldn't be dead now," Brenda spoke softly, saying exactly what I'd been thinking.

"On the contrary," the inspector responded swiftly. "If you had witnessed anything more, or been seen by Mr. Kumar or his passenger, I might very well be investigating three suspicious deaths at this point, rather than one."

I blinked. That put things in perspective, but I don't think it made either of us feel any better.

"I'm so sorry we can't be more help," I said.

The detective stood. "This has been extremely helpful."

"At least it seems to make it clear that foul play was involved in Kumar's death." I realized the cheap melodrama of the phrase 'foul play,' but I couldn't help myself from saying things like that around the inspector.

He gave me one of those frowns that are over so quickly you can't be sure they even happened. Then he looked at me curiously. "Do you think so?"

Well, yes—at least I had until he'd said that.

Jack came home late to find me in soaking in a hot tub. He'd brought up a bottle of Chianti and two glasses, and he poured while I told him how things had gone with the interrogation.

"It must not have been too bad," he observed. "At least Yahata left some skin on you."

I drew a leg up out of the bubbles. "Are you going to take the rest of it off?"

"Are you keeping anything else from me?"

"Nope." Really, I wasn't. At least nothing I could think of.

"Well then, since it's such nice skin, let's just dry it off." He held out a towel.

I sighed and took it, using it strategically as I got out of the tub. "I just wish I knew more about Kumar's death. The paper hardly had any details."

Jack regarded me with interest. "What would you like to know?"

I stared at him. "I think I'd like to know why Inspector Yahata tells you this sort of thing." But there was slim chance of that.

He sipped his wine. "A suicide note was left on Kumar's computer work, in an email that wasn't addressed to anyone."

I reached for my robe and followed him into the bedroom. "What did it say?"

He shrugged. "Something along the lines of the pressure at Zakdan getting to be too much and a realization that his life was empty and meaningless." He sat on the bed and crossed his legs at the ankles.

I watched his face. "You don't buy it."

He looked at me, and I could tell he was considering his answer. "I don't."

I plopped onto the bed next to him. "Why? What else do you know?"

He took a minute to dab at the wine my move had caused to slosh out onto his shirt.

"Jack! What else do you know?"

He took a deep breath. "I know that from every account I've heard, Lalit Kumar thrived on stress. He wasn't someone who would have issues with pressure. And as for his life being empty and meaningless, I know that he was in the process of adopting a child from an orphanage in Bangalore. The paperwork would have been finalized next month."

"Oh." I sat back. "How awful." Not just one man killed, but another life damaged.

"Yes." There was anger in Jack's voice. "And also not well known around Zakdan."

"So whoever faked the suicide note didn't know Lalit very well." I thought about it, and about the call I'd overheard on the night of Kumar's death.

"But," I said slowly, "the killer did know him well enough to call Lalit in the middle of the night, talk him into picking him up at a bar, and convince him to drive all the way across town."

Jack nodded, watching me.

"So it probably wasn't a close friend, or he'd have gotten the suicide note right. But it was an acquaintance who knew him well enough to exploit both the fact that he worked late and that he'd be nice enough to go to the bar in the first place."

Jack was still watching me.

"It was someone he worked with."

It was someone I was going to meet tomorrow.

It took me a few minutes to recover from my realization, but eventually I noticed that Jack had started talking again. It sounded like he was telling me about his day.

"…We got into Zakdan and did a few things that should make it possible for us to see what's happening to the codebase." He got up and stretched.

It took me a minute to realize he wasn't referring to breaking and entering. "You mean you hacked into the company computers?"

He shrugged. "Stokes did tell us to do whatever it takes."

"Are you going to tell him? How did you do it? What did you plant?" I assaulted him with these questions while following him down to the kitchen. There was a large box from Pizza Orgasmica on the island counter. Jack must have stopped on his way home.

"Are you familiar with the term 'spyware'?" He opened a cabinet for some plates.

"No, but I'm not surprised you are."

He grinned. "The stuff Mike writes is way beyond the sort of things that hackers use to spy on people's PCs," he informed me. "It's virtually undetectable and should tell us a lot."

"I've noticed that techie people use the word 'virtually' where normal people use the word 'almost.'"

He took a dripping slice of *ménage à trois*, a decadent three-cheese combo, and placed it on a plate in front of me. "What's your point?"

"I'd prefer it if you didn't get caught and murdered or sent to jail or something."

He looked me in the eye. "Right back at you, Pumpkin."

Chapter Twenty-one

Finally, it was show time.

"Good morning, working girl."

Jack's voice. I could tell by the mockery in it.

I squinted my eyes open. "Is it still dark out?"

"It's seven o'clock."

"That didn't answer my question." I pulled a pillow over my head.

"It's dim out," he conceded, cruelly taking the pillow away. "Not dark, just dim, and getting lighter every minute."

I rolled over on my back and opened my eyes. "I'm really going to do this?"

"You don't have to."

I looked at him, focusing. "I'm really going to do this."

He gave one brief nod. "Then you'd really better get up."

It was a little after eight by the time I made it downstairs in my I-work-in-an-office costume of hipster pantsuit from Banana Republic, stretchy cotton blouse from Ann Taylor, and I-can't-really-afford-these-but-I-love-them Via Spiga pumps that had been on sale at Macy's.

Jack greeted me at the bottom of the stairs with a gratifying whistle.

"You think?" I turned around, looking down at myself with some doubt.

"Just promise me you're keeping your wedding ring on."

I looked at it, then at him. "I told you once, it's for the duration."

"Then you have my permission to go to work." His mouth did that infuriating thing where it looked like it wanted to laugh but he wouldn't let it.

"You're enjoying this way too much," I told him.

"I have a few things for you." He picked up a black bag that I hadn't noticed leaning against the stairs.

"Is that Kate Spade?"

"It is. More importantly, it has a laptop in it. Mike sent a couple over to Brenda and Simon last night too."

"Oh, what a good idea!" I took the bag and opened it up. "And a new cell phone—oh! With a camera."

"All the cool kids have them."

All the cool kids probably didn't lose them as often as I did. I closed the bag and kissed him. "Thanks, Jack. You think of everything."

"We're not done." He took me by the hand and headed for the front door. When he opened it I was surprised to see an unfamiliar car at the curb.

"Did you take the Lexus in to be fixed? Whose is that?"

"Yours."

I looked at the car. Then at Jack. Then at the car again. It was a new VW Beetle. Lime green. I looked at Jack again.

"Why?"

He took the laptop bag from me and started down the path to the car. "Because I didn't think you'd like the bus."

"But...hang on..." I followed him, not quite sure I had a handle on what he was saying. "Do you mean I have to drive to work?"

"Many people do."

"But..." But I hate to drive. It's so demanding. You let your mind wander for five minutes and you could end up killing some random pedestrian.

And I particularly hate to drive in San Francisco. Because once you get somewhere you have to put the car somewhere, and that can take hours. Then you end up walking so far back to where you were going that you might as well have just hoofed it in the first place.

Jack was looking at me.

"Can't you take me in?"

He put the bag in the back seat and leaned against the car. "Very few mid-level consultants have drivers."

Okay, true, but... "Ha!" I held up my left hand. "I'm married, remember? So it would be perfectly reasonable for my husband to take me to work!"

"Perfectly," Jack agreed. "Except if someone is trying to kill me because I've been seen at Zakdan, we'd really rather not have anyone connecting us, right?"

Damn.

"Right."

He opened the driver's-side door. "So, do you want to take a look?"

I know when I've lost a battle. I came over and looked in the car.

"Oh, Jack, you put a flower in it!" A bright pink daisy in a little bud vase just to the right of the steering wheel.

He kissed me on the temple. "It was the least I could do." Then he shoved me in the car and closed the door.

He leaned in the open window. "You do know how to drive, don't you?"

I made a face at him. "I thought you knew everything about me." I turned the key and revved the engine.

"Okay, then I guess there's nothing else." He grinned. "Have a nice day, dear."

I think, at that moment, I kind of hated him.

I was scheduled to meet the rest of the A Team at a little café called Arugula near the Zakdan building. It was walking distance from Simon's loft, and an easy rendezvous place for Brenda, coming in off the Bay Bridge. This would be our last chance to get our stories straight before making our united entrance at Zakdan.

Assuming, of course, I'd ever be able to park.

As I got within a few blocks of the place, I started scanning the streets. Ideally, what I wanted was unmetered street parking someplace between the two locations. Which would be just coming up as I crossed Fifth.

Which is right when I spotted Flank.

He stood in the street near the curb, arms not quite able to cross against his massive chest, wearing a dark suit and sunglasses. His increasingly sparse ponytail blew around a little in the breeze. He looked more like a strip-club bouncer than a secretary, but at least he wasn't carrying an assault rifle. Probably.

I pulled up and rolled down the passenger window. "Flank? What are you doing?"

He crouched at the window, lowered his shades, and showed me a stunningly mismatched array of teeth.

I smiled back. Probably not my strongest effort, but it seemed the thing to do. "Flank?"

He made a sort of sweeping motion with both arms, gesturing to the sidewalk and the parking space he stood in. Then he said something unintelligible and looked proud.

"You saved me a space?"

The teeth appeared again. Then he resumed his don't-mess-with-me stance on the sidewalk.

I parked.

Maybe he'd be more useful than I'd thought.

I made my way to the café with Flank following about a half-step behind, and me turning every few paces to tell him not to do that. It fueled all sorts of paranoia. But apparently it was part of his bodyguard training, because he just kept stopping whenever I stopped, so eventually I gave up trying.

I saw Brenda had already gotten us a table. The café was one of those old brick warehouses that had been converted into chic hangouts for the digerati. Exposed brick walls, high ceilings, with a polished pine staircase leading up to an additional seating area. There was a long high table with stools running down the middle of the space, and tables and chairs that got progressively more comfortable looking the closer they were to the windows.

Brenda was in a comfy place, bless her. And she looked just right in one of her new outfits, a blue-gray skirt and loose jacket in a fine wool knit, with a slightly lighter shade of blue-gray shell in silk. Professional yet approachable. Comfortable yet pulled together. Brenda, yet not Brenda.

"Hi, Charley!" She clapped a hand over her mouth. "Should I call you Charley?" she stage-whispered as I got closer.

"You might as well." I plopped down in the chair next to her and set the laptop bag on the floor between us. "Jack and I didn't really finish discussing it." I could have told her that we'd been distracted by a bout of crazed lust, but it was probably too early in the morning for that kind of sharing.

"Discussing what?" Simon asked.

I jumped, not having noticed him on approach. Then I looked around for Flank. He'd taken a seat at the tall table where he could see us, the door, and just about everything else in the room. He nodded at me without disturbing his facial muscles. He was in position.

And he hadn't attacked Simon. That showed progress.

"What didn't you and Jack discuss?" Simon persisted. "And why aren't we drinking lattes?"

"The whole fake name thing," I explained. "And I don't know." I looked over to the busy counter. "Is this a stand-in-line sort of place?"

"It is," Brenda said. "And I stood in line before you got here. I didn't know how horrendous the bridge traffic would be, so I left plenty of time." She handed Simon a slip of paper. "They should call our number any minute. Would you…?"

He sighed elaborately and took the number. "Nothing ever changes, does it? Except my costume." He fiddled with the sleeves of the pinstriped Roberto Cavalli blazer he wore over distressed Diesel jeans and a pristine white shirt until we made sufficiently appreciative noises. Then he sat and leaned forward across the table conspiratorially. "And, of course, my name."

"You've decided to use a cover name?" Brenda grabbed his arm. "What?"

"Rex," he said, rolling the R a bit and savoring the word. "Rex Bannister." He grinned. "I thought I'd use my same surname in case anyone notices I look like that infamous local man-about-town Simon Bannister. I can claim to be a cousin or something if the subject comes up. But in the meanwhile I'm Rex."

He sat back, clearly pleased with himself.

"Why…Rex?" I hesitated to ask.

He blinked. "Isn't it obvious? So I can have the nickname Sexy Rexy."

Obvious. Sure.

Simon was spared our full reaction because our number was called. He went off.

"Are we all here?" Eileen's voice cut through the babble of the increasingly crowded café.

"All present and accounted for," I told her. "You, me, Brenda, Flank, and Sexy Rexy."

Chapter Twenty-two

Morgan Stokes stood in front of the stainless-steel-and-green-glass receptionist station. The lobby of the building was vast, with one ubiquitous brick wall providing a backdrop to an enormous fish tank, and three curving, swooping walls in deepest shades of red, purple, and yellow-gold—the colors of the Zakdan logo.

It was a space designed to impress, not only with how-successful-we-are, but with how-cool-and-funky-we-are as well.

"Hello, you must be Harry Van Leewen's team of consultants." Stokes" greeting was apparently for the benefit of the receptionist. It occurred to me that we probably should have come up with a name for our fake consulting firm.

Eileen held out her hand to shake his. "That's right. We're the team from SFG."

From where? Had I missed a page in the Fake Book?

"Great." Morgan handed her some VIP badges, and spoke to the receptionist, who looked roughly seventeen and wore the most severe eyeglasses I'd ever encountered.

"Lara, these folks will be here for the next week or so. Make sure they get everything they need." Then he hustled us onto the elevator before she could respond with anything other than a nod.

"The staff meeting is in ten minutes." Morgan checked his watch to be sure. "I've arranged for you to work from a conference room, so you can have some amount of privacy. Everyone at Zakdan works in cubicles, except the execs on the fourth floor, but I assumed you'd want a sort of a bull pen together. You'll need to wear your badges at all times. They're your keys for getting around in the building."

He illustrated this when the elevator doors opened on the third floor and we stepped out into a bright turquoise lobby. There were three doors, each with electronic card readers. He passed his badge in front of the reader at the door to the right, and ushered us in.

There was a field of cubicles ahead of us, a glass wall revealing a kitchen to our left, and a glass wall looking into a conference room on our right. Morgan led us down the hall and around the corner to the conference room door.

"You can put your things here for now—unless you'll need them for the meeting upstairs. Do your laptops have wireless? You should be able to get onto our network. There's a copy machine down the hall, and—"

"Morgan," I cut him off for his own good. The man had to breathe sometime. "We'll be okay."

I tried to believe it as I said it. And he seemed to buy it, at least briefly. He focused on the tabletop.

"Did you hear about Lalit Kumar?" he asked quietly.

Brenda and I exchanged swift glances.

"Just what we read in the paper," I answered.

"I'm so sorry," Brenda offered.

Morgan nodded, still looking down. "It wasn't a suicide."

"Are the police—" Eileen began.

"Don't talk to me about the police," he cut her off, his voice harsh. Then he looked at each of us, making eye contact one by one. "Clara didn't have an accident and Lalit didn't kill himself, and the only way I know how to find out what really happened is to trust you people." His voice cracked.

"You can trust us," Brenda said softly.

"We'll find out who's behind this," I heard myself promise.

He nodded and straightened his shoulders. "Right. Are you ready?"

As we'd ever be.

◇◇◇

The executive boardroom on the fourth floor was sleek and elegant, with lots of pale wood and huge wall-mounted flat panel video screens at either end. The table was shaped like a giant oval with the short ends chopped off. It had built-in speakers and a horrifying assortment of technical gear running the length of it, presumably for teleconferencing and video conferencing and all the other types of conferencing these people do.

I'd expected them to be…what? Tense? Depressed? Grieving for their two lost colleagues? Instead, I found the large leather chairs surrounding the table to be occupied by the most hostile-looking group of individuals I'd ever stood before. And for someone who's been in the theatre as long as I have, that's saying something.

"All right, everybody." Morgan ushered us to our seats. "Let's get started. I'd like you to meet the consulting team from SFG." He gestured to each of us in turn. "Eileen Scoto is the team leader. She'll be your primary technical liaison. Brenda Gee is our change management expert—"

Simon slipped him a note while everyone was acknowledging Brenda. Morgan glanced at it and went on smoothly. "Rex Bannister will be focusing on long pole issues…"

Okay, Morgan had taken the name change right in stride, but what the hell was a long pole issue? I didn't have time to figure it out, because it was my turn to give a little finger wave next.

"And Tess McGill is the project manager."

Tess McGill? Who the hell was that? From the way Morgan was looking at me I assumed he meant me, so I smiled in the general direction of the rest of the table, wondering where he'd gotten the idea.

And then it hit me.

Jack.

He'd come up with a false name for me. And it was vaguely familiar.

"Oh!" One of the Zakdan people squealed. It was a painfully young woman with straight blond hair and angular black glasses.

"Tess McGill—that's Melanie Griffith's name in *Working Girl*."
She looked around the table and seemed to sort of shrink back
into herself. "Oh, sorry. I didn't mean…"

"It's okay," I told her. "Don't worry. Everybody thinks it's
funny."

Particularly my husband.

Hilarious.

I told myself to focus as Morgan Stokes introduced the Zakdan
cast of characters and invited each of them to make a few
remarks. I mentally matched each person to what I already
knew about them.

Jim Stoddard: He sat at Morgan's left. Medium height,
medium build, bald spot. Dressed in khakis and a button-down
shirt with the Zakdan logo on the pocket. Looked annoyed to
be stuck in this meeting. He was the executive vice president of
Engineering. He was also the only one besides Lalit Kumar who
knew about Clara's proposed promotion, and he had a history
of drunk driving. I'd last seen him speaking into his cell phone
at Clara's funeral.

Millicent O'Malley: Known by her initials as MoM to all,
and I can't say I blamed her. I mean—Millicent? I looked at her
closely, remembering her as the schoolmistress who'd dished out
that slap to the hysterical girl at the funeral. Painfully thin with
cropped gray hair and tiny silver-rimmed glasses. Wearing a gray
turtleneck sweater that looked likely to swallow half her face.
Vice President of Engineering Services. I still wasn't entirely sure
what that meant. An old-timer at the company, she'd bounced
around among various groups on her way to her current position. Morgan adored her.

Tonya Ho: She sat mid-table behind a barricade of electronic
devices. A laptop, a phone, and I didn't know what else arranged
in a semicircle in front of her. Early thirties, with straight black
hair parted off center and pushed behind her ears. Glasses that
would have marked her as a member of the math club back in
junior high, but that seemed to be a popular look around Zakdan.

Wearing an outfit I'd seen at Banana, right down to the striped scarf. Vice President of Human Resources, she'd been with Zakdan just under a year. We had almost no information on her.

Bob Adams: Free of guacamole stains, but still a mess. Shaggy blondish-reddish hair thinning on top and an untamed beard. Wearing a much-faded tee shirt that stretched noticeably across a sizable midsection. I didn't recognize the logo on the tee shirt, but guessed it was from some software company that had crashed and burned long ago. Either that or his college rock band. Vice President of Quality Assurance. Bob had been with the company for close to a decade, and since his group was supposed to test the software and find any bugs in it, Jack had labeled him a "person of interest."

Troy Patterson: A slight build and a twitchy manner. Pale features, and straight blond hair worn in a sleek ponytail. He'd been at Clara's funeral too. I recognized the ponytail. Troy spent a lot on clothes, and was wearing a Helmut Lang suit and open-necked Thomas Pink shirt, unless I missed my guess. Simon was going to hate him. Or have an affair with him. Vice President of Marketing. Had a history of leaving jobs after three years. He'd been at Zakdan two and a half.

Krissy Livingston: The one who'd made the Tess McGill connection. And, I realized with a jolt, the one who'd made the scene at Clara's funeral. She was the only person new to the executive boardroom, which explained why she hadn't been covered by Brenda and Eileen's research. She'd been standing in for Clara since her death, but Krissy hadn't yet received an official promotion. And she didn't look comfortable in her seat. Acting Vice President of Client Knowledge.

I looked around at them as Morgan went on with his opening remarks. Did one of these people kill Clara?

Based on the gym receptionist's description, almost any of them could have been the figure in the gray sweats that night. Only Bob's beard made him ineligible. Okay, and maybe his physique. But any of the rest of them...

I snapped out of my mental lineup exercise when Eileen stood. It was time for her to give the speech she'd worked so hard on.

"At SFG, we believe that opportunity is the point at which luck meets preparation. Harry Van Leewen is in the position to provide you with a lot of luck. We're here to see if you're properly prepared."

She sat.

That was it?

Apparently it was, because Morgan adjourned the meeting, telling everyone that we'd be talking to them individually over the next few days. As soon as they'd filed out, I turned to Eileen.

"Three sentences? You gave a three-sentence speech after all that fuss yesterday? What happened to what we wrote?"

She shrugged. "I was in the moment."

Everyone's an actor.

"Well?" Morgan looked at us all expectantly. "What do you think?"

We glanced at each other. What did we think?

Simon was the one to speak up. "I think we should have gotten some cool glasses."

Chapter Twenty-three

We split up after the meeting, each pursuing our designated target of investigation for the day. I went back to our assigned conference room to check on Flank before tackling mine—Jim Stoddard, vice president of Engineering.

We'd decided to leave Flank out of the introductory meeting on the theory that the less attention we called to him, the better. It turned out that our decision had unexpected side benefits. I was stunned when I saw what the bodyguard had accomplished while we were gone.

All of our laptops were set up and humming away happily on the large conference table. Flank had positioned them facing the glass wall that ran the length of the room, so when we sat at them we'd be able to see the hall and across into the kitchen, and no casual passers-by would be able to glance in at what we were working on.

The conference room was rectangular, with the only door located on a second glass wall which looked out on a row of cubicles. So, given the fact that we were in what amounted to a fish tank, we were pretty well fortified.

Stacks of paper, boxes of assorted pens and pencils, pads of sticky notes, and every other possible office supply we might need were arranged tidily on a cabinet at the far end of the room. Also in the back corner was a high stool, positioned to give Flank a clear view of all approaches to the room.

The floor-to-ceiling white board on the long rear wall had "SFG Team" neatly lettered on it in purple marker, along with each of our names—fake or otherwise—below it.

"Flank, this is great! It looks like an office."

He mumbled something while handing me a printed sheet of paper. It was a floor plan of the fourth floor executive suites, with everybody's office labeled. Flank had circled Jim Stoddard's.

I took the floor plan and searched it, looking not for the circled office, but for Lalit Kumar's. Jack had gotten Harry's call about meeting him at Bix while in Kumar's office, and might have been overheard by someone in an adjoining room. And that someone had tried to run us into the wall of the Broadway Tunnel.

I found Kumar's office. Troy, the ponytailed guy, shared the rear wall, Bob Adams was on the left, and my afternoon appointment, Jim Stoddard, was on the right.

I handed the paper back to Flank.

It was time to go to work.

"What are your plans?"

I'd been seated in Jim's office for all of five seconds before he started asking questions. Luckily, I'd had a lifetime of evasiveness training.

"We're just in the evaluation phase now." A confident smile.

His left eye twitched a little. "What are you evaluating?"

I straightened my jacket. "Zakdan, of course."

The office was decorated with technical awards and pictures of Jim posing with various clusters of other geeks. Team photos from projects he'd worked on in the past, probably. No family. Was that significant?

He was looking at me narrowly. "What, exactly, do you think you'll find?"

A killer—but that's not what I said.

"We want to identify the tipping point," I said, recalling the name of a book Mike had listed in his bibliography. "We need to concentrate on what's going to push the needle."

That didn't sound quite right, even to me. Did you push the needle or push the envelope? I knew you didn't thread the needle.

My smile might have faltered a bit. Time for a change of tactic.

"What can you tell me about working at Zakdan?"

He sat back in his chair, putting his hands behind his head, elbows out. It was body language that said he had nothing to hide.

I didn't believe it for a minute.

"How was your day, dear?" Jack kissed me on the cheek.

Simon turned to Eileen. "He said it—you owe me ten dollars." Then, in response to the look I gave him, "What?"

"I can't believe you bet on Jack saying that."

"I can't believe I'm that predictable," Jack said.

"Nonsense," Simon told him. "You just always know your lines."

We'd rendezvoused at Rose Pistola after work, choosing the North Beach restaurant because it was close to Eileen's house, so she could pick up her son Anthony on her way there. Harry, Mike, and Jack had been waiting for us at a large table near the back. We'd lost Flank as we passed the massive antipasti bar on the way in.

"Who's that?" Anthony was staring at the very large bodyguard, who'd seated himself on a very small stool at the bar. "He looks like the bad guy in *Death Squad IV.*"

I looked at Eileen.

"It's a video game," she explained. Then she gave her son a menu and told him it wasn't polite to stare.

"God, I need a drink," I said. "No wonder everyone who works for a living has a substance abuse problem."

All the people at the table who worked for a living stared at me.

"Oh, you know what I mean. Let's get martinis."

Once we'd gotten our drinks and a bunch of antipasti to share, we got down to business.

"Simon," Jack kicked things off. "How did it go?"

"Not terribly well, I'm afraid." Simon nibbled at an olive. "I know I was supposed to spend the day in the company of the charming Mr. Adams, but I never seemed to be able to track him down." He picked up his glass, his hand shaking visibly.

"Do you think he was avoiding you?" I reached for a morsel of house-cured sturgeon.

"I don't know." Simon needed two hands for the drink. "He might have just been busy all day, but—"

"Simon, are you all right?"

Brenda's expression of concern was prompted by the sloshing of the liquid in Simon's glass.

"Fine," he assured her. "Fine, fine, fine. Perfectly fine. I might possibly have overdone the caffeine today. But I'm fine."

Eileen's eyes narrowed. "What did you do?"

"Well, since I couldn't seem to corner my quarry, I spent most of the day hanging about in the kitchen. I assumed all sorts of people would stop by during the day, and I'd just take the luck of the draw in who I talked to." He twitched. "Did you know they have an espresso maker in the kitchen?"

"How many did you have?" Brenda asked.

"I lost track at seven."

"You're not going to sleep for a week."

"Did you find anything out?" Jack brought us back to the point.

"Loads." He sat up and gave us a rapid-fire report. "Software engineers are apparently used to being treated like living gods, and the marketing people find that extremely annoying. The sales force all seem to have belonged to the same fraternity. Oh, and technical writers are far more entertaining than you might think. Every one of them is in a band or an artist's co-op or working on the Great American Novel of high-tech."

"Anything else?" Harry rumbled. I don't think he was interested in novels of high-tech, Great American or otherwise.

"Just that Zakdan seems to suffer from a serious shortage of eligible men." Simon looked pleased with himself. "I got three phone numbers before—"

"Simon!" Eileen's reprimand sent the rest of his drink flying.

"What? Aren't we supposed to be insinuating ourselves into the corporate culture?" He dabbed at the tablecloth.

"Anyway," Jack said. "You didn't overhear anything about Clara? Or rumors about Lalit Kumar? Or a software bug?"

"Not a word," he said. "Not a dicky bird, not a peep, not a—"

"We get the picture," I stopped him. "Eileen, how about you?"

She shook her head. "Nothing worth discussing, really. I spent most of the afternoon with Troy." The distaste she heaped on his name gave us a preview of her opinion of the man.

"He certainly doesn't suffer from low self-esteem. I'm the one who's undercover, and I'm the one who's supposed to be bluffing my way through this, but I swear that man spent half the meeting blowing smoke up my skirt."

"He's in Marketing," Mike said, as if no further explanation were required.

"Even so," Eileen said. "Although…I have to admit that, beyond the vast quantities of bullshit, he did seem pretty bright."

"But is he bright enough to plot two murders?" Brenda asked.

"Or sabotage the software?" I followed up.

She made a face. "It's hard to say. If you want, you can listen to the whole conversation. I brought my laptop to the meeting and turned on the microphone function before we started."

"There's a microphone function?" I asked. That sounded handy.

She nodded. "It's mainly for online conferencing, but you can record with it too. I think we should probably try to use it when we can."

That seemed like a good idea, assuming she could show us how it worked.

"Anyway," Eileen continued, "Troy's capabilities aside, I didn't really get a sense that he had a motive. I mean, his world doesn't really touch Clara's and Lalit's. He made it very clear that he owns the 'pre-sales' experience, and anything anybody else does is 'post-sales,' and therefore irrelevant. Oh—" she turned to Jack. "Did the Crime Scenes people find any long blond hairs anywhere?"

"Not that I recall. Why?"

"Because all the while we were talking, he kept taking his hair out of that ponytail, smoothing it all back, and putting the ponytail in again. He did it maybe ten times. It must be some sort of nervous habit."

"What do you think was making him nervous?" Brenda asked.

"Me." Eileen seemed perfectly comfortable with this answer. "The point is, if he does that when he's nervous, and he's the one who followed Clara to the gym…"

"There would probably be blond hairs at the scene," Jack finished for her. "I'll take another look at the report."

We took a pause from the debriefing while our entrees appeared. Chicken under a brick for those of us in the know, pumpkin ravioli for Anthony, and—predictably—terrorized steak for Harry.

When we'd all had our first bites, it was Brenda's turn.

"I spent the day with Tonya in Human Resources." She produced a small notebook and referred to it. "We didn't start out with anything specific. I asked her how employee morale is generally—"

"How is it?" I asked.

"Not good. After a while she started confiding in me about all the recent complaints the employees have been filing about each other." She glanced around the table. "I know we decided to concentrate on the execs at first, because they were Clara's immediate colleagues—"

"And because whoever is fiddling with the code must be doing so at a pretty high level not to have been found out," Mike said.

"Right. But, you guys, there's a lot of hostility at that company."

Damn right there was, if the atmosphere in that executive boardroom had been any indication.

"What kind of hostility?" Jack asked.

"Well, everyone seems to know how much everyone else makes," she told us. "And they get all kinds of complaints about that."

"That always goes on at big companies," Eileen said. "What else?"

"Everyone knows everyone else's business." She looked up from her notes indignantly. "Do you know you can log on to the email system and see everyone's calendars?"

"What?" I asked.

She explained. "Everyone has to use the same networked system for their email and calendars, and it's all public. So if you want to make an appointment with someone you can look at their calendar online and see if they're busy. And if they don't mark their appointments as private, you can see what they're doing and where they're doing it all day long."

That had to be the most appalling thing I'd heard so far. "So you could stalk your co-workers through their calendars?"

She nodded. "And people do. And they also complain about why they have to go to so many meetings when so-and-so doesn't, or why weren't they invited to a meeting that thus-and-such was. It gets awfully petty."

"Wow." I sat back. "I wonder—"

"Whether Clara put her gym plans in her calendar," Simon finished for me.

"I'll find out," Brenda said. "But that's not the big thing." She took a breath. "Clara was working with Tonya to fire someone."

We all stared at her.

"Who?"

"What?"

"How did you find out?"

Brenda shook her head. "I couldn't get anything more out of Tonya. She just let it slip. I asked her whether anyone had been fired recently, and she said that someone was about to be, but the person who was going to do it was killed." She put down her fork. "So I asked her if it had been the accidental death I'd read about in the papers, and she said yes."

Harry thumped the table. "Well, there's your motive right there. Whoever Clara was going to fire is the killer."

"What's happened to that person since Clara's death?" Eileen asked.

Brenda shook her head. "I'll keep working on Tonya for the details." She looked at Jack. "I'll find out who it was."

He nodded, then turned to me. "How about Jim Stoddard? Anything interesting there?"

I made a face. After I'd deflected the engineer's opening questions, I'd spent what were arguably the most mind-numbingly dull three hours of my life.

"Mike might have found it interesting, or you might have, but I was completely lost. Stoddard doesn't really seem capable of talking about anything other than computer code. Every time I tried to steer him into things like how he liked his job or what he thinks of his colleagues, he kept coming back to these monologues on the system architecture."

"What did you do?" Mike looked a little worried.

"I tried to seem interested." I shrugged. "And *that* was acting."

"So that was it?" Eileen said. "Nothing personal? Nothing off-topic?"

"Oh." I picked at my bread. "Not unless you want to hear about how he hit on me as I was leaving."

"Darling, he didn't!" Simon exclaimed.

"Seriously?" Eileen asked.

"How could he?" Brenda protested. "You're wearing your ring!"

I looked at Jack, who seemed a lot calmer than my friends.

"How did you play it?"

"Polite but firm."

"Good." He nodded. "No reason to alienate him now." He took a sip of water. "I'll just kill him later."

"Whatever," I agreed.

Harry cleared his throat. "How did Flank do? He was a help, wasn't he?"

I had to admit it. "He was a help this morning. I don't know what he did all afternoon."

"I saw him in the copy room," Simon volunteered.

"What was he doing there?"

"As far as I could tell, he seemed to be copying things." The quantity of alcohol Simon had consumed seemed to have evened out his caffeine buzz. "Heaven knows what he was copying. But he had quite an effect on some of the more skittish employees."

I'll bet he did. I was just surprised I hadn't heard any screams.

By the time Jack let us in the front door, I was ready to fall over. And it was just dawning on me that I'd have to get up and do it all over again the next day.

I was leaning against Jack, so I felt it when he suddenly tensed.

"What is it?"

"Someone's been in," he said quietly.

I looked at the little blinking keypad inside the door. "The alarm is still on," I whispered. "Are you sure?"

"I'm sure. Stay here." He left me outside the door, moving cautiously and keying in the code to disable the alarm.

Jack moving cautiously has a certain style that I normally enjoy watching. But I'm not normally watching him while standing in the dark in front of my burgled house.

At least the burglars couldn't have gotten away with much. We only had a bed and a table. And Harry's chair. Oh, wouldn't it be great if they took Harry's chair—

Then I thought I heard Jack laughing.

"Jack?" I took a step inside.

The lights came on, and I jumped. Jack was standing at the usually closed door to the library. Looking extremely amused.

"You've got to see this."

"What? Did someone break in?" I went down the hall.

"You might say that."

"But there's nothing in the library."

"There is now." He moved aside.

I peeked around him. In the corner of the room, looking like it had always been there, was a bar. Perfectly matched to the surrounding woodwork, perfectly sized for the space, and fully stocked.

I stared at it. "Jack?"

"I didn't do it."

"Then—"

"There's a note." He handed me a piece of stiff creamy notepaper.

Charley,

Everyone needs a drink when they come home from work.

—Harry

I looked up at Jack. "How the hell did he—"

"I have no idea. But I'd like to find out."

I was rattled. Seriously rattled. And not because Harry had been able to break into our house, or—more likely—pay someone to break into our house. No, I was rattled because I'd had just that thought about a drink after my first day at Zakdan. And to know that I'd been thinking like Harry…

I was rattled.

"What do you want to do?" Jack asked.

I eyed the thing. "Sweep it for bugs."

"Do you want a drink?"

"Not now." Since I was standing so conveniently close to him, I ran my hands up his chest. "We need to talk."

"I like it when we talk." He lowered his head toward mine.

"About Tess McGill." I poked him in the shoulder.

At which point he laughed at me, but since he was doing other, nicer things as well, I got over it.

Chapter Twenty-four

The big substance abuse problem in the workplace isn't alcohol after all. It's caffeine. This became glaringly apparent to me as Day Two at Zakdan progressed.

Jack propelled me out the door with a travel mug of coffee in the morning, and I met the gang at Arugula for cappuccino and strategy, Flank having again staked out the perfect parking spot.

"Before we get started," I addressed Eileen. "SFG?"

I hadn't remembered to ask her yet where she'd come up with the name for our fake consulting company.

She grinned. "Don't you like it?"

"I should probably know what it stands for—just in case I'm asked."

"San Francisco....something," Simon guessed. "San Francisco what, darling?"

"San Francisco nothing," Eileen explained. "It stands for Scoto," she pointed to herself, "Fairfax," me, "and Gee," Brenda.

"What about me? I don't even get billing?" Simon blinked.

"You would have, but SFGB starts to sound like a college radio station."

Brenda spoke up. "Shouldn't we get to work now?"

Right. Yes. Work.

◇◇◇

I had two appointments for the day. The gray-haired MoM in the morning, and the disheveled Quality Assurance guy, Bob Adams, in the afternoon.

But before any of that, I wanted to take a look at the Zakdan calendar system. That thing Brenda had said, about everyone being able to look at everyone else's calendar, had tickled something in my brain overnight. So after we got to Zakdan and the others went off on their assignments—except for Flank, who stood watch in his corner of our conference room—I settled in and opened my laptop.

I have a computer at the theatre, and I use email as much as I have to, so I at least knew how to get started. I clicked the icon that looked like a clock, and opened up the email and calendar program.

It was just that simple. Someone—Jack? Mike?—must have set up the laptop to connect to the Zakdan system. I saw my two appointments on a time grid of the day, and my email Inbox had eight messages. But I didn't stop to read them. I wasn't interested in my own data.

I went hunting around in the menus until I found a command that said "Open Other User's Calendar." I clicked it, and a small screen with a list of names appeared. Presumably everyone who worked at Zakdan.

I scrolled down until I got to the C's, and there she was. I clicked the name, and after a brief pause I was looking at Clara Chen's calendar. I paused a moment over the entry for 12:30 that day. Clara would have met with a wedding planner.

I shook my head, telling myself to hurry up before I was interrupted, and clicked the arrow that would take me back in time. After two weeks I stopped. Most of the meetings were engineering gibberish to me. Bug councils and UI reviews and the like.

But one appointment was perfectly clear.

Clara had met with Lalit Kumar on the day before she'd died.

Millicent O'Malley—MoM—appeared at the conference room door at exactly ten o'clock. She looked like someone featured in those stark winter paintings of prim New England townsfolk grimly skating on frozen ponds. Today again she wore a turtleneck, this time a loden green, over a long slim black wool skirt. She carried a green suede day planner notebook. I was a little miffed when I noticed it, because I have a fabulous hot pink Kate Spade day planner, but I hadn't judged it a sufficiently techie accessory to bring to the office.

"I thought I was going to speak with the team leader," MoM said. "Is she gone?" Her dismissive glance around the room indicated that I was a poor second best.

I glanced around too, for some reason.

"She had another appointment." I gave her my most I'm-a-competent-professional smile. "I hope I'll do."

I meant it as a joke, but she seemed to need a minute to consider the question. A flash of annoyance crossed her face, then she embraced the change.

"WONderful! Let's get some coffee." As if she'd been dying to get me alone for days.

I noticed two things about MoM: First, that she had completely ignored Flank. And that is not easy to do. He is the proverbial elephant in the room. And second, that she was more of a phony than I was. Once she'd decided that I was as close to the top of the SFG org chart as she'd get that morning, I'd suddenly become the most important person in the world to her.

She made little flourishing gestures as she led the way across the hall to the kitchen, and turned into a tour guide as soon as we got there.

"You have your choice of beans," waving her hand toward a line of canisters, each neatly labeled with the provenance and roasting methodology of the coffee beans contained therein. "And here's the grinder. Honestly." She lowered her voice conspiratorially. "You would not believe the amount of money they spent on this equipment. It's all Italian, and they actually hired baristas to come in and give us training when we got it."

Her eyebrows went up two inches, waiting for me to say "You're kidding." Then she shook her head as if they—whoever "they" were—were very naughty boys indeed.

"Now." She arranged herself at one of the small tables and scooted a chair around for me. "Tell me how I can help you."

She'd positioned the chair so my back would be to the door. I scooted it back before I sat down. We were alone in the kitchen, but I didn't count on it staying that way, and I didn't want to be overheard.

I mentally referred to my script. "I'd like you to tell me about your organization. Engineering Services?" I wished I'd brought the laptop with the recorder, or at least a notepad, but she'd swept me across the hall so quickly I hadn't picked anything up. "What exactly does your group do?"

"Well," she frowned. "First I should make it clear that I don't like the name Engineering Services. We are not handmaidens to the engineers." She verbally underscored the word "not."

"Okay…"

"I've only recently taken this position. Before the last company reorganization I oversaw all of Client Education—that comprises both Client Instruction and Client Knowledge."

I only understood one thing out of that sentence: MoM had been Clara Chen's boss.

"Client Knowledge," I said. "Isn't that Krissy's group now?"

"Yes." She wrapped her hands around her mug. "For now."

"Oh, you don't think she'll get the official promotion?"

"Krissy is a sweet girl." She gave me a sidelong glance. "But *really*."

Uh huh. Now the gloves were off. "What about the last person in that job? Didn't I hear something about…"

"Yes." She set her coffee down. "There was a tragic accident. We're all still in shock."

"How awful," I said. "Did you know her well?"

"I hired her." She gave me a tight, brave smile. "But I don't imagine that interests you. What do you need to know for your report?"

I needed to know who killed Clara, who faked Lalit's suicide, and who was planting bugs in the Zakdan code. But those were not the sort of questions best asked directly.

"I know Client Knowledge is what other companies call Tech Support," I told her. "But what's Client Instruction?"

"It's our Technical Publications department."

"The technical writers." I knew from the Fake Book that they wrote the user manuals. And, according to Simon, they had a wide variety of extracurricular interests.

"That's right," she said encouragingly. She may as well have patted my head.

"But now you run Engineering Services. How did that happen?" Had she had a falling out with Clara? Is that why she didn't want to talk about her?

She delivered a great sigh and turned into a martyr before my eyes. "Well, the web team was in trouble, and there was a new initiative that they just…" She gave me a stoic my-fate-is-to-take-care-of-those-less-competent look. "They needed me."

Right. The train wreck of a plan that Morgan Stokes had told us about. Something about cataloguing information? A paperless office—that was it. Doomed to failure, but that was beside the point.

"So Engineering Services is the web team." Now I was getting it. Maybe she hadn't had a falling out with Clara after all. Maybe she'd used her as a stepping-stone to get ahead.

"Oh, no," she protested. "No, I'm not involved with the web team anymore." The look on her face said she wouldn't want to touch that icky web stuff with a ten foot pole. "No." She straightened her spine. "Now it's Engineering Services that…well, I don't want to be indiscreet, but…" She shook her head, implying untold layers of corruption and mismanagement in Engineering Services.

"Thank goodness they have you to help out," I told her.

"She sounds like a piece of work," Eileen said.

We'd all gone to lunch at Eliza's, a hole-in-the-wall Chinese fusion place on Potrero Hill, figuring a quick comparison of the morning's findings might be better accomplished away from the office. Flank had ditched us to pick up a pizza from Goat Hill.

He was devouring it in the front seat of the little green bug, parked illegally outside Eliza's.

I'd been trying to capture my overall impression of MoM.

"Let's just say she's not my new best friend."

Brenda toyed with her Basil Chicken. "Well, pathologically condescending or not, the question is…"

"Could she be a murderer?" I finished.

They looked at me.

"It didn't feel like she was hiding a murder," I said. "It felt like she was covering insecurities of a breadth and scope I don't even want to think about, but…" I shrugged. "I don't know."

Eileen nodded and turned to Simon. "How did your talk with Krissy go?"

He took the last Crab Rangoon from the plate of appetizers we'd been sharing. "I hate to sound as catty as your friend MoM, darling, but my assessment is that Krissy is about as clever as a box of lint."

I expected Brenda to scold him, but she just leaned forward. "Really?"

He held up his hands in helplessness. "Try as I might, I couldn't get her to say anything remotely interesting. She walked me through the entire tedious Client Thingy operation as if someone had pulled the string in her back." He gave me a dark look. "Completely over-rehearsed, if you know what I mean."

"Does that make her stupid?" Eileen asked thoughtfully. "Or is she sticking to some script in order to avoid making a slip about Clara?"

"Did you ask her about Clara?" I asked.

"Mmmm." He nodded, his mouth full of Mango Beef.

"And?" Brenda demanded.

He swallowed. "She just said it was tragic and they were all still in shock."

"That's almost exactly what MoM said!" I nearly lost a prawn in my excitement. "Could they be in on it together?"

"Either that or it was tragic and they're all still in shock," Eileen said.

Okay, fine.

"But you have to admit that so far Krissy has the strongest motive," Brenda said. "After all, she gets Clara's job."

"Maybe," I said. "Depending on how much MoM has to say about it."

"Well," Simon said brightly. "If MoM is murdered next, we'll have our answer, won't we?"

We stared at him.

"What?" He blinked.

I turned to Eileen. "How did it go with Jim Stoddard? Did you have any better luck with him than I did yesterday?"

She made a face. "Not really. But you're not the only one he hit on."

"Oh, my God," Brenda said. "Would you believe Troy from Marketing hit on me too?"

"That place is a hotbed of sexual frustration," Simon mused. He looked at his watch. "When do we go back?"

We ignored him.

"Okay, but before the romantic overture, did you get anything useful out of Jim?"

Eileen shook her head. "It was the same as with you. He just wanted to talk about how brilliantly architected the software was and how much he liked my shoes."

They were very pointy shoes with very spiky heels. Did that say something about the Engineering VP?

Eileen looked at Brenda. "What was Troy's technique with you?"

She made a face. "He did the hair thing you told us about. Taking the ponytail out and putting it in again. I wonder if it's his way of preening? Like a male bird, sort of putting himself on display?"

The only thing I could say to that was "yuk," so I kept quiet.

"Anyway," Brenda went on, "I thought we decided yesterday that he doesn't have a motive. Is anyone going to talk to him this afternoon?"

"No." Eileen consulted her small electronic organizer. "I'm with MoM—I can't wait for that," she grimaced. "And you, Charley, are with Bob from Quality Assurance."

The bearded couch potato. I'd already written him off as a suspect because he couldn't have been the one at the gym with Clara, and I thought he was too chubby to have been the one dashing across the street in the rain to get in Lalit's car.

"Simon, you're with Jim."

"I wonder if he'll proposition me?" He wiggled his eyebrows. "Or if I should—"

"And Brenda, you're in Human Resources with Tonya again. See if you can get her to crack about who Clara was going to fire. I still think that's our best bet."

She looked up. "Are we ready?"

I wished people would stop asking that.

Chapter Twenty-five

Bob Adams. Vice president of Quality Assurance for the past two years, having risen through the ranks of code testers. Graduated from Brown—had everyone at Zakdan? Unmarried.

And not in his office when he was supposed to be.

I stepped inside the door. The entire wall along the corridor was glass, so I didn't think it was a good idea to actively snoop, but I did want to listen.

Lalit Kumar's office was next door, and there were two people in it. I'd seen them when I'd passed it on the way to Bob's. A man and a woman, who were apparently cleaning out the dead executive's personal items. Were they police? They seemed to be dressed a little more conservatively than most of the Zakdan crowd.

They were speaking quietly, but I could still hear the murmur of their voices, and I could tell one from the other. I was reasonably sure that if someone—say, Jack—had been speaking in a normal tone of voice into a cell phone, he could easily have been heard by whoever was in the adjoining rooms.

Of course, anyone could have been in those rooms. But they belonged to Bob, Jim Stoddard, and Troy Patterson.

The three men who were now my lead suspects.

I thought standing in an empty office might draw unwanted attention, so I decided to wander around the fourth floor executive offices, figuring Bob would probably show up eventually, and that I might learn something incriminating somewhere else in the meanwhile.

Since there seemed to be an espresso machine every ten feet or so, it wasn't hard to find gathering places. I went into the nearest break room, already occupied by two guys I hadn't met.

They both looked to be in their mid-thirties, shaggy-haired tee-shirt-and-cargo-pants types, which I recognized by then as the uniform of the software professional.

They were in the middle of an intense discussion, which left them oblivious to my presence. It wasn't difficult to eavesdrop as I made a cup of tea.

"Come, on—you can't be serious!"

"I'm totally serious. And I'm right, and you just won't admit it."

"But it's *wrong*! It's just wrong on so many levels I can't even begin to catalogue how wrong it is!"

What was wrong? Had I stumbled into a confession about someone planting bugs in the Zakdan software?

"Dude, just hear me out—"

"I'm not listening. You're insane, or you're high. And I hope for your sake you're high, because—"

"I am not high, and 'Smells Like Teen Spirit' is a perfectly legitimate rock anthem."

Damn. Not a confession.

"It is not! How can you even say that? 'Born to Run' is a rock anthem. 'Won't Get Fooled Again' is a rock anthem. Hell, 'Bohemian' fucking 'Rhapsody' is a fucking rock anthem—"

The other guy shook his head violently. "No, no, no. Listen, it takes three things to be a rock anthem. One: it has to be a voice of its own time—"

A late arrival brought the highly intellectual debate to a screeching halt.

"What's going on, guys?"

I jumped, not having noticed Bob Adams at the door.

"Hi, Bob," said the advocate for Nirvana.

"Hi, Bob," echoed the classic rock holdout.

"What are you guys talking about? Music?" He smiled too eagerly.

It was almost painful to watch. He was making such a strained attempt to show he was one of the guys, and the guys were so very clearly not interested.

"Yeah, something like that." Looking at the floor.

"Well, we'd better get back to work." With a brief, tight smile.

They began shuffling toward the door.

"Yeah, hey—any time you want to check out my CD collection, just come on by my office. I've got some killer stuff."

They'd moved past him, so he probably didn't see the look they exchanged. But I did, and I gathered they were not going to check out his killer stuff any time soon.

"Okay, see ya!" He turned to me, his overly bright grin still in place. "Great guys, huh? Oh! Sorry! I should have introduced you!"

I waved my hand. "Don't worry about it."

But he was worried. I couldn't tell if it was about his social faux pas, or the fact that I'd just seen him snubbed by the cool kids, or something else. But I got a definite whiff of something. And it didn't smell like teen spirit.

It smelled like desperation.

"Why? What's he hiding?" Eileen quizzed me.

We'd gathered back in the conference room after our afternoon interviews. Brenda, Eileen, Simon and I were at the table, Eileen typing our notes into her laptop. She planned on emailing them to Jack when she'd compiled them.

Flank walked the perimeter of the two glass walls—one the length of the room and the other, with the door, the width. This was his way of discouraging people from lingering outside or looking in.

"I'm not sure," I said. "But he's all bluster and no core, if you know what I mean."

Brenda nodded. "I see that a lot at school. It's usually someone who wants desperately to be perceived differently from how he sees himself."

"Doesn't everyone?" Simon asked.

I thought about the hour or so I'd spent with the Quality exec. "All through our conversation, Bob kept up this sort of double-edged attitude. I mean, he wanted me to see him as one of the guys. He mentioned several times that he couldn't believe he was a VP, because he still thinks of himself as a tester. But at the same time, it seemed really important to him that I walk away from the meeting believing that he's brilliant and a natural executive."

"So, if he's putting modest and brilliant up as his false front, does that mean he's really ambitious and stupid?" Simon enquired.

"Ambitious and stupid is a dangerous combination," Eileen observed. I'm not sure if she included that in the notes. "Anything else? Did he say anything concrete?"

I shook my head. "Nothing incriminating. He has this annoying habit of looking at you like he knows much more than he's telling you, but I wouldn't bet he actually does."

"What does he do when you press him on something?" Brenda asked.

"Just gets increasingly enigmatic. Which, come to think of it, did have the effect of getting me to change the topic…"

"But nothing concrete?" Eileen reiterated.

I sighed. "No."

Simon had already told us he hadn't been able to get anything from Jim Stoddard that we hadn't. And he seemed just slightly miffed that he hadn't gotten propositioned, but he chalked it up to the engineer's narrow-mindedness.

"How did you get along with MoM?" I asked Eileen.

She made a face. "I've already written up my notes, so you can look over the details with Jack and Mike later. The short version," she told us, "is that I think she's a corporate snake, but I don't know if she's capable of murder."

"Why not?" Simon asked.

"She seems...opportunistic," Eileen said thoughtfully. "Apparently, she's latched on to every new initiative to hit Zakdan in the last five years. But she's savvy—she can smell failure early, so she distances herself from doomed projects and gets out before they take her down with them. She'd make a good stock trader, but I don't know if plotting and planning are her strengths, and you need that to get away with murder, don't you?"

"I think the idea of us being here is that the killer won't get away with it," I reminded her.

"True." She paused and frowned. "But what about this—MoM isn't technical. For all her flitting around the highest ranks of the company, she has no programming experience and has never worked directly with the code. So if we believe Clara was killed because she discovered something about the bug planted in the software, and Lalit was killed because she told him about it—" which had become our working theory once I'd told them about Clara's meeting with Lalit on the day before her death "—I don't think MoM could be behind it."

"Great," I said. "So we have a couple cases of borderline personality disorder, but no valid suspects yet. Unless..." I turned to Brenda. "Did you get any good dirt in Human Resources?"

Brenda gave me a worried look. "I'm not sure I should tell you."

That sounded promising.

"Of course you should. What did Tonya tell you? Do you know who Clara was going to fire?"

"Yes." She still looked doubtful. "But I don't think we should leap to the conclusion that that person is the killer."

"Who was it?" Eileen demanded.

"Come on, Brenda," Simon encouraged. "Tell us."

She took a deep breath. "Okay, but seriously, let's not go rushing off—"

"Fine, fine, fine." I waved her concern away. "Who is it?"

I could tell she didn't like it, but she told us.

"Krissy."

We all took a while to recover from the news. None of us had the impression that Clara's replacement was a brain trust, but we hadn't pegged her to be the one walking the corporate plank.

"Why?" Eileen recovered first. "What were the charges against Krissy?"

"It seems to boil down to incompetence," Brenda told us. "Clara thought that Krissy had been promoted beyond her abilities, so she tried to give her extra training, but Krissy's attitude about that wasn't good. So Clara put her on a written improvement plan, and unless she lived up to the terms of it, she was on her way out."

"What were the terms?" Eileen had become sharply attentive.

Brenda shook her head. "Tonya put up a brick wall again. I could tell she didn't want to tell me as much as she had, but she had to talk to someone. It seemed like it was killing her that she knew Clara had been so close to firing Krissy, and now it looks like she'll get Clara's job."

"Doesn't Morgan know about this?" Simon asked. "Wouldn't Clara have told him?"

"Tonya didn't think so," Brenda told us. "She said Clara wanted to keep it strictly between her and Krissy and HR."

Eileen typed furiously on the laptop. If she wasn't careful, she'd be needing one of those wrist braces I saw every other person wearing.

"How long did Krissy have before Clara would have pulled the plug?"

But an answer to my question was preempted by an alarmingly strangled sound from the large man near the door.

"Yes, Flank?"

He gestured with his head, and we saw the danger: Jim Stoddard on fast approach. He hadn't come into the long hallway through the lobby door, so I wondered if there was a back door to the area somewhere. You never know when that sort of thing can come in handy.

Stoddard opened the glass conference room door and said, "Knock knock!"

Surprisingly, nobody said, "Who's there?"

Jim glanced uneasily at Flank, who stood menacingly at close range. He couldn't help the menacing part, but the closeness was definitely deliberate. Flank, apparently, wasn't a Jim Stoddard fan.

"Listen, there's a party tonight to celebrate shipping 7.3."

Which was largely meaningless, but we all made vague congratulatory sounds.

"You're all invited, and I hope you'll come."

How could he possibly look lasciviously at both Eileen and me simultaneously?

Simon apparently felt left out. "Where are we going?"

"Edinburgh Castle. Do you know it?"

One of the great dive bars of San Francisco. Of course we knew it.

"Seven o'clock, and Papa Zak is buying. Don't be late." He winked and left.

"Are we going?" Simon asked.

"It would be a good opportunity to observe people away from the office," Brenda said, but she didn't look thrilled at the prospect. "Although…"

"Although I'd sooner be poked in the eye with a sharp stick," Eileen finished for her. "I've had just about all I can take of that guy for one day."

Brenda nodded in complete agreement.

"Well, I suppose we don't *all* need to go…" Simon looked at me.

Ugh. "All right, I'll go. But I have to pick up Jack first and then I'm going home to change." Although I had no idea how to dress for a geek celebration. "I'll meet you there later. In the meanwhile, just take good notes."

"Notes! Right! I'm your man!"

Assuming we wanted our report on cocktail napkins.

Chapter Twenty-six

I'd gotten an email from Jack telling me that he and Harry had decided to get in some afternoon golfing in Lincoln Park. Since the Lexus was in the shop, and likely to be there for some time, he'd asked me to pick him up when I got off work.

My initial reaction had been…golf? It seemed a little damp for that sort of thing to me. Then again, the way Harry plays, more time was likely to be spent at the clubhouse bar than on the course.

I left Flank guarding the gang as they wrapped up for the day, and I headed across town in my little VW—which was starting to grow on me, but I'd never have admitted as much to my husband.

Something about driving in the fog made me thoughtful. Maybe it was the way the mist swirled around the streetlights in the evening dark, or just the fact that I was driving across town, in the city of noir, trying to figure out if I'd spoken with a murderer that day. In any case, my mind started wandering, and I found myself thinking about nerds.

Not to sound like a thirty-something-year-old fogey, but in my day nerds were nerds. Even at young ages, they were clearly identifiable by their short-sleeved dress shirts—worn all the way buttoned up—and their mechanical pencils. Some throwbacks still even sported those five-pound HP calculators with hundreds of colored function buttons.

Don't even get me started on their glasses.

The more advanced of them walked the halls of junior high discussing what they'd done on their Atari the night before, and exchanging computer printouts of Snoopy or the Starship Enterprise composed entirely of asterisks and dashes.

How times change.

The nerds had won the culture wars, and now geek chic was in. You only had to look at current trends in eyewear to know that.

But I couldn't help wondering, for someone like Jim Stoddard or Bob Adams—who were old enough to have been there for the origin of the species—was it all sweet revenge? Or was part of them still stuck in high school, watching the football players score with the pretty girls and seething with resentment?

I thought of Bob Adams' expression as the younger and infinitely hipper engineers had dismissed him in the break room. Even though he was an exec and they were lowly whatevers, he wanted their approval. He wanted to be cool.

Did he want it bad enough to kill?

The phone rang and I nearly swerved into an oncoming bus.

"Hi, Pumpkin."

"Hi yourself." I escaped with my life and made the turn from Van Ness onto Geary. "I should be there in ten or fifteen minutes, depending on traffic." And barring further disasters.

"Great. But I'm not at the clubhouse. They close at six. I walked up to the Palace of the Legion of Honor. I'm sitting on the front steps, so I'll see you when you get here."

"I'll try not to confuse you with the *Thinker*." Rodin's furrowed-browed figure was stationed in the outdoor courtyard of the museum.

"That should be easy. I'm in better shape."

I hung up on him.

◇◇◇

The fog got thicker as I headed out toward the ocean. The museum sits on a hill in Lincoln Park overlooking the Golden Gate Bridge and much of the city. A circular drive in front of it—complete with a fountain—has to be the classiest parking lot in the city. On a clear day the views are spectacular.

This was not a clear day.

I turned on my wipers once or twice before I got to the park entrance. I went up the hill through the golf course, and when I got to the top I could see that the fountain was off and the parking lot was practically deserted. What I didn't see was Jack on the front steps.

I checked the mirror to make sure nobody was behind me, then put the car in Park. I didn't really feel like getting out in the cold to go husband hunting.

The main entrance to the museum is at the far end of the *Thinker*'s courtyard, and an open portico is at the front. The portico is supported by a double row of columns, the rear of which has security fencing to keep people from wandering around when the museum is closed. There's a wide central walkway up to the building, with lawns, flowerbeds, and large horsy sculptures on either side.

I finally spotted Jack. He was on the portico, which presumably gave him some shelter. And he hadn't yet noticed me because he was shadowboxing, moving lightly on his feet and jabbing at the air.

He was probably only doing it to stay warm, but I had to admit he looked good in motion. He has this athletic grace thing, and—

I lost my train of thought, such as it was, when I saw something weird happen to the column just left of Jack. It was like a little puff of dust came off it, sparkling in the museum's floodlights. He hadn't noticed, but it happened again, this time a little higher, and I suddenly knew what it was.

Someone was shooting at Jack.

Another puff appeared on the column, this time taking out a chunk of it. "Jack!" I yelled as I put the car in gear.

There were iron posts at the end of the walkway, so I gave the wheel a sharp turn to the left and gunned the engine. I took out a floodlight, went sailing over five shallow steps, and tore up the lawn to the building. I slammed on the brakes and came skidding to a halt just in front of the portico.

"Get in!" I shouted. Which is when all the glass in the car exploded.

"Get out!" Jack yelled, pulling a gun from under his jacket and opening fire on something behind me.

I dove out of the car and stumbled to the portico. I took cover behind a column, staying low. Ridiculously, I had the car keys in my hand.

"Jack—"

"Stay down!" he shouted. "Are you hurt?"

I took a quick survey. Scraped in a couple of places, but not seriously. "No! Jack, who is it?"

He didn't answer. He was too busy shooting.

A bullet zinged by and chipped a corner off the large marble base of the *Thinker* behind us.

"Jack, they could hit the statue!"

He took a second to look at me like I was insane, then crouched behind the column next to mine as the shooter opened fire again. "I hardly think art preservation is our main concern right now, Pumpkin."

I winced as bits of marble fell between us. Maybe he had a point.

"How many bullets do you have left?"

"One."

Not the answer I was hoping for.

"What are we going to do?"

More bits of marble, coming from a different column. The shooter was moving.

Jack didn't answer. He just pointed the gun and shot.

Directly into the museum door, at the far end of the courtyard.

"Jack!" I couldn't believe he'd wasted his last bullet. But then the sirens went off and I got it.

Lights flashed, bells clanged, air horns went "whoop-whoop." It was fabulous.

In the middle of all of it, I thought I heard an engine fire up. Jack took a split-second look down the drive, then fell back against the column, the tension leaving his body.

He looked over at me. "Ready to go?"

I nodded.

He stood first, and waved an arm from behind the column. The theory behind which, I supposed, was that if it wasn't shot off we could proceed with our departure.

It wasn't shot off.

I stood shakily. When I turned and looked at the bullet-riddled little bug, I nearly sank down again.

Jack caught me. He held on for a moment, then said, "We have to get out of here."

I nodded again. I could do that.

He took the keys from my hand. "Maybe I'll drive."

Probably a good idea.

Chapter Twenty-seven

Traveling in a car with a missing windshield isn't exactly conducive to casual conversation. You have to yell over the noise, and if your husband suddenly stops at a light you may find yourself shouting things like, "Should I carry the gun while you're driving?" which can frighten the pedestrians.

So after one or two attempts, I gave up and concentrated on looking like it was perfectly normal to be roaming around town in a shot-up VW.

Jack took the lower road through Lincoln Park, then cut through the residential Sea Cliff area and turned into the Presidio. Once we were in the former military installation, he seemed to relax. There were hardly any cars on the narrow roads.

He headed downhill, and finally came to a stop in the deserted west parking lot of Crissy Field.

I looked around. There wasn't a soul in sight. With the fog and the drizzle and the darkness I shouldn't have been surprised that no joggers were out using the paths along the bay.

"Jack, what are we doing here?"

"Get everything you need out of the car," he told me.

What I needed was a stiff belt of whiskey. "What?"

He reached into the back for my laptop bag, and shook the broken safety glass off. "We're leaving the car here, Charley. Is there anything else you need?"

"We're leaving the car here?"

Being shot at gets my adrenalin going, but the same apparently can't be said for my mental powers.

"There are security cameras at the museum. The police are already looking for it. We need to leave it here and report it stolen right away."

"Oh." I looked around. I had my purse and Jack had the laptop bag. "I think that's it."

He got out. I had one more look around the interior of the car, took the only other thing I wanted, and got out.

"You're bringing the flower?" The bright pink gerbera daisy that had been in the dashboard vase.

"You gave it to me." I looked up at him. It's possible I wasn't thinking quite clearly yet.

He dropped the laptop and grabbed me. For an instant I thought we were about to get shot at again, but Jack just crushed me to himself, muttering all sorts of half sentences and muffled phrases that added up to something quite nice. When he finally released me the flower was a goner, but I felt completely restored.

"What are we doing now?"

He slung the laptop bag over his shoulder, grabbed my hand, and started walking fast.

"Jack, the Warming Hut looks closed," I told him. It was the little café at the end of the path where you could get a nonfat latte and feel virtuous after your workout. That is, if it wasn't locked and dark.

But he wasn't heading for the café. He was heading for the fishing pier. Probably the coldest, windiest place in all of San Francisco, so I shouldn't have been surprised.

"Jack?"

"I have to get rid of the gun, Charley. You stay here." He left me on the path and jogged out across the wooden pier, which stretched into the bay almost directly under the Golden Gate Bridge. When he got to the far end, he took the gun from his pocket and pitched it out over the water.

I had a bad feeling that I knew what he'd say when he got back, and I was right.

"Feel like taking a walk?"

◇◇◇

I can't count how many times I've gone running at Crissy Field. Its wide gravel path along the water is perfect on a sunny day. You don't even notice the distance from the east parking lot to the fishing pier and back. But I'd never done it in new Via Spiga pumps after getting shot at and ditching my car.

This time I noticed the distance.

But, by the time we made it the mile or so to the little bridge at the tidal marsh, the cavalry had arrived. Granted, it was in the form of Flank behind the wheel of an enormous black Hummer that Harry had recently acquired, but by that point I didn't much care.

"Harry must have sent him," Jack said. He'd spent most of our slog along the waterfront on his cell phone. First the police, to report the car stolen, then Harry, to make sure a second gunman hadn't targeted him after he and Jack had split up. Then Mike, and I don't know who else because my feet hurt too much by then to pay attention.

"Why the hell didn't Harry just give you a ride after golfing?" I asked. My uncle could have at least inconvenienced himself a little to spare my husband from being used for target practice.

"He ran into some crony on the course, and they decided to go to another bar when the clubhouse closed. I'd have gone with them, but the bar was in Vegas. They were taking the other guy's private jet."

Typical.

"He's on his way back now," Jack told me. "They said they'd turn the plane around when I called."

Great. Harry would probably be home before I would.

Flank got out of the car and did his best to cover all conceivable angles around us, performing an intricate series of commando/bodyguard stances while opening doors and shoving us in to safety. It was like watching a water buffalo attempt ballet.

I sank against Jack in the back seat, and his black leather jacket made a squelching noise. Or maybe it was me. Then Flank did something which was in flagrant violation of the law, for which I will always be grateful.

He handed me a flask of whiskey.

Once home, all I really wanted was a hot shower and to throw away my shoes. But I had a feeling everyone I knew was about to show up on my doorstep, so I settled for toweling myself off and changing into dry sweats before heading back downstairs to ask my husband a few questions.

Starting with "How long have you been carrying a gun?"

He was in his office, and—I don't know how he does this stuff—perfectly dry in fresh clothes. He gave me a distracted sort of look.

"On and off since I was about twenty-two."

I took a breath and told myself it wouldn't be helpful to kick him.

"How about if we just stick to discussing the gun that's at the bottom of the bay?"

"You'll have to be a little more specific."

"Jack!"

"Okay, okay." He touched something on his keyboard and the computer screen changed. Then he gave me his attention. "I started carrying that gun this week. And before you start giving me a lecture on gun control, I think you should admit that it came in pretty handy—"

"Why don't I have one?"

He blinked. "What?"

"I'm the one who's undercover. I think I should have one too. And I think you should admit that another one would have come in pretty handy—"

"Charley, the last time I gave you a gun you shot somebody. And as I recall, you didn't enjoy it."

True. Nevertheless… "That doesn't change the fact that another one would have come in damn handy tonight. And it might have come in damn handy in the Broadway Tunnel the other night too."

He did a sort of teeth grinding thing before he answered.

"You're telling me you would have opened fire in the middle of a crowded city street?"

"Well, of course not. Not if you put it like that. But—"

My argument was cut off by the sound of the doorbell.

Harry, probably. Flank would have raised the alarm for anyone else. I had the sneaking suspicion that our bodyguard planned to spend the night parked outside our house. And, for once, I didn't mind.

"We'll finish this later," Jack said, on his way to the stairs.

Damn right we would. I followed him, picking up the pace when the bell rang again, and thinking I knew exactly what I was going to say to my uncle for running off to Vegas and leaving Jack alone in the fog.

Jack opened the door.

"Harry—"

But it wasn't.

"Inspector Yahata," Jack said. "Thanks for coming so quickly."

My brain did that nuclear meltdown thing it does whenever I see the detective. How had he known it was us at the museum? I mean, okay, he probably heard it was our car involved, and maybe he thought the "it was stolen, officer" story was a little fishy, but—

Suddenly he was in my hallway and hitting me with that unnerving x-ray glance.

"Are you hurt?"

I had what promised to develop into nasty bruises on my knees and shins from the concrete floor of the museum's portico, and a few scrapes on my hands and arms from the whole exploding safety glass thing in the car. But I wasn't about to tell him that.

"I'm fine, naturally. Whatever do you mean?"

Why did I always end up sounding like a bad Blanche DuBois in a third-rate production of *Streetcar* when I was around this guy?

He tried a different question.

"What happened?"

Not big on chitchat, the homicide inspector. Which was just as well, because I'd transitioned into speechlessness. Something to do with the realization that Jack had been expecting Yahata.

They were both looking at me. It's possible one of them had asked me a question. But the sound of things clicking into place made it hard to hear anything else.

Jack looked a little concerned. "Charley, do you need to sit down?"

"What—" My voice was squeaky, so I tried again. "What—" Better. "The hell—" Much better. "Is going on here?"

Jack took a minute to consider his answer. "How about I make some coffee and we fill you in?"

◇◇◇

Yahata knew everything. What's more, he'd known all along. Because Jack had told him everything. All along.

It took more than a cup of coffee for me to make sense of that.

"So let me get this straight…Jack is working for you?" I stared at the inspector. We'd gathered in the kitchen, but the room's bright lights didn't help me read him.

He gave me a quick, slight smile. "Not precisely. The department has retained the services of MJC."

Mike and Jack's company. Okay. Now we were getting somewhere.

"To find out who killed Clara and Lalit?"

Yahata gave an infinitesimal shake of the head. "Not precisely. They have been retained to test, and—if necessary—recommend enhancements to the security of the department's information systems."

Right. That made perfect sense. Except… "Does the police department usually outsource that sort of thing?"

Jack looked surprised, maybe because he wouldn't have bet I knew what outsourcing was.

Yahata replied mildly, "'Usually' is not an applicable word in this situation."

Okay. Whatever.

"So how does our going undercover at Zakdan fall within the scope of what Jack and Mike are doing for the department?"

The inspector's jaw tightened. I'd hit a nerve. "By the slimmest of threads."

Jack explained. "The department's network uses the Zakdan enterprise system for information management."

I'd learned enough in the last week to realize what that meant. "So if there's a vulnerability in the Zakdan code, the SFPD computer system is at risk."

Jack's look said I'd made the connection faster than he'd expected. And that he was kind of turned on by it. "Exactly."

I finished the last of my coffee, thinking. Because of the above-board work that Mike and Jack were doing for the department, Yahata had apparently been able to make peace with the less above-board fact that civilians were being used to investigate the sordid goings-on at Zakdan.

"But." I spoke as if I'd been thinking out loud, which didn't seem to bother them. "Brenda and Eileen and Simon and I aren't really looking for the person who's sabotaged the code. We're looking for the killer. Which means…" I turned to the inspector. "You agree they're connected."

"I do."

Ah HA! Now we were getting somewhere. Now it was time to—

"It's time to call off the undercover operation," Jack said.

"*What?* Jack, we're just starting to make progress. I didn't even tell you everything we found out today, and—"

"And nothing," he said firmly. "You got shot at today. The operation is over."

"No." I shook my head.

"Charley—"

"Hang on a minute. I don't mean 'no' to ending the operation—although I do—"

"Charley!"

"I mean 'no' I didn't get shot at today. You did. I wasn't the one they were after."

"Really? Because as I recall we were both ducking for cover up there."

"You and Mike are the ones who went into Zakdan as the big time computer security specialists investigating the software bug," I insisted. "Don't try to tell me you didn't think that might draw the killer's attention to you. Well, it did. Nobody started shooting at me tonight until I drove up the lawn to get you. They were after you, Jack. Just like they were after you when they tried to drive us into the tunnel wall."

Inspector Yahata had been observing the exchange with undisguised fascination. Now, in the silence that followed my outburst, he looked at Jack sharply. And said something I never thought I'd hear.

"Your wife is right."

I stared at him as he continued speaking to Jack.

"The fact that the killer is aware of your involvement in investigating the glitch in the Zakdan software could be a valuable distraction. As long as you are the target of their hostilities, Charley's team might not be scrutinized. Your efforts provide a certain amount of cover for her efforts."

My first thought was that I liked the sound of "Charley's team." My second was that I didn't like "Jack is the target."

Then I had a third thought, and it was a doozy.

"Inspector, if you agree that there's a connection between the murders and the bug, why don't you have undercover cops or detectives or something investigating at Zakdan? Not that I'm complaining or anything, but—"

Something in the way he was looking at me made it impossible to continue. When he answered, it was with carefully chosen words.

"The fact that I agree there's a connection does not necessarily mean the department agrees there's a connection."

This was not exactly cheerful news.

My mouth went dry. "What does the department think?"

Yahata looked like there was a lot he wanted to say, but he didn't say anything.

Jack cleared his throat. "If I had to guess, I'd guess that there are some people who took Lalit Kumar's suicide as a pretty clear sign of his guilt."

I stared at him. "What? Why would he have killed Clara?" Then my eyes widened. Kumar was the chief technology officer, which presumably meant he had unlimited access to the Zakdan code.

"Lalit was behind the software glitch?"

"It's possible," Jack answered.

"It's one theory," the inspector nodded.

"And it's the one the police are investigating, isn't it?" I realized. "The only one."

"But if it's wrong, and if what you and Brenda saw in the rain that night was someone holding a gun on Kumar..." Jack began.

"Then we're the only ones who are still looking for the real killer," I finished.

And if our encounter at the museum was any indication, the real killer was seriously looking for us.

Chapter Twenty-eight

The upside to having my car shot to pieces was that I didn't have to drive to work the next morning. The downside was having Flank as my new chauffeur.

Jack categorically refused anything like getting his own bodyguard. I suppose half a lifetime of military training and extensive experience in clandestine operations can leave a man fairly confident in his own abilities.

But I was still worried about him.

He was worried about me, too. It crossed my mind that mutual worry might in fact be what marriage was all about. In any case, Jack was worried enough that he presented me with a small black .22 Smith & Wesson before we went to bed that night.

"How romantic."

He frowned. "You shouldn't ever have to use this. Flank should be around you when I'm not."

"I know."

"But the killer has seen you with me both times he's tried to get at me."

"I know." I swallowed. "But I'm telling myself that it would have been as hard for him to get a look at me in the tunnel that night as it was for me to see him."

Jack nodded. "And tonight? You're willing to bet that it was dark and drizzly enough that he didn't realize who you are? Because I'm not sure I am."

My uncle Harry had done his best to ensure that I knew my way around small firearms before my sixteenth birthday. So I took the gun, getting that familiar sick feeling in my stomach that came with handling instruments of death, and checked the chamber and the safety before tucking it into a pocket of my laptop bag. Then I looked up at Jack.

"If I were the type of woman to play things safe, I probably would have married some nice, boring investment banker."

"That would have made Eileen happy." He looked at me sideways.

"I'm not Eileen." I moved closer to him. "I married you, and you come with danger and guns and secrets, and sometimes that drives me crazy, but it's who you are." I reached up, wrapping my arms around his neck. "And I married you."

He pulled me close, and the last thing I remember him saying was "Damn right you did."

Naturally, Jack was gone by the time I made it downstairs the next morning. But he'd left a note next to a plate of fresh banana bread.

C,

Try not to drive Flank so crazy he has to kill you.

—J

Oh, ha ha.

The Hummer was parked at the curb. I really didn't think it was worth depleting the last remaining fossil fuels on the planet just to get to work in the thing, but it didn't appear I had any choice.

Besides, I didn't think Flank would fit into a hybrid.

He got out to open the back door for me, but I went for the passenger seat up front. He grunted something incomprehensible and held the back door open.

"I'm sitting in front, Flank. Someone may see us, and I might be able to get away with saying my car was stolen and you gave me a lift, but I wouldn't be riding in the back seat if that were the case, would I?"

He glared at me, which was a little unnerving, the look coming from beneath his Pleistocene-era brow as it did. But he gave in and shut the door.

It was going to be a long ride. And the conversation, I knew, would be minimal—mainly because Flank seemed incapable of articulate speech unless he had a gun in his hand. So I tried to concentrate on what I planned to accomplish in the day ahead.

Krissy was my highest priority. Now that we knew she'd been on the point of getting fired, she was the clear frontrunner for the role of Clara's killer. Luckily, I'd already scheduled a lunch meeting with her. If I played the scene right—

"You'd be safer in back."

I jumped.

Flank's eyes were on the road, and his right hand was on the gearshift. It was a massive gearshift, with a solid metal shaft and a leather-wrapped handle. Was it sufficiently…masculine…to have the same effect on him as a pistol?

"It's my job to keep you safe."

Apparently so. Wow. Flank could talk. Unfortunately, his topic was a little sulky, but that should be easily fixed.

"You're doing a great job," I told him. "Look how safe I am."

He frowned. "Should have been there."

I assumed he meant he should have been at the shooting spree last night. "No." I shook my head. "You're only supposed to be looking after us at Zakdan, and we've all been fine there. Besides, we figured out last night that the killer was after Jack, not me."

He didn't look reassured.

"You've been a huge help at the office. Saving me parking spaces, and making sure everything is organized…"

He lightened up a little, much to my relief. And I realized we'd never asked him whether he'd heard or seen anything suspicious at Zakdan.

"Flank, do you have any leads on the case? Have you noticed anything or overheard anything?"

He blinked a couple of times, then looked over at me. I don't suppose he gets a lot of call for delivering intelligence reports. Maybe some prompting would help.

"Have any of the other secretaries told you anything?"

He seemed to think it over. "They like to be called admins."

Oh. Okay. Duly noted.

"Are there any rumors going around? How do people feel about Krissy?"

He shrugged, and we stopped at a red light on Pine Street.

"How about Jim Stoddard? Any gossip about him?"

"Drinks too much."

"Really? Jim drinks?" Oh, but I knew that already. Brenda had found out about the engineer's old DUIs in her initial research. But it was good to know he still drank. At least, good in the sense that it offered the possibility that rampant alcoholism had led him into a life of crime. Maybe.

"What about the rest of them? Troy? Or Bob Adams? Or MoM?"

Something in Flank's reaction suggested we'd be better off taking the suspects one at a time. "Let's start with Troy."

The light turned and I gave him a minute to get things in motion again.

"Creep," he said. "Womanizer."

Fascinating. If the head of Marketing had that kind of a reputation, maybe someone had filed a harassment suit against him. And if that someone had been Clara...but wouldn't Morgan have known about that?

"Oh," I said. "What about Morgan? What do they say about him?"

Flank shook his head. "Poor guy."

"Are you saying that? Or do they say that?"

"Them. He was getting married."

I was stunned. "Are you saying it's common knowledge at Zakdan that Morgan and Clara were engaged?"

He nodded and made the left onto Golden Gate.

This was amazing. Morgan thought nobody knew. If the whole company was talking about it, the list of suspects could be huge.

"Bob." Flank interrupted my thoughts. "Loser."

I can't say I was surprised at the prevailing opinion about the head of Quality.

"MoM," he continued flatly. "Bitch."

My eyebrows went up, more at his use of the word than the consensus about Millicent O'Mally.

"Really?" But the higher-ups seemed to love her. Maybe she was only a bitch to the underlings. Which Clara had been once…

I shook my head. We were supposed to be finding people who might have hated Clara, not people Clara might have hated. "What about Tonya from Human Resources?"

"Gossip."

Not enough for my taste, she wasn't. "How about—"

But further conversation would have to wait for the trip home. Traffic had picked up and Flank needed both hands on the wheel.

"Do we have to guess where you were last night?"

Eileen asked the question as she handed me a copy of the *Chronicle*. I'd spotted her, huddled with Brenda and Simon over it, as I'd scanned the Friday morning crowd at Café Arugula.

I looked at the paper. The front page gave prominent space to the story of a mysterious shootout at the Palace of the Legion of Honor. Lots of bullets. No bodies and no suspects.

"Charley, are you okay?" Brenda asked.

Simon's eyes sparkled. "I'll forgive you completely for standing me up at that party last night, darling, but only on the condition that you tell us absolutely everything."

So I did. Which made us very late for work.

◇◇◇

"Ready for lunch? It's Mongolian Hot Pot day and there's usually a line."

Which is how I found out from Krissy that Zakdan actually had an on-site cafeteria. And that the Friday build-your-own-stir-fry event was an experience not to be missed.

The cafeteria was on the first floor at the back of the building. And Krissy had been right—there was a line.

I didn't really get a chance to question her in the crowd as we inched forward, putting raw veggies from a sort of salad bar into our bowls. The line moved pretty smoothly. The cooks seemed to know the drill. They'd probably been doing it for years. Except for one. I was almost sure it was his first day.

Because it was Gordon.

Jack's former partner and Harry's former chef looked at me as if we'd never met.

"Meat?" he enquired.

"Chicken," I accused.

How the hell had Jack gotten him in position so quickly? And what did he think Gordon would be able to accomplish from behind the cafeteria counter?

But my what-do-you-think-you're-doing-here stare provoked no response other than a slight glint of amusement in Gordon's unflappable expression.

"Hot and spicy, or mild?"

"What do you think?" I answered testily.

He reached for the hot sauce.

Whatever. I looked around the place. The get-your-lunch area consisted of a salad bar, sandwich bar, and grill station, in addition to the hot meal line where Gordon was igniting my stir fry. The eat-your-lunch area was a colorful space beyond the cashiers where it looked like the whole company was congregated.

The same corporate colors from the lobby were splashed around here. Tables shaped like ink blots in deep red and purple, minimalist acrylic chairs in yellow-gold and more red, with big abstract blotches of color on the walls.

"Tess?" Krissy poked me in the ribs, and I saw Gordon holding my bowl back to me.

"Have a nice day," I told him, and was rewarded with the briefest of grins before he turned to the next person in line.

I followed Krissy to the cashier and then to the seating area. She paused, looking around the crowded room, and for a moment I had a little first-day-in-the-high-school-lunchroom déjà vu.

"Who do you normally sit with?" I asked Krissy. I saw several of the execs all together at the far side of the room. Tonya, Bob, MoM, and Troy were at a table with several vacant seats, but Krissy was steering us away from them.

She led me to a small table in the corner, and answered as she unloaded her tray.

"Lately I've been taking my lunch back to my desk. I used to sit with them." She nodded in the direction of a loud group at a large central table.

They were noticeably younger and considerably more tattooed than the rest of the lunch crowd, and several looked as though they'd probably arrived for work on their skateboards.

"They're the customer service reps," she explained. "At least the ones we still have here. Most of that work is outsourced now."

"So they're the group you manage?"

"I used to manage just them, but since Clara…" She didn't seem to know how to end that sentence. "Anyway. Now I have the knowledgebase writers too, and I oversee the outsourced firms."

"That sounds like a lot."

Her shoulders had tensed. She tried to shrug but it came off more like a twitch. "I can handle it."

Right. Then why did she look like she was playing Ophelia on her way to the river?

"Why don't you sit with them anymore?" The gang at her former table looked like they were having a good time.

"MoM told me it wouldn't be appropriate, because of my new position. She says you have to draw the line firmly when you get to a certain level. She's been really helpful in all of this."

Right. I remembered her helpful slap at Clara's funeral.

I waved my chopsticks in the direction of the execs. "So are you supposed to sit with them now?"

She looked toward them. "Oh, sometimes…" Her voice trailed off and she toyed with her broccoli, keeping her eyes on her plate. "They don't like me."

"Oh, um…" This was not exactly the way I'd seen our conversation going. Time to change the subject if I wanted to accomplish anything other than making her cry.

I looked around the room for a distraction. Flank was sitting two tables over from us, devouring cheeseburgers and keeping an eye on things. I didn't think drawing Krissy's attention to him would have quite the calming effect I was going for. I scanned the crowd behind him.

"Who are they?" I gestured to a group of vampires in the far corner. At least they looked like vampires. Dyed black hair, pasty complexions, black clothes, and lots of eyeliner.

Krissy glanced over and made a face. "The Goths. They hired one in Creative Services six months ago and the next thing you know we've got a whole flock of them." She sniffed. "They think they're so cool."

"What does Creative Services do here at Zakdan?" Implying that I knew exactly what they did at the many, many other companies I'd consulted with.

"They work for Marketing. They do the artwork and design and stuff."

It was a wonder the Zakdan packaging didn't look like the work of Charles Addams.

I took a bite of spicy chicken. Krissy seemed to have given up on eating. The more time I spent with her, the more I just didn't see her as Clara's killer. She hardly had the demeanor of someone who'd killed to get ahead in her career. I decided to ask her a direct question.

"Krissy, do you like your new job?"

It turned out to be really the wrong thing to say.

◇◇◇

"She burst into tears right there in the cafeteria?" Brenda looked appalled. I'd found her in the conference room as soon as I'd been able to extricate myself from Krissy's emotional breakdown.

"It wasn't a burst so much as a slow leak," I explained. "She just started weeping, so I hustled her out of the lunchroom and got her to the nearest ladies room."

"What did she do then?"

"You know how all the bathrooms here have a room with all the sinks, and then a separate room beyond that with all the stalls?"

Brenda nodded.

"She ran ahead of me and locked the door into the far room. So I talked to her through the door."

Actually, I'd listened to her through the door. I found out later that Flank had taken position outside the bathroom to keep anyone from disturbing us in the middle of Krissy's confession.

A huge sobbing confession.

But not a confession to murder.

"She hates the new job. She hates that Clara was right about her—"

"She said that?" Brenda pounced on the information.

I nodded. "Told me all about how Clara had her on a performance improvement plan, and that she knows she's incompetent, and that she feels like a huge fraud, and that everybody knows she's an idiot—"

"That's so harsh," Brenda protested.

"She's just completely insecure, and in over her head, and has no idea how to get out of the mess."

"The poor thing! You know, I think that's probably pretty common. Places like this thrive on the insecurity of the employees. I've been reading all about it."

I'd found Brenda seated behind a stack of business books. It looked like she'd bought every item from Mike's suggested bibliography. And, apparently, she'd been doing her homework.

"I mean, I thought academia was bad, but this place has really opened my eyes." She pulled out a notepad. "There might be a paper in all of this. The effect of the corporate machine on people like that poor girl."

"Let's just not forget she's the poor girl we've been considering for the role of Clara's cold-blooded killer."

"Do you still think so?"

I made a face. "Not really. She may have had motivation to kill Clara, but she hasn't been here long enough to have planted the software bug, and I really don't think she's the one who's been trying to kill Jack."

Flank, who'd taken his usual stance in his usual back corner of the room, grunted. I took it as a sign of agreement.

"So where does that leave us?" Brenda asked.

With a new number one on my mental list of suspects. "Jim Stoddard."

She nodded. "If he's the one who put the bug in the Zakdan code—and he knew Clara found out about it—he has a motive."

"Right," I said. "Besides, I think he could have overheard Jack making plans to go to Bix from his office on the night someone tried to run us off the road."

Brenda scrunched her eyebrows together. "And he could have been the person we saw getting into Lalit's car," she admitted.

"Not to mention that if he was in the habit of hearing what goes on in Lalit's office, he might have heard Clara telling Lalit what she'd discovered about the bug when they had their meeting the day before she died."

"So we're concentrating on Jim," Brenda said with finality. "Okay, so—"

We were interrupted by Simon and Eileen, bursting through the door breathless and babbling.

"Did you hear?"

"Have you heard?"

"Do you know?"

"Can you believe it?"

"*What?*" I yelled.

Eileen got a grip first. "It's Jim Stoddard!"

"We know!" I jumped up.

"How did you find out? What happened? Did he confess?" Brenda joined the shouting.

"Confess? What are you talking about?" Simon said.

"About Jim being the killer!"

I saw the confusion on his face and got a sinking feeling. "What are you talking about?"

Simon and Eileen answered together.

"Jim Stoddard is dead."

Chapter Twenty-nine

"Please tell me he wasn't shot by an unknown gunman last night." Particularly if that unknown gunman might have been my husband, shooting back at whoever was trying to kill us.

Eileen shook her head. "Car crash."

"After leaving the party at Edinburgh Castle," Simon supplied.

"Drunk," Eileen concluded.

"Thank God." I sank down into a chair.

They all stared at me.

Perhaps I was being insensitive. "I mean…was it an accident?"

"Car crashes involving drunk drivers usually are." Eileen took a seat opposite me. "Why?"

Mainly because it seemed awfully suspicious for our lead suspect to be so conveniently disposed of.

"Do you know what I think?" Brenda closed her book. "I think we need to call Jack."

And maybe our new best friend, Inspector Yahata.

When I got home that evening, I followed the sounds of conversation and smells of garlic and basil to their source in the kitchen. Mike and Gordon were with Jack, who was stirring an immense vat of something on the stove.

"Hi, Pumpkin. Where's Flank?" Jack handed the spoon off to Gordon. He pulled out a high bar stool for me to take a seat at the kitchen island.

"On front door duty. What's going on? When did we get kitchen chairs?"

"They're on loan from Gordon's restaurant," Mike said.

"Oh." I turned to the chef. "So you're still planning on opening a restaurant? You haven't decided the Zakdan cafeteria has an irresistible charm?"

"It isn't the charm of the place I find irresistible," he said. "It's the fact that I get to observe such fascinating interactions." He dunked a piece of sourdough bread into the pot and it came out covered in marinara sauce.

"Like what?" Harry's voice, booming from behind me, was enough to make me knock over a bottle of olive oil.

"Harry." Jack caught the bottle before it hit the floor.

"What's going on? What have I missed?" Harry went over to Gordon and looked in the pot. "What interactions are so fascinating?"

"I was just telling these two—" The cook offered the bread to Harry and got out of his way. "—that Jim Stoddard had been having some fairly intense conversations over lunch this week."

"Really? With who?"

"Krissy on Monday, and whatever he was saying to her, she looked on the verge of tears by the time they left. Then Troy on Tuesday. They almost had a shouting match, but from what I could tell it was about how Troy was marketing their latest new product."

"Hang on," I stopped him. "Monday and Tuesday? We didn't even start the undercover thing until Wednesday."

Gordon looked over to Jack.

"*You* didn't start until Wednesday."

Right. So much for my husband's policy of telling me everything.

I turned my attention back to Gordon. "So, Wednesday?"

"Jim had lunch with Bob Adams on Wednesday. They both looked extremely agitated over something, Bob got increasingly upset throughout the conversation, but I didn't overhear what it was all about." He looked disappointed with himself.

"And yesterday?"

"That MoM woman. She did most of the talking."

I was about to ask a question when I heard Eileen calling from the front of the house. "Charley? Jack?"

"We're in the kitchen!" Harry bellowed.

Anthony came tearing through the door seconds later. "Hi, Jack. Can I go play on your computer?"

Eileen followed him in, Brenda close behind.

"Anthony, what do you do when you enter a room?" Eileen asked in her I'm-the-mother voice.

The boy rolled his eyes and turned to me. "Hi, Aunt Charley." Then he looked at the others. "Hi…everyone."

"I've got the pirate game all set up for you," Jack told him. "See if you can make it to Level Nine this time."

"Thanks, Jack!" He bounced once on the balls of his feet, then dashed out.

Eileen pulled up a stool next to mine. "Is that wine? What are we talking about? Have we heard anything more about Jim's accident?"

Brenda had joined Harry and Gordon at the stove. "Do you use pine nuts in your meatballs?"

Gordon nodded. "They're Jack's, and I think he goes a little heavy on the garlic, but—"

"Hello, darlings." Simon popped his head in the door. "Good heavens." he took in the vat of meatballs and the gathered troops. "Does this mean we're going to the mattresses?"

He may have seen *The Godfather* one too many times.

Eventually we got back to the point of the discussion. I was pretty sure we wouldn't have any more interruptions, because I was pretty sure everyone I'd ever met in my entire life was already in my kitchen.

Except Inspector Yahata.

"I spoke to Yahata today after you called," Jack told us. "According to the police, Jim Stoddard left the bar alone at around 12:45 last night." He looked at Simon. "Does that sound right?"

Simon brightened. "Did you see my statement? The police questioned me along with everyone else from Zakdan who'd been at the party last night. I must say, my particular officer was something of a disappointment. I mean—"

"Simon," Eileen interrupted him. "When did Jim leave the party?"

"Oh. Right. That." He beamed. "About quarter to one."

"And he'd been drinking heavily," Jack went on.

"Like a fish," Simon agreed. "But he wasn't sloppy. It wasn't to the point where anyone tried to take his keys away."

"Maybe they should have," Brenda said.

"So he wasn't stumbling drunk, but thinking about it now, would you say he'd had too much to drive?" Mike asked.

"Well, yes," Simon responded. "As the chap is now dead, I'd say perhaps he'd had a drop too much."

Jack cleared his throat. "Okay, so according to the police, he'd gotten in his car, which apparently he'd parked a few blocks away on the other side of Van Ness—"

"Hold on," Simon interrupted. "Wouldn't that be uphill from the bar?"

"Yes." Jack looked at him closely. "Why?"

Simon concentrated. "I could have sworn that as I got to the party I saw him coming from downhill."

"Did you mention that to the police?"

Simon swallowed. "Nobody asked me about the early part of the evening. They all just wanted to know what happened when he left."

"What did happen, Jack?" I asked. "How did he die?"

"He was in the intersection of Van Ness and O'Farrell when he was hit broadside by a truck that was carrying a load of new cars. The driver said he didn't see Jim's black BMW in the dark and the fog until it was too late."

"How is the truck driver?" Brenda asked.

"A broken leg and a bruise from his seatbelt, but he'll be fine," Jack said.

"What direction was Jim's car facing?" I asked. "Uphill or downhill?"

"Downhill. So if Simon really did see him coming to the party from the opposite direction, we have to ask how he got there."

"O'Farrell is a one-way street," Eileen said. "So either Jim was going against traffic or he'd come from uphill."

We all thought it over for a minute.

"Could it have been suicide?" I asked.

"You mean, overcome with remorse for having murdered Clara Chen and Lalit Kumar, the killer gets drunk and waits to be run over?" Simon shook his head. "I don't think so. He certainly didn't seem like someone about to top himself at the party."

"But," Jack said, "there are some things that don't check out about the accident scenario."

"Spill it, Jack." Harry had left his station at the stove and joined us at the kitchen island. He reached for the wine bottle. "What's suspicious?"

"Jim's lights weren't on," Jack told us. "And the driver of the truck swears that Jim was just stopped in the middle of the road."

"Which, again, makes it sound like it could have been suicide," Brenda offered. Then her eyes widened, and I could see she'd had the same thought I had.

"Or murder."

"Simon," Jack asked, "who else was at the party?"

Simon blinked a lot and did his best to recollect everything, while Mike popped open a laptop I hadn't noticed before and took notes. When they'd finished, we had a chart of our main suspects' activities.

Name	Arr Time	Dep Time	Actions
Jim	7:15	12:45	Looked harried when he arrived, and spoke with Bob first. Relaxed as the evening went on, and talked to just about everyone. Hit on several of the women, apparently unsuccessfully. Left alone.

Krissy	7:30	10:30	Looked miserable for most of the time she was there. Spoke to unidentified engineers and MoM. Left alone soon after Jim made a lewd suggestion that several people overheard.
MoM	???	12:50	Spent time with Krissy, Jim, Troy, and Bob. Didn't drink much.
Bob	???	11:30	Spoke with Jim and unidentified engineers. Drank heavily. Unidentified engineers insisted he take a cab home.
Troy	8:30	10:30	Came from another party and left for another party. Brought most of Creative Services staff with him, but didn't take them when he left. Spoke with MoM. Followed Krissy out?

MoM and Bob had both gotten to the party before Simon had arrived. He'd gotten to the pub at the same time as Jim.

"And you didn't catch the names of any of the engineers who were there?" Jack asked.

Simon looked uncomfortable. "There were rather a lot of them. And they were all sort of talking amongst themselves, so...no."

"Did any of them seem hostile to Jim?" Eileen asked.

Simon thought about it. "They all just seemed happy he was buying the drinks."

"What about the Creative Services people?" I remembered them as the vampires from the lunch room. "Anything weird there?"

"Aside from an absurd fashion sense?" Simon shook his head. "Nothing, really. Although their manager is a different story..."

"What?" We all looked at him.

"A body to die for, and the most amazing green eyes—what?" He noticed our collective sigh of disappointment.

"Simon." Eileen regarded him. "You're telling us you were in a room with the latest victim of Zakdan's maniacal killer—as well as every suspect we have in the case—for the entire evening, and you spent your time flirting?"

"Oh." Simon looked a little trapped. "Ah, well, you see…"

They all started talking at once again, and I saw Jack watching me from across the kitchen. He said something quietly to Gordon and slipped out of the room. I followed him to the hallway, and from there into the dining room. He shut the door behind us.

Since I didn't have any chairs in there yet, I had no choice but to lean against my husband in the moonlit room. "What do you think?"

"I'm not sure yet," he said. "Yahata thinks the police are going to call this an accident too, and Morgan Stokes is going a little nuts over that."

"When did you talk to Morgan?"

"This afternoon."

"Why wasn't he at the party?"

"He hadn't heard about it."

"That seems weird. I mean, it was a Zakdan celebration party."

"A lot seems weird." Jack tilted my face up to look at me. "How are you holding up?"

I thought about it. I'd been undercover for three days, had almost been killed twice, and now my leading candidate for the killer had become another victim. I closed my eyes and answered from my heart.

"Thank God it's Friday."

Chapter Thirty

Someone was yelling my name. I was driving in the fog without any headlights, and the car didn't seem to be moving. Who was calling my name?

Chip.

I opened my eyes. It was definitely Chip's yell. I'd heard him calling the cast to attention at the Rep often enough to recognize it. What I didn't know was why he was shouting my name, and why he was sounding increasingly panicked. Then I got it.

Flank.

I went to the window to find Flank assaulting the Rep's director on my front lawn. Pages of what were probably agonizingly bad plays were being blown all over the yard, and Chip didn't look like he had much fight left in him.

I opened the window. "Flank!"

He froze.

"Charley!" Chip shouted. "Call him off!"

I considered saying "down, boy" but since I was beginning to suspect Flank had a sensitive side, I opted for "Hey, Flank, cut it out. That's Chip—remember him from the theater?"

Flank took a closer look at the smallish wheezing man in his arms. Or, to be more accurate, in his headlock. Then he seemed to remember his manners and he stood Chip upright. I imagine he started mumbling unintelligible apologies, but I didn't stick around at the window to see how they worked it all out.

I had to call Simon.

◇◇◇

"If you're not here in twenty minutes I'll kill you."

"Good morning to you too, darling. What time is it? Has there been another murder?" At least he sounded awake.

"No, but Flank almost strangled Chip on my front steps. You remember Chip, don't you? And how you thought it would be a good idea for him to pick one of the plays for next season?"

"Oh." He yawned. Then, "Oh!"

"And how you thought we should meet with him on Saturdays to discuss the progress?"

"Um, yes, but…"

"Twenty minutes, Simon," I threatened.

"But Charley," he protested, "I'm still in bed." He lowered his voice. "And I have a *guest*."

"When don't you? But unless it's Tom Stoppard and he's written a little something just for us, I really think you'll have to make your excuses."

"You are in a mood today, darling. No, it isn't Tom Stoppard, but Zakdan's manager of Creative Services who's currently in my shower. And if you want to talk about creative services—"

"Simon!" I hissed. "Twenty minutes!"

"Oh, all right!"

◇◇◇

He showed up in an hour, most of which Chip spent in the downstairs bathroom, pulling himself together and applying a few well-placed bandages. I spent it drinking coffee.

Jack was gone, of course. It had been so long since I'd woken up next to him that I was beginning to suspect my husband of going off to a bat cave as soon as I fell asleep each night.

He probably didn't.

His note, in its usual spot on the kitchen counter, was customarily succinct.

C,
I'll be at Mike's. Don't forget Chip is coming over this morning.
—J

As if.

◇◇◇

"Where are we, darlings? What have we got?" Simon began the conversation.

"Did you read the plays from last weekend?" Chip, despite still being a little shaken from his Flank-related experiences, remained focused on the job at hand—finding a diamond in the dreck heap of plays we were slogging through.

"I did and I hated them," Simon answered.

I'd made Chip sit in Harry's comfortable leather armchair while Simon and I took the beach chairs.

"There was one," I said. "I didn't think much of it at the time, but now that I'm remembering it…maybe it had something."

"Which one?" Chip pulled out a pen.

"I don't remember the name, but it had the hostages. You know—the one where the guy goes in to the office and holds everyone at gunpoint for the duration of the second act."

"Wasn't it told from the point of view of the copy machine?" Simon wrinkled his brow.

"Right!" Chip began riffling through grass-stained pages. "With blow-ups of paperwork documenting the gunman's career projected onto the back wall of the set. We begin with the letter that offered him the job…"

"And end, predictably, with his pink slip," Simon finished. "Right." He frowned at me. "Darling, it was awful."

"Was it?" I know I'd thought so at the time. But it was the one that had stuck with me.

"Here it is." Chip produced a bedraggled manuscript from his pile. "*Copy This.*"

"Oh, yeah." It was all coming back to me. "It was terrible, wasn't it?"

"Well—" Chip began.

"What else have we got?" Simon began sorting through Chip's stack. "Good Lord, it just goes from bad to worse, doesn't it?"

I searched my memory for anything remotely interesting, but it seemed like I'd read the plays years ago. I could only really remember one other.

"What about the one where the guy is leading a double life?"

"Oh." Chip sat up. "He's a choir director by day, and a cross-dressing German cabaret singer by night. *Guten Abend, Sunshine.*"

"Darling, we all need to make peace with our inner Marlene," Simon told him. "But there's no need to subject an innocent audience to the process. And Charley." He turned to me. "Just because you're obsessed with deception and workplace violence these days doesn't mean our public will be."

"Well then." Chip got a little huffy, and I can't really say I blame him. "If you guys don't like anything so far, we'll just have to keep going. I've got another set of manuscripts in my car."

"Great." I gave it as much enthusiasm as I could possibly project. "And thanks for all your hard work. Now, who's up for lunch?"

I left them squabbling amicably and went upstairs to get shoes and a raincoat. Simon was probably right. I was obsessed with deception and workplace violence—which is the only possible reason I might have considered either of those plays. What I really needed was to find a script that would tell me who had killed Clara Chen, who had faked Lalit Kumar's suicide, and whether Jim Stoddard had been murdered by the time the final curtain came down.

I stared into my closet and thought about it. If I were writing that script, how would it turn out? Who would the clues lead to? Who was our red herring, and what slip did the real killer make?

I shook my head. It was a damn shame Jim Stoddard was dead. He'd been perfect for the role.

◇◇◇

Jack came home that night with takeout Thai food and candles. "I thought we might try eating in the dining room for a change."

So we put a candle in my fabulous French candlestick and sat cross-legged on the fabulous table—being careful not to scratch it—and it was just like an indoor picnic. It was fabulous.

"One of these days I'll get around to buying chairs and things."

He plucked a shrimp out of the Pad Thai. "Don't rush into anything."

Jack looks good by candlelight, so I was willing to overlook a little mockery.

"Besides," he said, "this works. Although I am tempted to make some sort of comment about Professor Plum having done it in the dining room with the candlestick."

"Resist the temptation."

He grinned. "Did you and the guys find a new play today?"

Which led to a whole long discussion of the horror which is the amateur playwright. And that led to a discussion of the plays we *had* decided to put on for the next season, before Simon had told Chip he could pick the last in the lineup.

It was all very nice, and it felt refreshingly civilized not to be chatting about forensics over dinner. Then I had to ruin the mood.

"Did you and Mike accomplish anything today?"

Jack nodded. "Mike's gotten a better understanding of the Zakdan bug. Turns out it's not exactly a bug."

"What do you mean, not exactly?"

He started gesturing with a stuffed chicken wing. "It's more like a virus. When it's triggered, it sets off a whole series of commands that destroy or corrupt all saved data, then it cripples the software. That's why it's so dangerous."

I swallowed. "How dangerous?"

"Remember the Y2K scare?" he asked. "When everybody thought all the computers in the world would go crazy on the same day?"

"The New Year's Day thing." That whole Millennium fever now seemed so quaint. "The killer wants to *intentionally* set something like that off? So everyone running Zakdan software would crash at the same time?"

"Not just crash," Jack frowned. "First it would corrupt all the data it could find, then it would bring the systems down. And we're talking about banks, hospitals, government offices…"

Like our very own police department.

"Then whoever is behind all this would be pretty ticked off at Clara for discovering it," I reasoned. "Which brings us back to who could have planted it, which brings us back to Jim Stoddard." Suddenly I lost my appetite.

"Mike is looking into the employment records of every engineer at Zakdan. There might be someone there who had the right skills and has been in the right place at all the right times. But something like this must have taken years."

Years. Great. It had better not take us that long to figure it all out. I was already beginning to hate the sight of the Zakdan building. And I only had enough outfits to see me through the next week.

"Jack." I poured some more wine. "Are we sure Jim was killed by the same person who killed Clara? And for that matter, are we sure the same person killed Lalit Kumar?"

"Anything is possible. But for what it's worth, Mike thinks it's likely that more than one person would have been involved in sabotaging the Zakdan code to this extent."

"So there might have been a gang? And now they're turning on each other?" Great. Just exactly how many maniacs were we dealing with?

Jack put his glass down. "Let's approach this from a different direction. Not starting with Clara, but starting with Jim. Who would have killed Jim?"

"Well." I didn't look at him. "I know of one person who said he was going to kill him."

"Who?"

I didn't want to say it, but I had to. Ever since it had popped into my mind I hadn't been able to shake it.

"You."

Jack went still. "Do you think I killed him?"

Suddenly I felt like an idiot. But I still wanted Jack to reassure me.

"It's just that you made a joke about it when we were at Rose Pistola and I told you he'd made a pass at me."

"It was a joke, Charley," he said evenly.

I nodded quickly. "Right. I know."

"And if you think about it, you might realize that I have a pretty good alibi. I was sleeping with you at the time."

"Sure. Of course."

But I never knew when he got up in the night. And I wasn't exactly sure what he'd be capable of if he'd thought I was in danger. And we'd been shot at that night, so maybe he'd been—

"Charley." Jack was looking at me steadily. I met his eyes.

"I didn't kill Jim Stoddard."

Something inside me released. Of course Jack wasn't a killer. I mean, maybe in his past that he never told me about…but not here and not now. Not Jack.

"Of course not," I said. "It's ridiculous. I was just kidding."

He pushed the food aside and reached for my hand. Then he slid me toward him across the smooth surface of the table.

"You have nothing to worry about, Pumpkin."

"I know."

"I'm harmless."

"I know."

"Like a kitten."

I stared at him. "Okay, I draw the line at kitten. You are so not a kitten."

"A puppy?" he grinned.

"Hardly."

"A fluffy—"

"Just shut up and kiss me, you lunatic."

Which he did, driving all but the most incoherent thoughts out of my head.

I located Jack's ear and whispered in it, "How about you be Professor Plum and I be Miss Scarlet, and we do it in the dining room?"

He looked at me. "With the candlestick?"

"Without the candlestick."

He grinned. "Deal."

Chapter Thirty-one

Monday morning. Back to the office.

I'd spent Sunday under the covers, listening to the rain and dragging myself through yet another set of manuscripts. Sooner or later I was going to have to break it to Chip that he probably wasn't going to discover the next Wendy Wasserstein lurking under a table in a corner of the Rep's office. But in the meanwhile he wasn't doing anybody harm. And it gave me an excuse not to obsess about the murders for an entire day.

Then, inevitably, Monday.

Eileen had drawn up a fresh list of interrogation assignments, based on the chart Mike had created Friday night. So we divvied up the work at Arugula, and agreed to focus on everyone's post-party movements on the night of Jim's death. Then we headed down the street to Zakdan.

Where the receptionist's desk was covered with flowers.

"Shit," Eileen muttered. "I knew it would be bad, but—"

"What's bad? What's going on?" And why was she looking so ticked off?

"Typical," Brenda said.

"Miss McGill? *Miss McGill?*"

Simon poked me in the arm and I remembered my name. I turned to the receptionist, who'd been calling me. She held out a huge bouquet of blood red roses. "These came for you. Looks like you've got a valentine."

Oh, Valentine's Day, right. That accounted for the florist shop in the lobby and the expression on Eileen's face.

"Who are they from?" Simon grabbed the card as we headed for the elevators.

"Who do you think? Eileen, haven't you gotten over your anti-Valentine's Day thing yet?"

"At what point in my four divorces would you suppose I'd have gotten over it?" she replied icily.

"It's a stupid holiday, Charley—I mean Tess." Brenda looked around to make sure nobody had heard her slip, but since the four of us were alone in the elevator, we were probably safe. "It's just an excuse for the candy companies and greeting card companies and florists to make you spend too much on meaningless—"

"My God, you two have never been more single," Simon said. "Personally, I'm wearing red satin boxers today, in honor of the occasion."

"I think that comes under the heading of 'too much information,'" I told him.

"Besides, Eileen." He ignored me. "What about Mike? I thought the two of you were…"

Were they?

"Mike who?" she asked.

Oh. So they probably weren't. "Mike Mike," I said. "Jack's Mike. I was kind of hoping that while you were collaborating with him on our Fake Books…"

She made a snorting noise that completely refuted any romantic leanings toward the man, and got off the elevator.

We followed.

"Hey, Tess," Simon began, as I swiped my card to get into our little corner of Zakdan.

"Yes, Rex?"

He waved the tiny envelope he'd taken from my flowers. "Why is this card signed 'Professor Plum'?"

I was saved from answering him by the sight of Flank on the other side of the door. He'd gone ahead of us from Arugula, presumably to check the conference room for bombs before we got there.

I revised my assumption when I saw the conference room. It was filled with balloons, hundreds of them, red and pink, round and heart shaped. Flank stood in front of the long glass wall with another dozen or so gripped in one hand, and an enormous box of Teuscher champagne truffles in the other.

He thrust both of them at Brenda, grunting something.

"Good God, man," Simon yelped. "You're in love with Brenda?"

Flank, for the first time since I'd known him—perhaps for the first time in his life—looked genuinely alarmed.

"Don't be an idiot," I told Simon. I knew whose handiwork this was.

"They're from Harry."

By late afternoon of a day filled with frustrations, I'd been stood up by Bob, listened to hours and hours of Krissy's increasingly tedious self-loathing, and strained my neck in the lunchroom while trying to eavesdrop on assorted conversations.

The only things I'd learned were that *The Simpsons* rock and I should look into getting a TiVo.

"Any joy today?" Simon pushed his way through the balloon-filled conference room. "Charley, what did you come up with?"

"A migraine."

"Eileen? Brenda?"

They both shook their heads.

"What about you? Any interesting scoop?" I asked him.

"Scads." He pulled up a chair and opened a bottle of water. "What would you like to hear first? Sex scandals, or imminent resignations?"

This sounded promising.

"I'll tell you one thing," Simon went on. "Morgan Stokes hasn't got a clue about what's really going on here."

"What's really going on here?" I asked. "I mean, aside from sabotaging the product line and killing the occasional co-worker. Because I think he does know about those."

"Does he know that Clara had an affair with the conspicuously ponytailed head of Marketing?"

"Troy?" Eileen stared at him.

Brenda sat up indignantly. "She didn't!"

"She did. Oh, I don't mean she cheated on Morgan," he clarified. "But she and Troy had a thing years ago, right after she got hired, and they managed to keep it a secret from just about everyone."

"You're kidding!" Eileen said. "How could she keep it a secret? How can anyone keep anything a secret in a place like this?"

"What could she have seen in Troy?" I asked. Which, I realized, wasn't really the point.

"I've got another one." Simon grabbed a balloon and started batting it around. "Bob Adams is leaving."

"Leaving? As in leaving Zakdan?" Eileen asked.

"As in leaving Zakdan, leaving San Francisco, leaving the Americas. He bought a sheep farm in Scotland and he takes occupancy in June."

A sheep farm? Scotland? I suddenly visualized the bearded Quality exec in a kilt, then really wished I hadn't.

"How in the world did you find that out?" Brenda asked.

He handed her the balloon. "Never underestimate the power of pillow talk."

"Simon, we saw you this morning," I pointed out. "Are you telling us—"

"That was hours ago," he said innocently. "And I did take a lunch break."

"In any case," Eileen cut off further explanation. "I'm guessing your source is the Creative Services manager—"

"Chris," Simon supplied. "Yes."

"And Chris works with Troy, so…"

"So was in a position to observe certain compromising incidents with Clara which left little to the imagination," Simon said. "All long ago."

"And the sheep farm?" I asked. "Bob?"

"Bob was careless with the faxes he left lying around." Simon shrugged. "People will look."

People will.

"You're right," Brenda said. "Morgan Stokes has no idea what's going on around here. I mean, aside from all of this new stuff, he didn't know anything about Clara's plan to fire Krissy, he didn't know Jim was throwing a party on Thursday night—even though it was a company party—and he had no idea that everyone knew he was engaged to Clara."

"And he thinks everyone adores MoM as much as he does," I added. "When I have it on reliable authority that half the company thinks she's a bitch." I nodded to Flank, at his usual station in the back corner, to acknowledge his reliable authority. He looked pleased.

"It's because he's the boss," Brenda said. "What's that old expression about speaking truth to power? Something about when you speak truth to power, you should do so from a distance…"

"I thought it was 'speak truth to power, and power will listen,'" Eileen said.

"I wouldn't count on that," Simon commented. "But I have a good one. 'All great truths begin as blasphemies.' Shaw. And then there's—"

"I think we're straying from Brenda's point, Simon," I told him.

"My point," Brenda said, "is that nobody tells Morgan the truth about anything. Maybe because they're afraid of him, or maybe because they're trying to get away with something, but I think mainly because they're so busy trying to figure out what he'd like to hear."

"So the truth gets lost," I agreed.

"Truth is stranger than fiction," Simon said. "Sometimes."

◇◇◇

Things started looking up when I got home and found a note from Jack.

C,

Meet me upstairs. Bring the champagne.

—*J*

The champagne in question was a bottle of Veuve Clicquot, resting on ice in a silver bucket on my kitchen counter.

I heard the sound of running water when I got to the third floor, and figured out Jack's plan for the evening when I saw the candles around the tub. The fact that Jack was already in the tub, up to his chest in bubbles, was another dead giveaway.

"I take it we're not going out tonight." I set the champagne bucket on the step leading up to the oversized bath.

"Valentine's Day," he scoffed. "It's amateur night."

"And that makes us what? A pair of old professionals?" I raised an eyebrow.

"Not old," he corrected. "Just seasoned."

He reached over to turn off the taps.

I sat on the edge of the tub. "I didn't get you a present," I told him. "I forgot about Valentine's Day."

"Which is one of the many ways in which you are the perfect woman."

That was nice.

"Except…" He reached for the bottle. If I was going to stay even slightly focused he'd have to stop reaching for things. It causes my mind to wander.

"Except?"

"You have too many clothes on." He poured.

"Oh." I took the glass he offered and looked around the room. Fluffy stacks of towels, creamy marble surfaces, extremely flattering lighting. "I think this is my favorite room in the house."

"That's because the only thing necessary to furnish it is terry cloth. Are you going to get in, or do I have to come out for you?"

I could have told him about Clara and Troy. I could have told him about Bob and the sheep farm. I could have told him that the bubbles were leaving certain areas of his anatomy completely vulnerable.

Instead I did the sensible thing.

I got in the tub.

Chapter Thirty-two

I wandered downstairs the next morning wrapped in a heavy silk kimono, fully expecting to find a note from Jack in the kitchen. But when I got to the second floor I could have sworn I heard noises coming from his office.

I poked my head in the door. "What are you doing here?"

"I live here," he answered.

"But you're usually...what have you done to this place?"

The room had been completely transformed. An entire wall of shelving was filled with neat stacks of books and miscellaneous things like ceramic pots and Indonesian-looking carvings. Low-slung chairs in clean modern lines were arranged around a coffee table on a kilim area rug. The wall behind the desk held filing cabinets and a set of deep bookshelves.

"I went to Ikea," Jack said. "What do you think?"

"How did you do all this?" I tried to take it in.

"I had some things in storage." He pushed his chair back from the desk. "Do you mind that I did it?"

"It's your office." I noticed an Asian tapestry hanging on the wall behind me. "And it's gorgeous. Do you want to do the rest of the house?"

He grinned. "That's your project."

"I don't know." I looked around. "This seems to be another of your hidden talents."

"I thought all my talents were pretty obvious." He came up behind me as I was looking over his book collection. "And yours are pretty stunning too. Just think what we could accomplish if we—"

"Hey Jack, you're out of—"

Whatever we were out of was lost in my yelp at the sudden appearance of Mike at the door.

"Oh," Jack said. "Mike's working here today."

If I were a cat, I'd have been clinging by my claws to the ceiling. As it was, I tightened my kimono and turned around. "So I see."

"Hi, Charley. I just made coffee. Want some?" Mike put a tray with a coffee pot and three mugs on the table. Three mugs.

"Is Gordon here too?"

"He should be, any minute," Jack said. "Mike wants to show him some photos of a couple of the engineers who've been at Zakdan the right amount of time to have planted the virus."

"So he can watch them in the cafeteria?"

"Among other things."

Mike went to Jack's desk and picked up a folder. "This is for you to take in and show to your gang. It's got the names and photos of the four guys we're interested in."

I took the folder. "I'll see if Simon can place any of them at the party." I checked the clock on Jack's desk. "And I'd better get moving. I don't want to be late for work."

"There's something I never thought I'd hear you say," Jack grinned.

I suppose there really is a first time for everything.

I completely chickened out of asking Brenda what she'd done the night before, and whether it had involved my Uncle Harry. Probably because I was afraid she'd tell me. At least the conference room was blissfully free of balloons, so the whole V-Day discussion never even came up.

Flank couldn't find a place to park and he refused to let me go to the café without him. So we were gathered around the Zakdan conference table before I had a chance to show Simon the photographs of the four engineers Mike had come up with.

"Maybe…" He flipped through them. "Maybe…possibly…I don't think so."

"That's a help," Eileen said dryly.

He shrugged. "Sorry, darling, but these are grim little head shots and I was in a dark bar when I might have seen them."

The head shots were grim. They were copies of the photos on the engineers' security badges, taken from the employee database.

"They look like mug shots," Brenda said. "Every single one of them looks guilty of something."

Flank made a growling noise and I quickly shut the folder. It's good to have an early warning system when two of your walls are made of glass.

We saw what had set him off. MoM was on approach, and she began making may-I-come-in gestures when she saw we'd noticed her.

Eileen waved her in, and as she entered she tucked her day planner under one arm and pressed her hands together in supplication. "Please forgive the intrusion."

Which forced us to say things like "It's no intrusion—" and "Please, sit down," until she did.

"I know this is *wildly* inappropriate." She pushed up the sleeves of her slate gray turtleneck as if she were about to deal us all a hand of poker. "But I heard you're going to share your findings on Friday, and I just couldn't wait to see what you have to say."

She must have recognized our expressions as stunned, because her eyes widened. "Oh *no*, I shouldn't have said anything. Wasn't I supposed to know?"

Hell, we didn't know. What was she talking about?

"Where did you hear that?" Eileen asked.

She retreated into the depths of her sweater, pulling the neck up to cover her mouth and nose. Then she peeked out again. "Was it a secret? Everyone's talking about it. It's on your calendars."

Someone should tell her she couldn't pull off coy.

"No," I said. "Of course it's not a secret. We just…"

We just what?

"We just don't think it would be fair to everyone else if we gave you a sneak preview," Eileen finished for me. "But, as long as you're here, there are a few follow-up questions I'd like to ask you. Is now a good time? How about if we go to your office?"

I silently blessed Eileen for taking MoM off our hands. She'd tapped something on her laptop, and turned the screen toward me as she stood to hustle MoM out of the room.

I looked at Eileen's computer when they'd gone. It was opened to her calendar and, sure enough, there was a meeting scheduled for ten o'clock on Friday.

"'Presentation of SFG Findings,'" I said. "Who put that on there?"

"I wouldn't know how, even if I'd wanted to," Simon said. "But it's on my calendar as well."

"And mine," Brenda said. "I think whoever put it there wants us gone."

Flank grunted in agreement.

We'd been given a deadline.

I saw Bob Adams at the espresso machine in the kitchen across the hall. "I think I'll go have a chat with the future sheep rancher."

"Better you than me," Simon said.

I told Flank I wouldn't stray out of his sight, and went over. The kitchen had a high arched window that overlooked the CalTrain station. Bob was staring out of it, sipping a latte. He was wearing baggy pleated jeans and another ancient tee-shirt that stretched across his midsection. This one had a drawing of a large hairy beast on the back, and a cryptic slogan—*If you don't get it, you might as well be herding Yak.*

I didn't get it, but I'd learned in my time at Zakdan that the more obscure the saying, the more the engineers loved it.

"Hi, Bob."

He jumped and looked over, a little foamed milk clinging to his facial hair. "Hey. I heard you're going to be presenting your findings on Friday."

"Word gets around." Especially around Zakdan.

"Any chance you'll tell me what you're planning on saying?"

As if I knew.

"I really can't."

He nodded and looked back out the window.

"I was sorry to hear about Jim Stoddard," I said. "You two must have worked together a long time."

He left the window and sat at one of the tables. "I guess you just never know, do you?"

"No, I guess you never do."

I sat with him. Surely I could do something to save the conversation from disintegrating into funeral-parlor platitudes.

"Who do you think will get his job?"

My remark was sufficiently callous to startle him. He glanced up, then got an uncomfortable look on his face as he gestured toward the glass wall of the kitchen. "Probably one of them."

Half a dozen men in brightly colored spandex were clumping through the hallway between the kitchen and our conference room. They wore the heavily logoed jerseys and pedal-ready shoes of seriously pretentious cyclists. They'd just come through the lobby door and were peeling off gloves and loudly commenting on each other's riding abilities as they made their sweaty way along.

"Who are they?"

"The biking club. They meet twice a week in Mill Valley and ride in together."

"Mill Valley? The one on the other side of the bridge?"

"They like to do at least a quarter-century before work."

Twenty-five miles on a bicycle is not my idea of how to spend a morning. Neither, I could tell, was it Bob's.

The cyclists were spilling into the kitchen now. "Hey Bob, you missed a great ride today," one of them called out.

"Yeah, you should join us some time," another one smirked.

Bob flushed, which was not a look that worked well with his reddish hair. He sat up a little straighter and sucked in his belly. "Yeah, sounds good. Maybe I will."

"You'll need to get a new bike, dude. They don't allow training wheels on the Golden Gate." The wit who said this looked around for someone to high-five him.

Bob turned a shade darker. "They're really great guys," he muttered to me. "We just like to give each other shit."

The Quality exec might not have been a glorious physical specimen, but I can't stand jerks—particularly of the jock variety.

"I get it," I murmured to Bob. "They're assholes."

He choked on his last gulp of coffee.

Suddenly I didn't blame Bob for wanting to go hang out in the highlands and get away from all of this. It didn't seem sinister at all. It seemed—

Then I forgot all about Bob. Because I realized I'd seen four of the sweaty cyclists before.

In mug shots provided by Mike.

"So what?" Eileen demanded. "So they ride bikes together—that doesn't mean they've conspired to bring down Zakdan."

"Maybe not," I told her. "But you have to admit it's suspicious. I mean, all four of Mike's suspects are best friends? They hang out together outside of the office? Don't you think that's worth looking into?"

We'd reconvened to compare notes before leaving for the day. I'd had an uneventful lunch with Troy and had spent most of the afternoon trying to catch my new four suspects doing something incriminating together. But unless you could call sitting in meetings and working in their cubicles incriminating, I'd come up empty, except for the discovery of a back stairway to our little corner of Zakdan and a handy shortcut to the ladies room.

"I'm not sure it's exactly suspicious," Brenda said. "The reason Mike identified them is that they've all been working at Zakdan a long time, and they're all senior engineers, so it doesn't seem that odd that they'd hang out together."

"But I'm completely willing to keep my eye on them," Simon volunteered. "Where did you say they took their showers?"

Bob had told me about the locker rooms on the second floor, but I didn't think sending Simon on a stakeout would be terribly productive.

"Never mind," Eileen said.

"Uh oh." I'd been toying with my laptop, and hadn't realized I'd spoken out loud until I noticed them all staring at me.

"I just got an email from Morgan Stokes," I explained.

"What does it say?" Brenda asked.

"He's in New York for a series of meetings this week, but he heard about our presentation on Friday and he's changed his plans so he can be here." I looked up. "He wants to know if it means we've identified Clara's killer."

Eileen was the first to speak. "Well, it looks like we're giving a presentation on Friday. Does anybody have a copy of Power-Point?"

I had a lot of questions. Was going ahead with the meeting on Friday the right thing to do? What could we possibly say about our "findings"? Who had set up the meeting in the first place—was that person the killer?

And what the hell was PowerPoint?

Chapter Thirty-three

Wednesday night at my house, chaos ruled.

Mike had shown up with three guest geeks and a small flotilla of computer equipment, all of which he deposited in the library to work out a few remaining secrets of the universe while he went upstairs to share something with Jack that I was clearly not technical enough to appreciate.

Not that I minded.

Eileen had shown up with a gigantic green chalkboard, on loan from Anthony's private school, which she positioned against the fireplace in the living room. She and Brenda then began drawing an enormous chart of suspects and facts, taking Mike's who-left-Jim's-party-when spreadsheet as a springboard. They were currently arguing over whether Tonya Ho, of Human Resources fame, even merited being added to the list.

Anthony, who had accompanied his mother, was on roller blades. I realized I had only myself to blame, and it did look like fun as he swooped down the hallway from the kitchen and shot across the living room floor, but his activities weren't exactly conducive to clear thinking.

Harry was in the kitchen, having been driven out of his position behind the bar in the library by the arrival of the guest geeks, none of whom had accepted his offer of a flaming rum punch. He was currently stirring something he called "grog" in a large pot on my kitchen stove, on the theory that the ex-navy men in the crowd would find it irresistible.

"Do you really think this is the time to get them drunk?" I asked.

"Everyone's mental machinery needs a little lubrication from time to time, Charley."

Harry was lubricated enough for all of us, but then he usually is.

◇◇◇

The doorbell rang, and I opened the door to find Simon chatting delightedly with a pizza delivery man.

"Darling, this is Tony. Do you know he stopped off at a mini-mart to pick up some energy drinks for the profs on his way here? Wasn't that delightful of him?"

Energy what for the who?

"Hi." Tony handed me four boxed pizzas and held up three six-packs, variously labeled Monster, RockStar, and Full Throttle. "That'll be seventy-two dollars."

I looked at Simon.

"I didn't order it, darling. I just ran into the man on the way to your door. Where's Eileen?"

He moved past me smoothly, and Tony the delivery guy spoke again.

"The profs ordered it. Said they were working on a wicked juicy bug here."

I was beginning to get it. Although the term "wicked juicy bug" initially conjured up a mental image of something icky with thousands of legs, I was willing to bet it had more to do with the Zakdan code and the three guest geeks in my library.

Sure enough, one of them stuck his head out with perfect timing. "Tony! Dude! Thanks!"

Geek No. 1 and his cohorts swarmed out, relieved me of the pizzas, took the energy drinks from Tony, and vanished behind the library door again.

Tony looked after them with stars in his eyes. "They're so awesome."

Uh huh.

"Are they your professors?" I asked him. He looked vaguely student-ish.

He gave me one of those looks the young reserve for the hopelessly clueless. "They're just the three best hackers in the entire world, is all."

Of course they were.

"Give me a minute," I told him. "I have to go find my purse."

On my way to the kitchen for some cash, it occurred to me that this had been an unfortunate choice for Flank's night off. I could have used him on door duty. It also occurred to me that I really didn't want to find out how Harry's grog mixed with Monster cola in the systems of the world's best hackers.

Anthony skated past me. "Aunt Charley, you have the coolest house ever!"

At least I didn't have to worry about the furniture getting broken.

"Charley, where do you keep your coconuts?" Harry demanded as I entered the kitchen.

"In the cabinet right next to my machete," I told him.

I opened the drawer near the telephone, pulled out the phone book, turned to M for Money, and took one of the hundred-dollar bills I keep there for just such emergencies.

"You know, nobody likes a smartass," my uncle told me.

"I have to disagree with you there, Harry." Jack had come in behind me. "Charley, who's that guy in our front hall?"

"Tony the pizza man," I told him. "He's a big fan of the profs."

I left them and went off to pay the guy. I got to the door just as Gordon was coming in, loaded down with a giant tray of something that smelled garlicky and fabulous.

"Charley, why is there a pizza delivery car in front of your house?"

I gave Tony the money and sent him on his way. "Because the best hackers in the world ordered some delivered to my library. What's that?"

"Enough Fettuccini Ricardo to feed an army. I can't believe you ordered pizza!"

"I didn't!" I protested. "And that smells amazing. Why don't we take it to the kitchen, and—"

He went off muttering, and I was about to close the door when I heard my name called from somewhere outside.

"Charley!"

"Martha?" What was the Rep's costume designer doing here? Had Simon called her in for some sort of emergency fashion consultation?

She made her way up the front path in a swirl of black knitwear, her long loose hair whipped by the wind.

"I'm sorry I've taken so long to get to this, but it's really the first chance I've had. Is this a good time?"

"For what?"

She was taking something out of the large black bag she wore crosswise over her chest. "For your ritual purification ceremony, remember?" She produced what looked like a large clump of dried herbs tied together with red string at one end.

"My what? What's that?"

"A sage wand. I'm here to do your smudging!"

Right. Not here for fashion. Here in her capacity as my friendly neighborhood Wicca. And now that I thought about it, I did remember saying something like "oh, sure" on our clothing expedition when she'd offered to come purify my new house.

"Um, Martha…"

"Oh, there are a lot of people here." She pushed past me and started looking in rooms. "That's not really…well, never mind. We'll make the best of it. Do you have a match?"

"Uh, no, and—"

"Who needs a light?" Harry boomed from behind me. He held out his ever-present cigar to Martha. "Will this do?"

"Oh…" She looked a little taken aback, which was nothing compared to how I was feeling. "It's a bit unorthodox, but in a pinch…"

She lit the sage, which began putting out a pungent gray smoke. She started waving it all around, looking serious.

Anthony careened around the corner from the living room and came to a sudden stop. "Aunt Charley, why is there a witch in your house?"

"A Wicca, dear." Martha wafted the sage toward him, then asked Harry where the heart of the house was. He led her off to the kitchen. Jack passed them as he came out.

"Do I want to know?"

I shrugged.

Anthony skated up to Jack and grabbed hold of his arm. "Hey Jack, can I go play the pirate game on your computer?"

"Sure. Ask Mike to come down, okay?"

The boy zipped to the bottom of the stairs, then clumped his way up.

"Anthony! Take your skates off on the stairs!" Eileen called from the living room.

I went back to the still-open front door and looked out.

"Who are you expecting?" Jack asked.

"Just Groucho and Harpo and the boys."

He closed the door and turned me around to face him.

"We'll figure it out, Charley," he said. "Things are a little crazy, but we'll figure it out."

I looked beyond him down the hall and into the kitchen, where Martha was waving a sage wand over Gordon's fettuccini, while the cook looked on darkly and Harry attempted to hand him a drink. To my left I could hear Simon and Eileen bickering about the viability of Troy as a killer, and to my right I swear the hackers were having a power belching competition.

"If you say so, Jack."

The doorbell rang. I took a deep breath, turned, and opened it.

"Hi. Are you Charley? I'm Kevin Allred. Morgan Stokes asked me to stop by with some samples. I'm his interior decorator."

Perfect.

◇◇◇

Harry's grog turned out to be a surprisingly good accompaniment to Gordon's fettuccini. And after sufficient quantities of both, following the departure of the decorator and the witch, with the hackers still closeted in the library, the rest of us were finally able to get down to business.

"Darlings, I don't think we have a clue." Simon spoke first, after we'd all taken rather longer than was needed to study the chalkboard chart that Eileen and Brenda had put together.

"We have plenty of clues," Eileen corrected him. "We just don't know how to make sense of them."

"And we're about to be given the bum's rush out of Zakdan," I didn't need to remind them. "Without being any closer to figuring out who killed Clara, Lalit, or Jim, and who planted the ticking time bomb in the Zakdan code."

Brenda turned to Mike. "Can you figure out a way to turn it off?" she asked him. "I mean, even if we can't figure out who put the virus there, can you figure out how to fix it so it doesn't go off?"

"We've got a team working on that," he told her. I assumed he referred to the pizza fans in the library. "But isolating the trigger in the current code is one thing, and disarming it in every application that's ever been deployed on a Zakdan system is something else again."

Jack was leaning against the far wall, his arms crossed and a look of concentration on his face. This is the part where I expected him to have the blinding realization that would make everything clear. This is the part where he should look at the chart, smack his forehead, and say, "Why didn't I see it before?" This is the part where he was supposed to solve everything.

"Jack?" Harry was watching him. "What do you think?"

Jack frowned. I held my breath.

"I think it may be time to call it a night."

Okay, not what I had hoped for.

"Do you think if we had more time…" I suggested.

"Maybe we should search everyone's offices," Simon proposed. "We still have tomorrow, right? So if we just create a series of diversions…" He looked around and apparently picked up on a noticeable lack of enthusiasm.

"That isn't necessary," Mike told us. "We've already…um… we kind of…"

I turned to Jack. "You broke into Zakdan and searched everyone's office?"

He moved closer to the chalkboard. "Not everyone's."

Oh, well, all right then. He was only guilty of selective breaking and entering. I was just about to launch into something approaching a diatribe when we heard Anthony yelling from the top of the stairs.

"Jack! Hey, Jack! Can you come help me?"

Eileen waved Jack away and went out into the hall. "Anthony, don't yell in the house!" she yelled. "And take off your skates."

"But, Mom…"

"Now." Her voice held the kind of authority that makes investment bankers quail.

She came back in and started gathering up their things. People with children, I'd noticed, rarely travel light. "Sorry, everyone, but I think we'd better be going."

"I'll go see what he wanted," Jack said.

"You don't have to do that," Eileen told him.

"It's no bother." He left, and the rest of us started wrapping things up for the evening.

It was not a happy group. I was pretty sure everyone else was feeling exactly as frustrated as I was. Nobody likes failure, and I couldn't tell any more whether Harry's loud assurances that it would all make sense in the morning were examples of optimism or denial.

When everyone had gone I went upstairs to take a long shower. I passed Jack in his office on the way up. He had called out his goodbyes but hadn't made a reappearance downstairs. He still hadn't come to the bedroom by the time I toweled off.

I went to his office. He was still in front of the computer.

"What's so fascinating?" I looked at the screen over his shoulder. A group of rowdy pirates was making somebody walk the plank. But every time the tattered sailor got to the end, he popped back to the beginning again.

"You're playing the pirate game?" I asked him.

"Anthony found something," he said.

"Treasure?"

"Better. A bug." He looked up at me. "And this game was developed with Zakdan tools."

I blinked and looked back at the screen. A parrot kept repeating, "Dead men tell no tales. Dead men tell no tales."

Maybe not, but from the look on my husband's face, this game had told him something.

Chapter Thirty-four

The offices of Zakdan, Inc. were deserted by three o'clock the next afternoon. The entire company had been invited to a memorial service for Jim Stoddard. Whether they'd all actually gone to Trinity Episcopal was a matter of speculation, but they'd certainly cleared out by the appointed time, and that left us with an opportunity. One that I was having a hard time convincing Brenda and Eileen to take advantage of.

"But Charley," Eileen reminded me, "Mike and Jack already searched everyone's offices."

"But they don't know everyone as well as we do," I argued. "We might be able to notice something they missed."

Simon joined us in the conference room, closing the glass door behind him. "Don't bother," he said. "I had the same idea. I've been up on the fourth floor, and everything interesting is locked up tight."

"You actually tried to break into someone's office?" Eileen's eyebrows went up.

"Morgan's."

"He's not a suspect!" Brenda looked shocked.

"Why not?" Simon demanded. "I mean, why is it that we've never suspected his motives in all of this?"

"Mainly because he's the one who asked us to investigate it," I reminded him.

"Still." Simon slouched into a chair. "I have a feeling about him."

"Now that's interesting," Brenda said. "I was reading another of those business books last night, and the main thesis was that, regardless of how well we delude ourselves into believing we're all critical thinkers, most of us make up our minds about most of the important things in life in a split-second, gut-instinct flash." She looked around the room.

"I read that book a few months ago," Eileen said. "It certainly explains some things about politics. Do you realize—"

"Politics aside," Brenda interrupted. "I want to try something. I'm going to ask each of you a question, and I want you to answer—don't think, don't justify, don't do anything but answer—with the first thing that pops into your head."

Why not? Nothing else had worked.

Brenda stood, and did a good imitation of a cobra about to strike.

"Eileen, who killed Jim Stoddard?"

"Bob Adams." Eileen answered immediately, then gave Brenda an astonished look. "I can't believe I said that."

"But you did," Brenda answered. "Simon, quick, who wrote the software virus?"

"Jim Stoddard," Simon replied. "I know it makes no sense, but if you want my gut reactions—"

"Charley," Brenda cut him off to turn to me. "Who killed Clara?"

"MoM," I answered. Then my jaw dropped. "But I really don't think she did, I mean…why would she?"

Brenda sat down again, looking defeated. "I have no idea. According to the book, that should have given us a really clear indication."

"It did that," Eileen said. "It just gave us all different ones. And probably one of us is right—but which one?"

We were not a cheery group.

"Well, I have one clear indication," I stated. "And it's that we should pack up our stuff and finish this sham of a presentation at my house over big sloppy martinis."

"That seems appropriate," Simon agreed. "Now, if only we could think of a way to get everybody drunk tomorrow when we deliver the bloody thing as well."

I stood as my laptop was shutting down. "Flank, will you go get the car while I run to the restroom? We have a lot to bring home with us tonight, and we parked miles away."

Which was a slight exaggeration, but he roused himself from his station in the corner and made a noise that I decided to interpret as "No problem, Charley."

I went with him as far as the elevator, then used my card key to get into the ladies room. Reflecting, not for the first time, that perhaps Zakdan took the whole security thing a little too far.

The room contained three sinks and a vanity, with a door leading to the bathroom stalls beyond. The door was closed. And on the vanity was a book.

I looked at it for a minute before it clicked into place. A green suede day planner. And every time I'd seen it before, it had been in the possession of its owner, Millicent O'Malley.

MoM.

I didn't think. I didn't plan. I went on pure gut instinct.

I took the book and ran.

◇◇◇

"What in the world are you doing?" Brenda looked at me with wide eyes.

I'd burst through the door from the hall, gesturing wildly through the glass for the length of the conference room, until I got to the door on the far side.

"Open your laptops and put them in a line." I came in and started positioning the computers to shield the back corner of the table from any prying eyes.

"Why? What are we hiding? And who's left in the building, anyway?" Eileen asked.

"MoM." I held up the book. "And we're hiding her planner."

"Oh, well done, darling!" Simon pushed his laptop over. "Let's have a look."

"I can't believe you did that!" Brenda reached for it.

"I know," I admitted, putting the book on the desk, concealed from any casual observer by the laptops. "I can't either."

We crowded around, in Flank's usual position. If anyone came through the hall door we'd see them through the glass in plenty of time to hide the book.

"This is all my fault," Brenda said. "If I hadn't asked you all those stupid questions—"

"Never mind," I told her. "What's done is done. We'll just take a look at it, and when we're finished, Simon can go put it up in the fourth floor kitchen. She'll think she left it there."

"That's assuming it doesn't contain her diary, in which she confesses to being a homicidal maniac," Simon said. "And why am I the one carrying the incriminating evidence all over the place?"

"It's hardly incriminating." I was leafing through months of neat writing on calendar pages. "At least so far."

"That's because you're looking in the wrong place."

I yelped, Brenda screamed a little, and Eileen slammed the book shut.

MoM stood at the door.

Chapter Thirty-five

"Act casual," Simon whispered. "She can't have seen what we're doing."

It was worth a shot.

"Hi," I said too brightly. "We were just packing up. Are you going to Jim's memorial service?"

"That would be a little hypocritical." She closed the glass door behind her and leaned back against it, putting her hands in the pockets of her raincoat.

"Oh, really?" Brenda's tone was too bright as well. We were overacting.

"Were you on your way out?" Eileen asked.

"Yes, but I need my book first."

We assumed various looks of blank incomprehension.

"Book?" Simon enquired politely.

"The one somebody just took from the ladies room. Probably you." She looked at Eileen.

Why probably Eileen? Why wouldn't she think I'd done it? I mean, what did that make me?

"Sorry?" Simon tried a slightly befuddled smile.

She stood up straighter. "I'm not an idiot. I came around the back way and I could see my planner perfectly well behind your computers."

The back way. Great.

Eileen was quietly and almost motionlessly tapping something on her laptop, and Simon, giving up the pretense, began leafing through the book. He stopped when he got to the Accomplishments tab.

"Good lord."

There was a pocket on the back of the divider page, and in the pocket was a plastic card. He pulled it out.

Clara Chen's gym card.

◇◇◇

It took us all a minute to remember to breathe again. Then I spoke.

"You killed her."

MoM's expression didn't change.

"But why?" Brenda asked. Then, angrier, "*Why?*"

"Don't get carried away," Mom said impatiently. "It wasn't my fault. She had an accident. I liked Clara. I'm the one who hired her. I was her mentor."

"So…" Simon still held the ID card. "What happened?"

Her face twisted. "It was a bad day, all right? It was late, and I'd found out that the project I'd been working on was getting cancelled. I'd been killing myself, and for what? So they could throw everything I'd done for them away? *Again?*"

Brenda spoke. "But Clara wouldn't have been the one to cancel your—"

"Oh, no." MoM cut her off, her voice bitter. "She never did anything. She just floated up through the ranks, everybody's darling, never doing anything wrong—"

"You were jealous," I said.

"Don't oversimplify," she snapped. Then she took a deep breath and straightened her coat, pulling the belt a little tighter.

"Look, I just ran into her in the garage that night. We'd both been working late. I'd gone jogging before it got dark, and then gone back to the office to finish some work. Clara and I hadn't had a chance to catch up for a while, and she said she wanted to ask my advice about firing that idiot Krissy."

She looked at each of us. "Clara still needed me. She still turned to me when she had a problem." It seemed important that we acknowledge this.

"What happened then?"

She shot me a hostile look. "After we talked about Krissy, she started telling me how happy she was. How everything was going so well for her. That she was getting married." MoM spoke the word with distaste. "That she was being promoted." She compressed her lips.

"And you couldn't stand it," Brenda said softly.

MoM ran a hand through her cropped gray hair. "Nonsense. I was delighted for her. I told her if I hadn't still been in my running sweats I would have taken her out for a drink to celebrate. But as she was on her way to the gym…" She shrugged.

"You manipulated her into asking you along," I finished for her. "And then you killed her in the steam room."

"It was an accident," MoM insisted. "We were just relaxing and talking, and she got up to push the button for more steam, and she slipped."

"I don't believe you," Brenda said.

"I don't care," she answered flatly. "That's what happened."

"And she hit her head on the bench?" I asked.

Had the coroner been right all along? Was there really no murder?

"But you meant to kill her," Eileen spoke up. "Otherwise, why didn't you leave your name on the gym guest pass?"

MoM looked insulted. "I see no reason to give every living soul my personal identification information. So when the girl behind the counter gave me a card to fill out, I just waited a moment and handed it back to her blank. She didn't even notice, she was so busy gossiping with Clara. She just tossed it into a drawer and handed Clara our towels."

"It's possible," I said slowly. "The receptionist said she didn't really notice you."

MoM's eyes narrowed. "Of course not. Who would notice me when the glorious, young, beautiful, brilliant *Clara* was around?"

"Not that you're bitter or anything," Eileen said.

She flushed. "Oh, you think you know me?" Her voice held disgust. "You don't know me."

She turned a challenging stare on each of us.

"Do you have any idea what it's like to be a woman over fifty? We're *invisible*. And working in a place like this? Where I'm older than anyone else in the room every day of my *life*? Where they think of me as their *mother*?" She stopped, shaking with hostility.

"Well, to be fair, dearie, you do rather play into that," Simon drawled. "I mean…MoM?"

"Shut up!" she snapped. "Don't you call me that, and don't you *dare* condescend to me!"

Her voice sent a chill through the room. I waited a beat before going on.

"What happened in the steam room?"

MoM regarded us, her chin held high. It was a moment before she spoke.

"She slipped. The idiot slipped and then sat on the floor laughing about her bruised butt. About how Morgan was going to think it was sexy. About how she hoped it would fade by the time she went on her honeymoon to Maui."

"So you pushed her," I said.

"I did no such thing! I reached out to help her—"

"Right. I've seen the way you help people. First you create a disaster, so then you can come to the rescue. What did you say to Krissy at Clara's funeral to trigger her hysterical outburst?"

I was just going on a hunch, but at that moment I was sure MoM had set Krissy up for that slap.

"I don't know what you're talking about."

"I'm talking about you, and your manipulations. If Clara slipped in that steam room it wasn't an accident, and if she hit her head it was because you pushed her."

Her eyes flashed. "So what if I did? So what if I took her by that little-girl ponytail and crushed her skull into the bench? Who's going to prove it?"

Brenda sank to her chair, her hand over her mouth.

"I think—" My voice came out in a croak. "I think that membership card proves something."

She froze.

"That was your one mistake," I said softly. "The missing card was the one thing that said it couldn't have been an accident. So what I'd like to know is—what was so important for you to take from Clara's locker? Why did you need her card?"

MoM was still motionless, her face flushing but her eyes growing colder. When she spoke it was like the sound of crushed ice.

"Krissy's file."

"Krissy?" Eileen said. "What does she have to do with this?"

MoM glanced at her dismissively.

And suddenly, I got it.

"You knew Krissy would get Clara's job," I said. "And you knew she'd collapse under the pressure, leaving the way clear for you to step in and save the day."

I'd been watching the scenario play out ever since we'd gotten there. I just hadn't realized what was going on.

"Why did you keep Clara's ID card?" Simon still held it. "You had to know it was evidence."

Her mouth twisted. "I'm allowed one mistake, aren't I?"

But I didn't think it had been a mistake. She'd wanted to keep the card. She'd been proud of it. Hadn't she filed it under Accomplishments?

She straightened again, and glanced at the wall clock. "Well, I have to admit I didn't plan for this today. Which leaves us with a problem."

"What are you going to do now?" Eileen asked. "Kill all of us?"

She blinked. "If I have to." The she pulled a gun out of her pocket. "And I think I have to."

I stared at the gun. And I remembered suddenly that I had a gun too. It was in my laptop bag, which was in front of Brenda on the table. I began to move slowly toward it.

"You can't possibly plan to murder us all and expect to get away with it," Eileen said.

"I know that," she snapped. "You're coming with me."

"Oh, no we're not," I said firmly. I've seen enough episodes of Oprah on the subject to know that when a crazed killer invites you for a ride, the smart thing to do is decline.

"I have the gun." She waved it. "That means you'll do what I say."

My bag was in reach. "Like hell we will—"

I might have made a mad grab for my gun if the two glass walls of the conference room hadn't suddenly exploded.

There was an ear-splitting crash as the glass shattered and disintegrated. Everyone in the room screamed and dove for cover. But when the dust cleared and we crawled out from under the desk there was only one person with any serious damage.

And she was on the ground, with Flank standing over her.

Chapter Thirty-six

I assumed it was wishful thinking when I thought I heard Jack's voice. A side-effect of the ringing in my ears. Then I heard another voice.

"Are there any casualties?"

Inspector Yahata.

Jack and the inspector were both standing in the doorway to the elevator lobby, both surveying the damage, both holding guns.

"Stay put," Jack said when I started toward him. "This isn't stable."

I followed his gaze to the ceiling, where crackling sheets of glass still hung between us. Safety glass, thank heavens, but that didn't make getting caught in a shower of the stuff any more appealing.

"Is she dead?" Brenda asked. She was looking at Flank.

He shook his head and crouched over MoM's body, applying pressure to a fast-spreading stain on her shoulder. She was covered in broken glass.

Yahata pulled out a cell phone and started speaking into it in urgent, clipped tones, which probably meant an ambulance was on its way.

"Well." Simon brushed himself off. "You three certainly know how to make an entrance."

"Who shot her?" I asked. There were a lot of guns around.

"Me," Flank grunted. "Saw her gun."

"Where were you?" Eileen asked. "Did you get my messages?" She looked from Jack to Flank.

"What messages?" Then I remembered her surreptitious typing. "Is that what you were doing on the laptop?"

"I sent SOS text messages to Jack and Flank," she said.

"You're a genius," I told her.

She picked some glass out of her hair and looked modest.

"I was at the Hall of Justice with the inspector when I got the message," Jack said. "And you are a genius." This to Eileen.

The Hall of Justice was only a few blocks away. Still, they must have done the whole lights and sirens bit to get here so quickly.

"We were outside the door coming up with a plan when Flank..." Jack surveyed the extensive wreckage. "...took action."

"Came up the back stairs," Flank said. Which explained why we hadn't seen him in the hall. He must have been behind MoM in the hallway, which accounted for the fact that his shot had shattered both conference room walls, as well as the kitchen's.

Flank was still crouched over MoM's body. "She's waking up."

Jack and Yahata crunched their way through the broken glass to her, skirting the perimeter of the room.

"It's fake," Flank said, handing MoM's gun to the detective.

Yahata took it, and turned it to read the inscription on the barrel. "To MoM, for all her great work on *Sniper*."

"I'll be damned," Jack said. "That was the first game ever developed on Zakdan software. This must have been a team gift."

Right. She couldn't have gotten a tee-shirt like everybody else.

"Charley, you're bleeding." Brenda came closer to look at a cut on my arm.

"So are you." From several scattered cuts on her hands and arms.

Simon had a small cut on his forehead. "This had better leave a damn sexy scar." He reached up to touch it.

"Come on." Jack was suddenly next to me. "Let's get out of here."

◇◇◇

Several hours later, in the cafeteria of San Francisco General, Inspector Yahata found us cleaned up, bandaged, and drinking lots of coffee. All of us except Flank, that is. He hadn't been hit by any glass, so he'd gone to the police station to surrender his gun and make a statement. Although if they made him surrender his gun first, I didn't know how they'd ever get an intelligible statement out of him.

But that wasn't my problem.

"How is she?" Brenda asked the detective.

"Well enough to give us a statement." He sat, producing the familiar small notebook and glittering silver pen.

"Is a statement the same thing as a confession?" Brenda asked.

The detective's eyes flashed in Eileen's direction. "Had it not been for your recording, I believe she would have insisted that Ms. Chen's death was accidental."

"What recording?" Brenda and I asked simultaneously.

"You clever thing," Simon said. "You recorded the whole thing, didn't you?"

Eileen shrugged. "After I sent the text messages, I turned on the computer's microphone. It seemed the obvious thing to do."

"For you, maybe." I stared at her.

Brenda put her hand over Eileen's. "Thank you."

Jack cleared his throat. "Did she have anything to say about Lalit Kumar or Jim Stoddard?"

Damn. I'd completely forgotten about them.

Brenda's hand flew to her mouth. "Oh, she must have killed them. At least, she must have killed Jim. Remember when we asked if she was going to his memorial service? She said it would be hypocritical."

"But why?" Simon asked. "Don't tell us she was jealous of him too?"

"If I had to make a guess—" Jack looked at the inspector closely. "I'd say Jim knew something about Clara's murder."

Yahata hesitated, seeming to consider several thousand things at once before speaking. "He saw them in the garage on the night of Ms. Chen's murder."

"And he didn't go to the police?" Brenda protested. "What a bastard!" She looked shocked at her own outburst.

"He tried to blackmail her." I looked to the detective for confirmation, which came as a minute lift of his eyebrows.

"How did she kill him?" Eileen asked. "I mean, how did she make it look like an accident?"

Yahata looked at Jack. "How would you suppose?"

Jack thought about it. "He was already drunk. So she probably followed him to his car and offered to drive him home. Maybe she gave him more to drink, or maybe she just talked to him for a while until he passed out."

"Literally boring him to death," Simon muttered.

Jack, having learned the technique from me, ignored him. "Then she could have driven the car into position, heading downhill on O'Farrell, gotten out, and released the brake so it rolled to a stop in the middle of Van Ness, where the road flattens out."

"And waited for the inevitable," I finished.

We all looked at Yahata. "It might very well have happened that way," he acknowledged. Which was not the same thing as telling us the details of MoM's confession, but it was as much as we were going to get.

"You put it best when we first met her," I told Eileen. "She's opportunistic. With both killings, she saw the opportunity that presented itself, and she took it."

Eileen nodded. "Which is why she probably still thinks none of it was her fault."

"Hang on." Brenda's eyes widened. "What about Lalit Kumar? And what about the shooting? That wasn't opportunistic. That was a deliberate ambush."

"But, be fair," Simon said reasonably. "Charley did provoke it by stealing—"

She waved her hands. "No, not today. The shooting at the museum. At Jack and Charley. The same night Jim Stoddard was killed." She looked at Jack. "If she wasn't killing people because of the software bug, why would she have wanted to kill you? And if she didn't even have a real gun, how could she have?"

She turned to Simon. "Wasn't she at the party before you? So how could she have been shooting at Jack and Charley all the way across town?"

Brenda was right. It couldn't have been MoM. So who? And where did Lalit Kumar fit in?

"Well, darling, people have been known to shoot at Jack before," Simon suggested. "Maybe that didn't have anything to do with dear old MoM."

All eyes turned to my husband.

"Eileen," he said. "I may need to make a few changes to your PowerPoint presentation tomorrow."

The presentation?

Oh.

Chapter Thirty-seven

We were in the executive boardroom, as scheduled, at ten the next morning.

After all, the show must go on.

Even if, as we now assumed, MoM had been the one to schedule it.

Jack and Mike had left for Zakdan ahead of us. They, along with Bob, Krissy, Tonya and Troy, were already in position by the time we got there. We were still undercover, so I wasn't entirely sure if I was supposed to know Jack or not, but I had a hard time not staring at him.

Jack looks good in Armani.

Brenda, Eileen, Simon and I took our places and waited for Morgan's arrival to ring up the curtain. Nods were exchanged. Conversation was murmured and minimal.

"Does anybody know where MoM is?" Krissy's high voice cut through the quiet.

Nobody who knew was telling.

Things were starting to get fidgety when the door opened again. All the Zakdan execs sat up taller and began straightening their clothes when Morgan entered the room. But that was perhaps less because of Morgan, and more because of the man striding in next to him.

Harry.

His cigar was a flagrant violation of state smoking regulations, and his hula-girl shirt was a slap in the face to corporate dress codes, but his wealth guaranteed that the staff of Zakdan would sooner die than point that out to him.

Morgan made a round of introductions, and I did my best not to react when Harry winked at me. Or maybe it was at Brenda, but it was in our general direction.

"I don't know about anyone else," he said with a broad grin, "but I'd like to hear what these folks have to say about this place."

He looked at Eileen. "You ready?"

She nodded briskly, rose, and flipped a switch on the conference table's elaborate center console. Suddenly the screen of her laptop was replicated on large flat-panel monitors mounted at either end of the room, and the SFG logo was on display.

The SFG logo had been created the night before by her ten-year-old son, but it looked good enough for the purpose of the meeting.

"The evaluation of Zakdan has had two distinct branches," she began. "As you all know, the SFG team has concentrated on understanding the business models and overall viability of the corporation as a whole."

Heads nodded on the Zakdan side of the table.

"Concurrent with our efforts, the consultants from MJC have been conducting an investigation of the core technology and intellectual property of the company."

That caused a little ripple of something. I thought Bob was going to speak up, then he just stuffed his hands into the pockets of his baggy jeans and looked sulky.

Eileen continued. "I think it would be the most effective use of our time to turn things over to Jack Fairfax and Mike Papas, of MJC, for a discussion of their technical findings."

"Excuse me," Troy spoke. "Was Jim Stoddard aware you were examining the code?"

"Yes," Jack answered for Eileen. "He was very aware of our activities."

"Morgan," Troy addressed the CEO, "I really think if we're going to proceed with this we should have some representative of the Engineering function here. Have you named Jim's replacement yet?"

Morgan stared at the Marketing VP. The phrase "not yet cold in his grave" could have been written in script on the wall behind him.

"It's a little premature, Troy. And we do have a representative of the Engineering function here. We have Bob."

Bob looked like he'd just found an electric eel in the bottom of his latte.

"Bob?" The scorn in Troy's voice was clear.

"Yes, me." The Quality Assurance VP got over his shock and sat up a little straighter. "Coding and testing go hand in hand. Both functions, working together, make up an Engineering organization."

Score one for Bob.

"In any case," Harry rumbled, "I'd like to hear what you came up with, Jack." His eyes glittered.

Jack nodded. "What we came up with was a deliberate and systematic effort, occurring over years and across multiple releases, to implant a sophisticated series of delayed-release viruses at the most fundamental levels of the Zakdan code."

It took a minute for everyone to realize what he'd said, mainly because he'd spoken so casually. He might just as well have been remarking "gosh, it looks like rain" instead of informing them that their company was sitting squarely on a time bomb.

Krissy reacted first. "Excuse me?"

Jack looked at her. "My colleagues and I specialize in system security. And it became obvious to us that some individual or group has been planting increasingly complex viruses in every product released by Zakdan for the last decade."

She stared at him for a minute, then shook her head. "That doesn't make sense. We would have known about it. We would have gotten Tech Support calls."

"Not if the virus hadn't been triggered yet," Mike told her. "The only calls you got were the results of accidental triggers that set off small corruptions in individual applications. The pattern wasn't obvious, but it was there."

"But how could someone do that?" Krissy protested.

"Yes, how?" Troy challenged. "It doesn't even sound possible."

"It would take planning and patience and access to the code at the highest level," Jack explained. "It's exactly the sort of scenario that Homeland Security has been concerned about."

"Homeland Security?" Tonya echoed.

Mike spoke up. "Terrorist cells have been known to operate for years, with a single goal, working in isolation for the day when they can unleash something of a scale that would otherwise be inconceivable."

"Terrorist cells?" Bob's complexion had taken on an alarming purple cast. "No way. There's no way terrorists could have gotten access to the code."

Jack looked at him. "As a matter of fact, our liaison from the SFPD agrees with you. He feels it's a simple criminal affair."

Inspector Yahata, right on cue, slipped into the room. A frisson of electricity circled the table.

"Hello, Inspector." Harry pulled out the chair next to him, clearly enjoying the unfolding show. "Have a seat."

"So the only question remaining—" Jack's voice made several people jump— "is who had that kind of access, over that period of time, to the Zakdan code?" He looked around the table. "Inspector, do you have any thoughts on the matter?"

Yahata sat with his hands, fingertip to fingertip, on the table before him. "Our investigation has yielded evidence that Jim Stoddard, the late executive vice president of Engineering, was the mastermind behind the plan."

"No way," Krissy murmured.

"Stoddard appears to have long nursed a resentment towards the original founders of the company, Zak Bridges and Dan Maceri, with whom he was a student at Brown," Yahata continued. "He was deeply hostile toward them for what he perceived as their condescension in offering him a job when they were in the early phase of the company. He believed himself to be a far more gifted programmer than either of them, and that it was his genius that was ultimately responsible for the success of the company."

"You're shitting me," Troy said. "You are absolutely shitting me. How could you know that?"

I didn't think the inspector cared for his language. "Jim Stoddard, like many egomaniacs, kept a journal."

It was probably just my imagination that he looked at Harry when he said "egomaniac."

"Why?" Tonya asked, her eyes huge. "Why would he have done something like that? He can't have just wanted to bring all the systems down—was he going to hold up the company for ransom or something?"

"If that had been his motivation," the detective replied, "he would have had ample opportunity to act upon it."

"Then why?" Krissy wailed.

Harry said one word.

"Power."

They all stared at him.

Jack spoke. "It gave Jim a tremendous sense of power to know that he had his finger on the button."

"But I still don't understand how it can have gone on for so long," Krissy said. "I mean, why wasn't this virus discovered? Why didn't anyone find it in all the testing over all the—"

She stopped, and turned to stare at Bob.

I'd been watching him turn from purple to very, very white. And now that everyone was looking at him, he went a shade paler.

"You said it, Bob," I spoke to him. "Coding and testing go hand in hand."

His eyes flashed, and he looked at Inspector Yahata.

"Jim would have been nothing without me."

Jackpot.

Chapter Thirty-eight

Bob stood, and swayed on his feet for a moment. Sweat darkened circles under his arms and around the neck of his tired tee-shirt. He patted the pockets of his baggy jeans as if he was looking for something.

"Are you all right?" Brenda asked. She pulled a pack of tissues from her purse and reached over to hand it to him.

"Don't!" I yelled, but it was too late.

Bob grabbed Brenda by the arm as he pulled a gun from his pocket. He yanked her toward him until they stood together, his gun to her head. He looked as surprised as she did, then both their expressions changed.

He was as terrified as she was.

Harry, Eileen, Simon and I had all leapt to our feet as it happened. Now Bob gestured to us with the gun. "Sit down! I'm in control here." He swallowed, then looked at Harry.

"Who has the power now?"

His voice shook, but there was a feverish light in his eyes.

"Mr. Adams," Inspector Yahata spoke calmly. "This is not something you want to do."

"Don't tell me what I want!" he yelled, and we all cringed as Brenda squeezed her eyes closed.

Bob licked his lips. "I'll tell you what I want. I want a helicopter. On the roof. Now."

Yahata regarded him evenly. "I'm not in a position to get that for you. But if you hand me the gun—"

"I am," Harry cut the detective off. "I can get you a helicopter and whatever else you want. Just stay calm and don't hurt anybody." The expression on his face when he looked at Brenda made my heart stop.

Bob's eyes darted back and forth between Yahata and my uncle.

I hadn't brought my gun to the meeting, figuring that between Jack, Mike and Inspector Yahata, we'd have all the firepower we needed. So why weren't they doing anything?

"I'm going to reach into my pocket for my cell phone," Harry said. "Nice and easy, and I'll get you the best goddamn helicopter you've ever seen."

Bob nodded quickly. "Do it."

Harry reached into one of the vast pockets of his cargo pants and came out with a sleek black cell phone. "See, nice and easy. Now you just think about what else you want. You just name it and I'll get it for you."

I shot a look toward Jack, who kept his eyes trained on Bob. He spoke evenly.

"What do you want, Bob? Because I don't think this is anything you ever wanted."

"Just be quiet and let me think," Bob snapped.

"Okay," Jack said. "Sure. But this can't be how Jim told you it would all turn out."

Bob laughed, a little too hysterically for my taste. "Jim told me it was about the money," he said. "All these years, it was about the money. Jim said the Zakdan board would pay anything for the bug fix, once they knew what we were capable of doing. We were going to make more money than God."

Harry, who had more money than God, nodded as he dialed his phone.

"Enough money for you to get away from everything," I said as soothingly as I knew how. "Enough for you to buy that sheep farm in Scotland."

He stiffened. "How do you know about that?"

"I think it's a great idea." I kept my voice soft as my mind raced. "It sounds beautiful. The hills and the heather…"

He relaxed slightly as we heard Harry speaking into his phone about a helicopter and giving the location of the Zakdan building.

"This is all your fault," Bob said to Jack. "If you hadn't come along, Jim wouldn't have gotten so crazy."

Jack nodded. "He knew we'd found out about him."

"He should have killed you," Bob told him. "He should have killed you just like he did Kumar."

Jim had killed Lalit Kumar. That made sense. Lalit had been a nice guy. So nice a guy that he'd go collect a drunken colleague at one in the morning if he called and said he needed a ride. Jim, with his history of drinking, had probably done it before.

"Kumar knew about the bug," Jack said.

"That stupid bitch!" Bob spit out. "She was too stupid to know what she'd found, but Jim heard her telling Kumar all about it."

"Clara," Morgan spoke. "She told Lalit?"

"Yes, Clara," Bob snapped. "It was just lucky for her that she had that accident before Jim got his hands on her." He swallowed. "Jim would have made her suffer."

Brenda made a little sound, and Bob tightened his grip on her.

"But he did get his hands on Lalit," I said.

Bob looked at me, and there was pride in his voice. "He was brilliant. Not just in how he shot Kumar to make it look like suicide, but the way he got the note onto Kumar's computer. Jim could access any computer at Zakdan remotely. It was—"

"It was obviously faked," Jack finished the sentence. "And it didn't fool Inspector Yahata here for one minute."

"Shut up!" Bob yelled. "He should have shot you in your car the first night he tried to get you. But he thought he had more time, and he wanted to make it look like an accident."

"So he just stole a big truck and tried to slam into us?" Jack said. "This is your brilliant mastermind? A drunken teenager might have tried the same thing."

If he was deliberately trying to make Bob crazy, it was working.

"Shut up!" he yelled again, squeezing Brenda tighter. "Would a drunken teenager have listened in on your cell phone call to know where you were going that night? Would a drunken teenager talk to everyone you'd met at Zakdan until he found out you live in Pacific Heights? Would a drunken teenager have known the city streets well enough to realize that you'd have to take the tunnel to get to the restaurant from that neighborhood? And be cunning enough know exactly where to wait for you?"

Right. That explained why Stoddard had never made an attempt on us at the house. He only knew our neighborhood.

Bob was still talking, but shifting his attention. "He should have killed you the second time—and he would have, too, if she hadn't come along." He gestured at me with the gun.

The hatred when he looked at me was like a physical thing. "Jim was tapping into your email. He read everybody's email." He looked back to Jack. "He knew where you'd be that day."

"Is that Jim's gun?" I asked, my eyes fixed on the weapon held to my best friend's head. "The one he used at the museum?" If so, it must have had a silencer then.

Bob nodded. "He gave it to me at the bar that night when he told me what had happened."

"Did it ever occur to you that, by giving you the gun, your partner was trying to frame you for attempted murder?" Jack asked.

Bob looked like his head was about to explode. "Don't say that about him! You didn't know him!"

"True," Jack agreed. "And now I never will."

Tears came to Bob's eyes. "You didn't have to kill him!"

"I didn't," Jack said softly. "He just had an accident."

He was probably right not to get into the whole MoM thing at that point.

Bob's eyes widened. "No, you killed him. Don't lie to me!" He looked over to Harry wildly. "What's happening with my helicopter?"

"It's on its way," Harry said, showing both hands, one still holding the phone. "Just tell me what else you want. Anything you want…"

"Money," Bob said. "Lots of it. Twenty million dollars."

"Done," Harry said, and began dialing another number.

"Fifty," Bob yelled. "Fifty million."

Harry nodded and spoke into the phone.

"If you want money," I said, "you've got the wrong hostage."

Brenda's eyes widened. "Charley—"

"Take me," I said. "I'm worth a lot more than she is. Harry's my uncle."

Bob looked confused.

"Really," I told him, my words tumbling out. "Harry's my uncle and Jack is my husband and I'm rich and I'm a much better hostage." I'd also rather die than see Brenda get hurt because of a situation I'd put her in.

"Take me."

"Charley, don't you dare—" Brenda began.

But Bob acted quickly. He rushed toward me, pushing Brenda to the side, and grabbed me by the elbow, pressing the gun to my temple.

"Charley!" Harry yelled. "Brenda!"

Bob's movement had been the signal for all hell to break loose. Everyone who had been frozen suddenly sprang into action, shouting and trying to get someplace else. Troy knocked Krissy down in his race to the door.

"All right!" Jack shouted above the chaos. "That's enough!"

He reached over and grabbed the gun from Bob's hand, neatly snapping his wrist as he did so.

We all stared at him, including Bob.

Jack looked at me. "You don't think I'd be crazy enough to let him bring a loaded gun into the room, do you?"

Which just set off another round of shouting. Bob, as Inspector Yahata moved in to handcuff him. Brenda, punching me in the arm and asking how dare I do such a thing, Harry, babbling incoherently as he pushed his way over to scoop Brenda and me up in the same crushing hug, and me, as soon as I was free, yelling at my husband that he might tell a person what the plan was once in a while.

Then Eileen and Simon were jumping up and down and hugging, and Troy, Tonya and Krissy were looking at us like we were insane, and Morgan was shaking Mike's hand and seeming much older than when I'd first met him.

Jack put his arm around me and pressed a kiss to my forehead. "That was a truly stupid thing to do." He handed the gun to Yahata.

"Look who's talking. When did you empty out the bullets?"

"Right before the meeting," Mike answered, slapping Jack on the back. "I distracted Bob while Jack slipped into his office."

"And you knew where to look for the gun...?"

"It might not have been my first time in his desk drawer," Jack said.

"Hey!" Harry yelled. "Who wants to go for a ride in a helicopter?"

I looked up at Jack. "I think I'd just as soon go home."

"Right!" Simon hollered. "We're going to Charley's house! Last one there drinks the cheap champagne!"

As if I'd ever serve cheap champagne.

Chapter Thirty-nine

The Four Seasons at Langkawi. The most gorgeous, relaxing, sun-soaked beach resort I had been able to book on no notice. The web site had said Langkawi was an archipelago in the Andaman Sea, and while I had no real idea where that was, it sounded just about far enough away from Zakdan, Inc. to make me happy.

Jack and I were on our honeymoon.

About damn time.

The room, all gloriously polished wood and clean, simple furnishings, had one wall that swung open completely, revealing a private deck and a pristine white beach beyond. It was exotically beautiful, a genuine tropical paradise.

And it was raining.

"They said this only happens in September and October." I pulled a hibiscus-print sarong around myself and sat up to look out at the meteorological anomaly that hadn't let up since we'd gotten there.

"You can never trust a weatherman," Jack stated. Which was a slightly sore subject, since he sometimes claimed to be one, but as he was naked and in bed next to me, and at least close to a beach, I let it pass.

"What did Brenda have to say?" He propped himself up on one elbow, making strategic adjustments to the sheet.

I might have wanted to get away from it all, but that didn't mean I wouldn't call home every day. I'd spoken to Brenda that morning.

"Morgan Stokes offered her a job at Zakdan," I told him. "He wants her to come work with Tonya in Human Resources, and lead the effort to draft a new corporate code of conduct. The salary is *huge*."

Jack's eyebrows went up. "Is she taking it?"

I shook my head. "Not a chance. She says in academia at least the backstabbing is all verbal. And she's still taking that group of students to Europe."

Jack looked at me carefully. "Is Harry going with her?"

I looked at him more carefully. "I didn't ask."

I was slowly adjusting to the fact that there might—okay there probably was—a relationship between my best friend and the madman who'd driven me crazy most of my life.

It was likely to be a long period of adjustment.

Jack wisely changed the subject. "How's Eileen?"

"Brenda says she's swamped since she went back to work. Oh, and Anthony keeps asking her if they can go see Mike's office with all the computers." I reached for the room service menu. "He now officially wants to be a geek when he grows up."

"There are worse things," Jack responded. "And he's on the right track. If he hadn't found that bug in the pirate game, we might not have been able to trace the virus back as far as we did."

Jack and Mike had decompiled the pirate game and apparently found something like a signature in the virus that predated anyone but Jim Stoddard at Zakdan. They'd known then that the exec had to have been behind the years of sabotage. And that his long-time colleague, Bob, must have helped him cover it up.

"But you'd have known about Stoddard anyway," I said, flipping through the menu. "I can't believe he was stupid enough to keep a journal—or at least, if he was such a genius, he might have put it in code or something."

The silence from my husband was profound. I looked at him.

"He didn't keep a journal, did he?"

Jack shrugged. "Yahata had to say something to get Bob talking."

I stared out at the rain-soaked beach. "Do you think Mike and the hackers-for-hire have finished cleaning up the code yet?"

"They'll never get everything out of applications that have already been deployed, but they should be able to strip the virus from anything that gets shipped in the future. And they'll take out all Mike's spyware while they're at it."

"But the virus is still out there? Lurking?"

Jack nodded.

"And whose finger is on the button now? The three best hackers in the world?" Somehow, that didn't give me a warm glow of security.

"No, only Mike knows all the components of the trigger."

Mike. I was going to have to remember to be nicer to him.

I tossed the menu aside and stretched.

"Don't tell me you're not hungry?" Jack said.

"I just remembered we have all that fruit."

There had been a gorgeous platter of tropical fruits, most of which I couldn't possibly identify, waiting for us when we'd checked in. I went to get it, and brought it back to the bed, along with a sharp knife.

"What do you suppose this one is?" I poked a green spiky thing with the knife.

Jack took both dangerous objects from me. "I have no idea." He cut in. "But it smells good."

He gave me a sliver of fruit on the point of the knife. Whatever it was, it was yummy.

I sighed happily and stretched out next to him.

"This is more like it. Being fed exotic fruits by a naked man in the tropics. This is how I should spend my life."

"You'll be bored by Tuesday," Jack informed me. "And I'm not entirely naked. Don't make this any more depraved than it already is."

"A sheet doesn't count," I told him. But he may have been right about the boredom thing. Paradise is great in small doses, but I was already starting to think about what Kevin Allred, the decorator Morgan had recommended, might be doing to my house.

I rolled over toward Jack. "Whatever shall we do next, to keep away the tedium?" I used my huskiest voice and wiggled my eyebrows for emphasis. "Since it's still raining—"

"I thought we might read something."

I blinked. That was so not where I had been going.

Jack was looking through the fruit again. He hesitated over a mango, and I willed him to choose it because mangos are so juicy, and I could think of some fabulous ways to deal with that problem, given our current state of undress.

He was still talking, I noticed. "Since it's raining, and since I need at least a few more minutes to recover before we do what I suspect you want to do with this passionfruit..."

Passionfruit, mango, whatever.

"...maybe you want to read something?"

"I didn't bring any books."

He nodded. "Neither did I, but I brought a play. It's the weirdest thing. I don't know how it got into my luggage—which the TSA would not be happy about—but there it was."

He licked his fingers clean, reached around to the other side of the bed, and came back with a manuscript.

I looked at the cover.

"*Power.*"

I continued reading.

"By Harry Van Leewen."

I stared at my husband. "You have got to be kidding me."

He grinned. "You'd be surprised. It's not bad."

There was only one possible response.

"Damn."

To receive a free catalog of Poisoned Pen Press titles, please contact us in one of the following ways:

Phone: 1-800-421-3976
Facsimile: 1-480-949-1707
E-mail: info@poisonedpenpress.com
Website: www.poisonedpenpress.com

Poisoned Pen Press
6962 E. First Ave. Ste. 103
Scottsdale, AZ 85251